CLOSE TO YOU

GEN X SERIES

CARY J HANSSON

ABOUT THE AUTHOR

Cary is a fifty something mum of three, an ex-dancer, actress, waitress, cleaner, TV presenter, double-glazing sales rep, fax machine operator ... You name it and she's cleaned it, served it, sent it or sold it.

She writes stories about ordinary people, living lives of extraordinary courage and indestructible humour. She promises only one thing: no knights in shining armour. Her characters save themselves, as in the end we all must do.

She is also a certified practitioner of Writing for Wellness.

To learn more visit: https://www.caryjhansson.com/

All characters in this publication are fictitious and any resemblance to real persons, living or dead, is purely coincidental.

Cover design and illustration by Jojo Ford Illustration

Created with Vellum

1

CLOSE TO YOU

by

Cary J Hansson

2

'Good afternoon. You've reached piñatas, pizza, and Pinot Grigio. Party Girl is here to help!'

'I don't say *Pinot Grigio*!' Clutching her phone, Jo threw her handbag onto the passenger seat and fell into her car. As she did, the waistband of her trousers sliced flesh. 'That's better,' she breathed, slipping the button.

'Chardonnay, then.' On the other end of the line, Diane laughed. 'I couldn't get through my kid's birthday parties without one. Not that you'd know. You were swanning around Singapore back then. Are you wearing your lucky trouser suit? AKA, the Tomato Outfit?'

'Of course.' Jo angled the rearview mirror. Her face had flushed almost as red as the trouser suit. It was excitement, she guessed, or a hot flush. Preparing for the worst, she leaned forward and struggled out of the jacket.

'So?'

Jo smiled. 'Well... It's funny you should mention them.'

'Birthday parties? Why would that be funny? Kids high on sugar is your business. Most people would run a mile, but––'

'Piñatas.'

'Because?'

'Because... I've just promised Nikki Lembit, married to Andi Lembit, Norwich United striker, the world's biggest football-shaped piñata!'

Diane squealed. 'You got the gig! Tell me you got the gig, without telling me you got the gig!'

'I got the gig!' Drumming her feet on the floor of the car, Jo grinned. 'You didn't seriously think I wouldn't?'

'Not for a moment! Who else could pass off a Shetland pony as a unicorn and get away with it!'

'The average age at that party was eight.' She plugged her phone in and turned the ignition. 'And actually, that's why Nikki Lembit called. She saw the pictures in the paper.'

'Of course she did! The whole of East Anglia did! How much did that ad cost?'

'A fortune.' Jo sighed. 'But it was worth it. I'm moving up, Diane!'

'You are. And no one deserves it more. You've worked so hard.'

Taking her lipstick from her bag, Jo studied her reflection. The ad had cost over five hundred pounds. *Jo Swainson of Party Girl makes every dream come true.* Toby, her husband, had been horrified. She'd been determined. After three long years of screeching kids' parties and flimsy back-garden marquees, she'd had to push forward.

'You're a determined woman, Jo.'

Stubborn, Toby had said during one of their recent rows.

'Once you make a decision, you really go for it.'

'That's one way of putting it.' *Unable to compromise.*

'So? Nikki Lembit wanted a unicorn?'

Jo laughed. 'It's a gender reveal, Diane. Of course she

doesn't want a unicorn. She was just impressed because she thought I'd supplied one.'

There was a long silence. 'And how did you break it to her?'

As she opened the lipstick, Jo looked back along the drive to the impressive house she'd just come out of. She was thinking of the way Nikki had looked at her as she'd started to explain... Like a child waiting to be told the Tooth Fairy isn't real. Through the silence, she could hear Diane smiling, waiting for the punchline.

'You didn't shatter her dreams?'

'No,' she said. On a day like today? Just as she was on the verge of achieving dreams of her own, why would she shatter anyone else's? 'You'll never guess what the budget is,' she whispered, and slaked on a layer of cherry red to nearly match the tomato red.

'Five grand?' Diane whispered back.

'Higher.'

'Ten.'

'Higher.'

'Bloody hell, Jo! I'll wheel over an ultrasound scanner myself for half that!'

'I know.' Jo laughed. 'And that's not even the best bit.'

'What is?'

'Football is a team sport.'

Diane giggled, little snorts escaping through the phone line. 'Actually, it's a game of two sides.'

'And eleven players a side.'

'With similar budgets?'

'With similar budgets.' Throwing the lipstick back into her handbag, she pulled out a packet of Cadbury's Animals, stuffed a parrot into her mouth and put the key into the ignition.

'What was that?' Diane snapped. 'An elephant?'

'A parrot.'

'How many points?'

'Less than a bloody elephant, that's for sure. They're skinnier. Like you. Anyway, I'm starving.'

'You're rushed off your feet, that's why. How's Renée going? Saved your marriage yet?'

'My marriage isn't in trouble!' She turned the engine and put the car into reverse, stretching her arm across the passenger seat as she backed into a three-point turn. Renée was her new virtual assistant. More artificial than that unicorn/pony and not nearly as intelligent. And Diane was only joking. It was true, Toby had been upset about the ad, and he did mutter about the weekend mornings she spent *just checking on an order, just updating the website.* But given the size of the mortgage they had taken on, it wasn't surprising he was worried. And anyway, after years of supporting him on overseas postings, this was her chance. She couldn't wait to get home and tell him! With a footballer's wife as a client, Party Girl was poised to launch into a whole new universe. The new house was the right move. Once they got the summerhouse, she could move her work boxes into it. That would help. Brushing crumbs from her trousers, she said, 'That reminds me. I've provisionally booked a date for my birthday.'

'Forty-nine, eh? You're catching up!'

As if Diane could see her, Jo nodded. With five years between them, she would of course never catch Diane up, but still... Forty-nine. Nearly fifty. The number felt slightly unreal. Another year and she *would* be fifty, and that *was* unreal. 'I'm going for a Vegas evening. Roulette wheel. Craps table, the works! I'm going to hire a croupier. Or two.'

'Sounds fantastic!' Diane said. 'What does Toby think?'

'I haven't told him yet.'

'Oka-a-y.' Diane said, stretching the word.

'You know what he's like. He'll never get around to anything. I've been organising my own birthday parties for years.'

'Mmm.'

The pause Diane left had Jo looking at her reflection again, thinking of Diane's comment. *Saved your marriage yet?* It wasn't surprising she should have said it. Jo had done her fair share of complaining recently. But her marriage wasn't in trouble. Strained, perhaps. Once they'd decided to say no to any more overseas postings and put down roots there had been a lot of adjusting to do. 'I'm looking at the first Saturday in September,' she said, swallowing down the last of her biscuit. Whatever the difficulties they were having, it was all the more reason for a party.

'September… Oh, Jo. That's going to be difficult.'

'Is it?' Jo looked at the console, the green light of an open telephone line. 'I thought Emma's due date was August. That's why I thought September would work.'

'It is. But she's going to want me for those first few weeks, to help with Esme apart from anything else. And Rachel's due in June. They're like buses, these babies. All coming at once.'

'Will you go over?'

'It's looking that way.'

'I see.' The car came to a halt. Diane would soon be a grandmother three times over. Her daughter Emma was expecting her second child, and over in Chicago, Emma's younger sister, Rachel, was expecting her first. Slowly Jo moved the lever into drive, the silence that had arisen in their conversation a river she had come to know well. It had meandered through her life these last twenty years: her friends and their children on one bank, Jo, childless, on the other.

'I'm sorry, Jo.'

'No. Don't be. It's fine.' But she was bitterly disappointed. As the children had grown, the river had begun to shrink. Friends had become more available. And she was proud of the way they had all held on. Her years overseas; their years nappy bound. In particular, Diane and she had picked up almost where they had left off. Monthly meet-ups, the occasional weekend. Until now that is. Diane already minded one grandchild on a weekly basis; with the arrival of two more, her time would be even more restricted.

'Anyway, we need to celebrate today at least!' Diane said brightly.

'Absolutely.' She couldn't bring herself to add anything more.

'Talk tomorrow?'

'Yes. Talk tomorrow.'

As she sat looking along Nikki Lembit's huge driveway, resentment rose, sharp-elbowed with pettiness. Her birthday party wouldn't be half as much fun without her friends. Maybe she should postpone. This, she thought wryly as she pressed on the accelerator, was the irony of not having children. People thought it made life flexible. The reality was that at times her social life had been shaped as much by other people's children as their own lives had been. It was always her diary that had had to be flexible. School term dates were that rigid, she was glad not to have had to abide by them. Well, maybe Toby and she could fly off to the Seychelles instead. It wasn't her idea of a birthday party, but he'd mentioned it in the past. And he was always saying she went ahead and decided without him. They could discuss it together. Tonight. Over champagne.

'Siri!' she called, opening the window. 'Play messages!' She felt lighter than air, buoyed up with optimism. She'd stop for the bottle on the way home. He wouldn't be able to complain about her deciding without him this time. She indicated left, and was just about to pull out when Siri's disjointed voice rang though the car, loud and harsh.

Hello. This is the Royal Norfolk Hospital. Could you call back please on this number at your earliest convenience?

Jo slammed on the brakes, her hands floppy with fear.

Toby.

Dead in a ditch.

She snatched her phone and swiped the screen open. Displayed along the bottom were five missed calls, all from the same number. She swiped again, and when the crisp voice rang through, *Accident and Emergency,* she went dizzy. 'I'm returning a call,' she managed. 'This number has rung me five times in the last hour.'

'Can I take your name?'

'Jo Swainson. Joanne Swainson.'

'Bear with me.'

Her foot was trembling so much, she had to lift it clear off the pedal. She sat, staring straight ahead, waiting for the line to open up again.

'It's your mother,' the voice said, a moment later. 'Roberta Carter. I'm afraid she's had a nasty fall. She's in surgery at the moment. Can you get down here?'

3

Her throat was dry and her toes itched and, although she hadn't seen her mother in nearly three years, now it was all Jo could do not to turn away in disgust.

One step off the kerb and she had lost her balance, fallen face first, handbag and its contents scattered. Her right eye was a sunken crater, bruises dark as a midnight sky spread across her cheek, deltas of veins pulsing beneath paper-frail skin.

Holding onto the rail at the end of the bed, Jo put her fist to her mouth, bile at the back of her throat.

'Mrs Swainson? I'm Doctor Dandicott. Are you OK?'

'JoJo.' Jo whispered, the name, the moniker, escaping before she could stop it.

'JoJo?'

'Jo... one is enough. Yes. Jo.' And hitching her trousers up, she felt herself blushing to realise the top button was still undone. She turned away to fix it.

Dr Dandicott didn't react. 'Will there be anyone at home to take care of your mother when she's discharged?'

'Take care of her?' He had a nice face. Round cheeks that reminded her of a puppet, small horn-rimmed glasses. But Bobbi had a fracture of the orbital ridge and had broken a bone in her lower arm. The arm had been operated on; the fracture would heal, the bruises fade. If there was anyone in the world that didn't need caring for, it was her mother. Something she'd made clear for as long as Jo could remember. 'I'm not sure I understand,' she said carefully. 'She'll be staying in hospital for a while, won't she?'

'Until she's recovered from the operation, yes. But she's going to find things difficult. Is there anyone at home?'

'At home?' Her mother was in a geriatric ward, every bed filled with old people who had watched her as she'd walked its length. She could feel their eyes on her still, piercing the fabric of the curtains that surrounded Bobbi's bed. Waiting, listening for her answer. 'My father's dead,' she said quietly.

Dr Dandicott nodded.

Blood rose in her cheeks. Her relationship with her mother, or the lack of relationship, was a hard knot, far too entangled for where this conversation might be leading. 'My mother lives alone,' she said and because there was nothing more to add, she turned away from the doctor and tried to smile at the nurse standing on the other side of Bobbi's bed.

The nurse did not smile back. Instead, she picked up an empty jug. 'I'll get this topped up. She was speaking to the doctor but looking at Jo.

No one spoke. Dr Dandicott turned to the computer trolley, and his fingers on the keyboard seemed loud as he typed.

Perhaps, she thought, he was making a list. Noting down her cold, unfilial attitude. Her shoulders were hard and round as doorknobs. Well, she had a list herself. Memorised, not written. The countless times Bobbi hadn't had an answer. For not being there. For leaving in the first place. For not being a mother.

The tapping stopped. The doctor looked up. 'Your mother was very confused when she came in, Jo,' he said gently.

'That's not surprising, is it?' she said. 'If I'd just banged my head, I think I'd be confused as well.'

Was the flicker of emotion that passed through his eyes one of impatience? She was sure of it. She watched as he pushed the trolley to one side. Turning, he put his hands in his pockets and looked at her. 'When your mother was admitted, she underwent an AMTS test. It's an abbreviated mental health test. Standard procedure with patients her age. I'm afraid to say this, but your mother's response was very low. She has some memory loss. Now that could, of course, be down to the TBI.'

'Which stands for?'

'Traumatic brain injury.'

Jo flinched, so blunt were the words. Almost, she thought, as blunt as the blow that would have caused them. Traumatic brain injury. Chastened, she turned to Bobbi. 'Was it that bad?' she whispered, and instantly regretted it. Of course it was that bad. Her mother's face made that clear. Her toes went itchy again. It was hard to imagine.

'We don't know too much yet,' the doctor said, his voice a tone softer. 'When she's recovered from surgery, we'd like to run more tests.'

'Of course.' She nodded. 'Of course.'

'But I should make it clear now, the memory loss could well have another explanation.'

Jo looked at him.

'There's the possibility of dementia,' he said.

'Dementia?' she parroted.

'I'm sorry. I know it's hard to hear. But with you being the only family... now is the time to ask if you have any jurisdiction over your mother's affairs.'

Jo stared. She had almost nothing to do with her mother's life, and her mother had almost nothing to do with hers. And that, for as long as she could remember, was the way they both preferred it. *As long as she could remember* being from the day she came home from school to find her mother gone. The day she'd tiptoed across to the empty armchair and sat and pulled her socks up tight over her knees and waited, feeling not sadness, not fear. Just relief. Relief that, along with her mother, the low cloud that hung over her home was gone. And shame. And guilt, because even as a young child she knew it shouldn't be like this. 'I'm not sure what you mean,' she said.

Dr Dandicott nodded. 'Well. If your mother's problems are due to a TBI, we won't know the extent of the damage, or how the recovery will be, for quite some time. And if it is a form of dementia, that's a condition that has only one direction. If you don't have jurisdiction, it might be a good idea to get it put in place sooner rather than later. It will make things much easier for you. You'll be able to make decisions on her behalf. Rivers, I'm afraid, don't flow back out of the sea.'

'Rivers?' Her nod was slow and considered. The doctor was a poet? She looked at his lanyard. *Doctor Paul Dandicott. Consultant Geriatrician*. Late thirties? Forty-five at the most. He had his tests, his TBIs and AMTs, or whatever they were called. Still, he was getting a little ahead of himself. Jurisdiction. *Dementia*.

'You'd be able to handle your mother's finances, make medical decisions on her behalf. It's a serious decision, getting power of attorney, but I mention it because...'

As the doctor's voice grew smaller, her thoughts drifted. She hadn't seen her mother in so long that this talk of Bobbi willingly handing over financial and medical responsibilities to her felt as fanciful as... as Jo willingly accepting them! They rarely spoke, hardly ever met. She didn't like it and she wouldn't have voiced it, but she couldn't even have said that she knew her mother, and likewise, Bobbi did not know her.

Dr Dandicott smiled. 'Well,' he said, as he drew back the curtains around the bed. 'It's something for you to think about. We can talk again, especially when we know more about your mother's condition. Maybe,' and he gave her a brief, warm handshake, 'in the meantime, have a look into the question of getting power of attorney.'

4

Jo stood alone by the bed. Sun poured in through the high windows, bleaching the walls and the floor and the beds and their occupants alike. Outside, on a long telephone wire, a row of small black birds bobbed together, riding the wind. Hitching her bag up her shoulder, she smiled at the woman in the bed opposite. The woman stared back, her eyes unblinking, her pale arm reaching to lift a glass from the bedside table. She felt she should help. At least offer to help. The water wobbled as the woman brought it to her lips. Squeezing her eyes shut, Jo turned away. She wanted to leave. There was an image in her head of what she wanted to get back to. Home, in her lovely new house, with her husband. Champagne glass in hand, papers on lap, fine-tuning the details of Nikki's party. But every minute in this twilight world and that image was bleaching too. She wanted to turn and run. She couldn't. Not so soon after the doctor, so soon after arriving. Not with all these eyes on her.

Hooking her bag across the arm, she sat down on a chair

at the foot of her mother's bed. From the air-conditioning unit a low hum vibrated like the chanting of a mantra. If she sat here long enough, she'd fall asleep. Wake up under a white sheet herself, with white hair.

The thought had her pulling out her phone and scrolling through her emails. There were two enquiries about children's birthday parties, and another about an engagement party with a proposed budget of three hundred. *Would that be sufficient?* the enquiry had finished on. *No*, she mouthed. She sat back, phone in her lap. There was still no response from Toby. She'd messaged on the way to the hospital, and although he wasn't the best at replying promptly, he wasn't usually this bad. Hopefully he would at least have read the message, and would be delaying dinner.

And then she willed herself to do it. She lifted her chair and moved it closer. Bobbi's face was a mess. The fall would have hurt. She tried to imagine. The force going down, the brutality of it, her mother crumpled by the roadside, handbag flung open. That's what admissions had told her – that the ambulance driver had had to pick up her mother's purse and glasses, her crinkled handkerchief.

Will there be anyone at home to take care of your mother when she's discharged? The doctor's words had felt like a judgement. Had sounded like an echo. Her father's echo. *She should be here to care for you. It was her job to care for you.* Words uttered by him in the heat of anger, put into cold storage by her. Lips pressed together she leaned forward and tucked the sheet close around her mother's neck, gentle as if she were wrapping a child in a scarf. Bobbi was so small, so frail of skin, so reduced of muscle, but how could Jo begin to care for someone who'd never cared for her? This was why she'd stayed away. Meeting her mother's emotional distance with a geographical one. Encouraging Toby to accept every overseas posting he'd been offered. Because after her father had died, who did she have to stay for? She eased back into her chair, looked down at her hands and noted how they shook. 'I can't do it,' she whispered, a hard-edged something sticking in her throat. She couldn't leap in now and start making decisions on behalf of a mother she hardly knew. And she could not go back. She could not be that child again. Coming home every day to someone who did nothing but sit and stare out of the window. A blue-and-green checked armchair.

Slowly, she stood, hesitated and then leaning in close brushed her lips against her mother's forehead. For all she knew, all she remembered, it might have been the only kiss between them. 'Goodbye, Mum,' she managed, and as she went to pull her hand back, she felt the squeeze. Feeble and faint, but real.

'Joanne.' Bobbi's lips didn't move.

Jo stared. How could her mother have spoken if her lips hadn't moved?

'I've a few of your mother's things here!' The voice behind was sharp and loud and bright. 'All over the pavement!' it said cheerily.

She turned. The nurse had returned, and she was holding up Bobbi's handbag. 'She's awake!' Jo said, looking back at Bobbi. 'She just spoke.'

'I don't think so!' The nurse laughed. 'She'll be sleeping a long time yet.'

Her mother's eyes had remained closed, her breathing steady. Had she imagined it? She looked down and pulled a tiny thread from her blouse. She hadn't imagined it. Her mother had said her name. Why would she imagine that?

'This is your mother's.' The nurse stretched a blue

handbag towards her. The strap had frayed and the leather was scratched. 'We popped everything that had spilled out into a plastic bag,' she said, and moving to the other side of the bed, she began straightening the sheets, tucking them in. 'Perhaps you could pick up a few of her things? Mum's going to be with us a while. She'll need a couple of nighties. Hairbrush. Any medications.'

'Medications?'

Straightening up, the nurse nodded. 'Your mother takes a few different ones. Enalapril for her blood pressure, a statin for cholesterol. Probably explains why she was so dehydrated, poor dear. They forget to drink.'

'Of course. Yes.' And for the second time in less than ten minutes, she felt her cheeks warm. Her smile was too bright, her nod too vigorous. The nurse knew, of course she did. She knew that Jo hadn't a clue what medications Bobbi took.

'It would be nice for her to have a clean nightie in the morning.'

Keeping her head down, she put Bobbi's handbag on the table at the end of the bed. She did not want to look the nurse in the face again. In front of her, she felt like a child. The same guilty child unable to look her father in the face all those times the questions had gone further. When he'd had a drink, which in the end, became every time. *Don't you miss your mother? Aren't you sad?* Questions that stung. That even at that tender age, she'd known were impossible to answer correctly. She pressed her lips together and concentrated on the bag, unknotting the plastic with clumsy hands. It rustled as she emptied the contents. A purse, a set of keys, a pocket diary, three years out of date, a packet of tissues, an old Nokia phone, and a plastic headscarf rolled tight into its neat packet. A plastic headscarf?

The nurse shook her head. 'My goodness, I haven't seen

one of those in years. I didn't even know they made them any more.'

'They probably don't.' She opened the purse. Three pound coins, some silver, tokens for shopping trolleys. In the back envelopes she found one five-pound and one twenty-pound note. And a photograph, which she took out. The colours had faded and there was a crease along the top one-third from where the paper had pressed against the leather folds of the purse. It had obviously lived there a long time. It was a picture of a baby, new-born, she thought, as she studied it. Swaddled tight in a blanket, the tip of the nose visible, eyes shut.

Moving closer, the nurse peered over Jo's shoulder. 'Ah, bless,' she said. 'Grandkiddy?'

Her shoulders went stiff. 'There are no grandchildren.'

The nurse shrugged. 'You, then?'

Jo frowned. Was it her? Her heart expanded and contracted, a movement faster than light. If it was her, it didn't make sense. Keeping a photograph of the baby that grew into a child that you walked out on?

'Can I see?' The nurse already had her hand out. Large, with wide chubby fingers. 'So sweet,' she said as she took the photograph.

Jo looked up, and as she did the nurse and the ward lost focus, and her vision narrowed to a line of pencilled handwriting on the back of the photograph.

The nurse handed the photo back and Jo turned it over, impatient to read what she thought she'd just read. There it was: April 1982.

'Bless her.' The nurse smiled. 'My mum's just the same. She's got this photo of me and my brothers. I'm about three, hair sticking up like a toilet brush. Carries it everywhere.'

'It isn't me...'

'What isn't you?'

Surprised, Jo looked up. She hadn't been aware that she'd spoken out loud. 'That baby,' she said now, staring at the date on the back of the photograph. 'I would have been...' She counted the years on her fingers. 'Seven years old. That baby isn't me.'

5

Forty minutes later, she was parked outside Bobbi's bungalow, ready to do her duty and collect the few personal possessions that would make Bobbi's stay in hospital more comfortable. As she sat watching traffic rush by on the busy road, she thought what she'd always thought, every time she visited. Why had her mother moved here? Of all the places she could have gone when she'd left the peaceful seclusion of her father's cottage, why here? The noise, the traffic, the constant buses. The contrast was so marked on those childhood visits, it had always seemed like a deliberate choice on her mother's part. A carefully chosen rejection of him, his lifestyle and, by extension, Jo. These were bad memories. Things she hadn't thought about in years and didn't want to start thinking about now. Shaking her head, she opened the car door and immediately had to whip it shut again as a van sped by. No, she'd never understood.

Bobbi's keys were in her handbag. It took Jo three attempts to get the right one. The smell, when she finally got the door opened, was pungent and immediate, instantly recognisable as the stench of decay. Head down, sleeve pressed against nose, she jammed the door open and went inside. All the pegs on the coat-rack were empty. Bobbi's jacket was with her at the hospital.

It was keenest in the kitchen, a sweetly foul scent that hit the back of her throat and made her gag. She found the key to the back door and shouldered it open, almost falling down the back step where she stood, filling her lungs with fresh clean air, a long moment passing before she was ready to turn and go back in.

Looking around the first thing she saw was a fruit bowl tucked away in a corner of the worktop. Mould had furred over what had once been... oranges? She took the bowl and opened the cupboard under the sink, ready to tip the contents. But the bin was already overflowing, scraps of furred food littering the bottom shelf. Lifting it free from the holder, she put the bag on the floor, shook it to free up space and emptied the oranges, covering her mouth as a cloud of lilac dust rose up. She knotted it closed, dumped it outside, and stood, hands on hips, taking in the scene. Crockery had been spread all along the worktops. A pile of plates, amongst which she found three still smeared with the remnants of congealing food. A stack of bowls. Knives, forks and spoons. Three cups and three saucers, laid out as if Bobbi had been expecting guests. She bent to open a cupboard. It was empty, but stuck to the inside of the door, sellotape peeling back, was a faded yellow post-it note. Jo's lips moved as she read the tiny scroll of Bobbi's handwriting: *Bowls and Plates.* She opened another cupboard. *Cups.* But again, the cupboard was empty. *Cutlery.* Empty. *Cans.* This cupboard wasn't empty, and she had to push the first row aside to keep counting. Fifteen... yes there were fifteen cans of baked beans.

On she went, opening doors and reading through the labelled contents of her mother's kitchen, some of which were still in place, most of which had been spread along the bench. Bobbi, it seemed, had forgotten where it all went, forgotten those discreetly hidden notes she'd so carefully written out and taped to the inside of each cupboard. Or maybe she couldn't trust herself to remember. Maybe it was easier to leave everything out. Jo didn't know.

She moved across to the microwave and opened it. Inside was a bowl of soup, shrunken and forgotten. On the dresser a pile of unopened post. Mostly bills, with the exception of one stiffer envelope that bore a Canadian stamp and had *Season's Greetings* scrolled into the postmark. Cobwebs hung from the ceiling corners; the grouting was sticky with grease. On the hob stood a lone saucepan. She lifted the lid. A pale potato floated in water so stagnant looking it might have been there a week. An A5 wipe-clean pad had been propped up against the wall, *MONDAY* written in spidery capitals. But it was Thursday.

Overwhelmed, she walked to the sink, turned and looked through the window to the back garden. The grass was overgrown, knotted through with frothy chickweed and white-headed clover. Along the border dishevelled shrub roses were sprouting green shoots among last year's hips. It made Jo sad to see it so neglected. Her mother had nurtured this garden with more constancy and care than she had anything else in her life. Dr Dandicott had been careful with the word, measuring out his words, as if she'd known their value. But she hadn't. Within the orderly confines of the hospital ward, she hadn't even believed. She did now. The unwashed plates, and misnamed days? The unopened Christmas card? The fog of confusion her mother had been living in was crystal clear and the doctor was right. Bobbi's mind was failing, and she couldn't come back. Not without someone to care for her.

Her throat went dry. She turned to the cupboard above the kettle and opened it, relieved to find glass tumblers. But the water was almost at her lips before she saw the film of orange floating on the surface. The glass was filthy. Throwing the water away, she left the glass on the drainer and turned again to a room that sang her guilt. Every plate and post-it note an accusing finger. How long had this been going on? This slow disassembling of her mother's mind?

She didn't know. She couldn't even have guessed.

The last time she had seen her mother was Mother's Day, nearly three years ago. Toby and she had been back from Malaysia only a few months and in a fit of optimism she'd booked a lunch and extended an invitation. They were home for good, and she was preparing to launch her business, and she thought she would try. But the moment they had walked through the doors of a pub teaming with children and mothers, a place that oozed happy family vibes, she'd understood the depth of her mistake.

The meal had been eaten in an uncomfortable silence, not a single question asked about Malaysia, or her business idea.

Don't let it get to you, Jo, Toby had said afterwards.

I don't think she even likes me, Jo had replied, and he hadn't disagreed.

A month had slipped into six. She'd sent flowers on Bobbi's birthday, and Bobbi had rung back, and Jo had missed the call and then she hadn't rung again. Summers had sailed past, an autumn and a winter with nothing beyond an exchange of Christmas and birthday cards.

Breathing deeply, she tipped her head back and pinched the bridge of her nose. She was here to collect a few essentials. There was nothing more she could do. There probably never had been. She closed and locked the kitchen door to the garden, took a shopping bag from the back of a chair, and went into the bedroom.

Only she couldn't get over the threshold.

There she was, a grown woman, unable to take a step further into a room frozen in time. A room she remembered. The white melamine wardrobe, the chest of drawers with its brass handles. The angled mirror and padded stool. The blown-glass ornaments on the window ledge. What had the nurse said? Nighties, pants, bras, dressing gown. But things in drawers were sacred. If anyone went through the top drawer in her bedroom, what would they find? A necklace with a broken clasp. The card from her father's funeral service. She took a step in and then another, moving to open the top drawer, relieved to find only a tumble of underwear. Working quickly, she pushed socks and pants aside and found a rolled-up nightie. Just one. She threw it onto the bed, and reached in again, and this time her hand settled on something cool, flat. An envelope.

On the outside that same date, April 1982. On the inside, wrapped in a piece of tissue, a lock of hair. Baby-fine hair, from a baby. The shock was electric, pushing her back onto the bed. It had to be connected to the photograph.

And now her hands were paddles as she churned through her mother's most personal belongings. Socks and pants, stockings. What she was looking for, she couldn't have said. What she found was only the static of stockings catching on fingertips, brushing against plywood.

Slowly she put everything back, picked up the envelope again and went to the kitchen where she stood looking around that room she hadn't set foot in for years. *You'll be able to make decisions on her behalf,* the doctor had said. She almost laughed. If the doctor's words had felt unlikely at the hospital, they felt ridiculous now. How could she make decisions for a woman she didn't know? Because she didn't. Turning the envelope over, her lips moved as she read the date again. April 1982. She didn't remember a baby, she didn't remember her mother expecting a baby. But there was one thing she did know, one thing she was absolutely sure of. Whoever this baby was, tucked away for years in the folds of Bobbi's purse, it had stayed closer to her mother than she had ever managed to.

6

The sun was low by the time she pulled into the driveway of her own house. It had made shimmering orange rectangles of the front windows, as if what they reflected was a citrus ocean, not an early summer sky. Elbows wide, she leaned across the steering wheel to look at the house she had fallen in love with on the first visit. Their forever home. Solar lights glowed all along the front pathway, and by the door her solar-powered butterflies, wings spread in welcome. Toby had had to be persuaded, but, as far as she was concerned, there couldn't be enough solar-powered butterflies in the world, welcoming people home. Plus, no one else had them because they were new this year. The trade catalogues, he had often joked, were why she'd gone into the party business in the first place. Justification for hours spent leafing through fairy lights. But they made her happy. Making her home a home made her happy. She looked across at his car, parked on the road. He'd have an early start tomorrow, and wouldn't want to be disturbing her in the morning to move her car from the drive. How considerate he still was. And how warm and inviting her home looked. Compared with her mother's.

The silence rose like water. Then from the branches of the Wych elm at the end of the garden a wood pigeon let out its low melancholy call and it sounded to Jo like the question that had haunted her whole life. What had she done, to make her mother leave? What had she done to not be worthy of her love?

The bird called again. It could call all night. There would be no answer because as she had come to accept, there was no answer.

7

She dropped her keys in a bowl and took off her shoes. Dumped her bag on the hall table and stood looking at it. Not tonight. She wouldn't tell Toby everything tonight. Conversations about her mother tended to go awry, and she understood why. Within the realm of normal, Bobbi was inexplicable. Years ago, watching a late-night movie, in which a mother had turned to her son and said, *I have never loved you,* Toby had yawned, declared the script unbelievable, and taken himself off to bed. But Jo had watched to the end, a morbid curiosity carrying her through, because she'd known. Sometimes parents didn't love their children

She leaned to the mirror and pulled the skin backwards at her neck, instantly lifting her face. As she released the skin and her jowls returned, she sighed. Today she had actually felt gravity. The world pulling her down. Well, not tonight! Something easy on the TV. A good murder! Dinner on her lap, lean against him – that was all she wanted. *I'm home,* she called because the lights were off, and she assumed he must be upstairs. Tipping her head back, she waited, not just for his answer, but to take the kind of moment she often did. She was home. In the home she had created and filled with light and beautiful things. Large canvas paintings of open landscapes, forests and oceans. Open doors, open plan. Everything a home should be. *Did you get my message?* she called into the darkness. Messages. She'd sent three explaining what had happened, where she was. *Toby?*

There was no answer, and standing in the hallway she realised that something she'd been expecting was signalling its absence with a low rumble in her belly. Food. That was it. She couldn't smell food cooking. Her brow wrinkled with irritation. Weeknights were Toby's domain. If he'd changed his mind, he could have told her, responded to one of the texts she'd sent. She'd have picked up takeaway.

Hunger pricking, she went into the kitchen and opened the fridge staring at a packet of cheese and a pot of hummus. Takeaway would take at least thirty minutes, and right now she was so hungry she could eat her arm. She reached for the cheese.

'I'm here, JoJo.'

Jo turned.

And there he was. A silhouette, she hadn't noticed, sitting on the other side of the island.

'Why are you sitting in the dark?' she said, and flicked the light switch. 'And why have you got your jacket on?'

'Jo.' Toby slipped off the stool, his eyes fixed on her with an intensity that turned her stomach upside down. She could see how scared they were, his eyes. And that scared her.

'Why have you got your jacket on?'

He looked down at his hands. 'I'm sorry about your mum. I'm really sorry, it's the worst timing.'

'Timing?' Her hand balled to a fist. There was another emotion in his eyes, something she couldn't name.

'Jo, I'm sorry. This is really hard.'

'What's hard?'

'I'm leaving.' And when he looked up, she knew what it was that she hadn't been able to name. *Pity.* His eyes were scared, and full of pity. *For her.* She felt her mouth twitch and she wanted to laugh. She was a child at a funeral, about to laugh, because under the circumstances it was the last thing she should do. The only thing to do. She'd come home, expecting him to have cooked and he hadn't. But that was OK. They could still get takeaway. 'I don't understand.'

'I know.'

What did he know? Blood rushed in her ears. She had come home. Tomorrow, they'd made arrangements to go and look at summerhouses. They were going to find a landscaper, for the garden. It was going to be perfect. Their home.

'There's someone else,' he said and looked straight at her.

She looked straight back at him, and his head wobbled and she saw then how difficult it was for him to say the things he was saying. Which made it real. Her heart raced, colours flashed. 'We're going to buy a summerhouse,' she whispered.

'There's... I've met...' He stopped talking and his eyes said *don't hate me.*

'You didn't reply.' She was thinking of the texts she'd sent. Of course he didn't. What would he have said? *Can you get home as quick as possible please, I'm leaving you. No dinner tonight, sorry, I'm leaving.* 'I've been at the hospital.'

'I know. I'm sorry. About your mum.'

Her mum? Jo looked across her kitchen. Her vibrant

kitchen with its abundance of bonhomie. *Eat, Drink, Love* in neon pink. A pot of rich-leaved basil on the table. Olive oils and artisan vinegars. Wine stocked and displayed. And as she looked, she forgot that her husband had just told her he was leaving, and she forgot because she was thinking of her mother's face, the bungalow and its dying post-it notes, the photograph of a baby born a year before her mother had walked out.

'You and me, JoJo... It's been difficult for a while. You know that.'

'Is it the butterflies?' She turned to him.

'*What?*'

That was it. The last time they had argued, it was about the solar butterflies. 'I know you didn't want them. You said—'

'It's not the butterflies.' He closed his eyes. 'I've met someone else. I'm sorry.' And again he looked at her and his mouth didn't move, but his eyes were on their knees.

'Do I know her?'

Toby opened his mouth. Nothing came out.

'Do I know her?'

He nodded. 'Her name is Wendy. We met when... She's... the conservatory. She works for the company...'

She thrust her head back and stared at the ceiling, hand splayed on her chest because breathing was suddenly something she felt she had to remember to do. 'How long?' she whispered. The conservatory had been put in eight months ago.

He took a step forward.

She took a step back. 'How long, Toby?'

'Some time,' he managed.

Some time. Too long for it to be a mistake, a fling.

'I didn't mean for this to happen, JoJo. I'm sorry. I didn't realise…' His voice trailed off. 'Until it happened, I didn't realise how much I wanted a family.'

Family? Lowering her chin, Jo stared at him. Something about the way he was watching her filled her with anger. In one sentence he'd gone from guilty to innocent, accused to accuser. '*She's* pregnant?'

'I'm sorry. I wanted you to know before anyone else. We're having a baby.'

We? Now she did laugh. Now she threw her head back and snorted loud as a hog. *We!* 'There's no *we* about having a baby, Toby!' she said loudly. 'What you mean is, *she's* having a baby. *She* is.'

'Yes,' he stammered. 'I mean, she is. Wendy's pregnant.'

'And until this happened, *you* didn't realise how much you wanted a family?'

'Don't…'

'*Don't what?*' The rage that surged was a hand at her throat. Pressing her lungs, leaving her with a voice thin and sharp and mean as a blade. 'You were going cycling. In the Alps,' she sliced. Then, another, quieter cut. 'You'll lose your deposit.'

Picking up his phone, Toby turned away. 'I can't do this. I didn't want it to be like this. I thought you'd be back. I was hoping––'

Four *I*'s in one sentence. She counted again, silently in her head. *I can't do this. I didn't want it to be like this. I thought you'd be back. I was hoping.* Yes – four! A red mist descended. He was leaving her and still, it was all about him. '*My mother fell!*' she shouted. 'I'm sorry if that has inconvenienced you —' And when he didn't answer, she flung a cupboard door open, grabbed a glass and sloshed an inch of red wine in. 'Well,' she hissed, watching as he stood watching. 'Don't worry, Toby. I'll try and remember to get it right next time!

I'll tell my mother that the next time she has an ambulance take her to hospital, can she please do it on a day when my husband isn't leaving.' But she was talking to his back now, following him out of the kitchen. 'Twenty-five years! Are you doing this? Toby... Please...' Still he didn't answer, and everything that happened after, happened in a series of slow-motion images that Jo knew she'd never forget.

The confused half turn as he looked for his keys, the bend at his knees as he reached for his suitcase. *His suitcase.* Jo stared. She'd walked right past it as she came in, hadn't even seen it. She watched in silence as he opened the door and walked out, butterfly wings showing a kaleidoscope of rainbow colours in the gloom of the evening.

8

Renée, her virtual assistant was typing...

Good morning. What can I help you with today?

Jo's fingers hovered over the keyboard. She had been going to ask Renée to create the graphics for her spring newsletter. Pastel colours. Cheerful images, that kind of thing. But she couldn't find the right letters to tap out the right words. Three days since Toby had left and she hadn't told anyone. Not even Diane. She'd lost count of the times she'd picked up her phone and failed to call, sitting instead with it heavy on her lap as she'd sat and stared out of the window. Words – the right words – to start the conversation, hadn't come. If her life was a movie, she could ring and be shrill with hysteria and Diane would be sassy and smart and they'd arrange to meet somewhere with tasteful décor to talk it out, over chilled wine. If she was eighteen, she could ring and be incoherent with tragic weeping and Diane would be outraged and full of expletives on her behalf. But it was real life, and she was going to be forty-nine any moment, and she didn't feel hysterical or tragic. She felt stunned. As if she existed in a state of calm so deep she could pinch herself and not feel it, pass a mirror and be surprised at her own reflection. It was shock of course. A detachment that had borne her from bed to the kitchen and no further. That had had her lying awake through three long nights, staring at the ceiling, listening to the many sounds an empty house makes. He was gone. He really was gone.

And yet the situation felt no more real than the day he walked out. This was what she really needed help with. Accepting reality. Leaning back, she stared at the screen.

Nothing feels real, she typed.

Ground yourself.

Renée's response was instant.

Grounding techniques can help you reconnect with the present moment and your surroundings. Some methods include:
Deep breathing
5-4-3-2-1 technique

Jo lip-read the words.

Can ghosts ground themselves? she typed. *Because that's how I feel.*

The concept of ghosts grounding themselves is not widely recognised. However, let's explore this idea from different perspectives.

Why am I asking you? Jo typed. *You're even less real than I am.*

But she didn't press send. It felt too cruel. Instead she backspaced until the message had been deleted, picked up her coffee and spun the chair to the window. At the end of the garden the lilac tree was showing its first blooms. He was gone. He was gone, and she was on her own. Forty-nine – almost. Jowly. Alone.

The tin-sharp notes of her ring-tone, Kool & the Gang's *Celebrate Good Times,* burst through the quiet, grounding her in a way a hundred 5-4-3-2-1s couldn't have managed. She picked up her phone and looked at the name flashing across the screen. *Nikki Lembit.* So far, she'd ignored three calls from Nikki, each time responding with a swift *I'll get back to you. I'll call. Sorry, super busy right now.* If she didn't pick up she might lose the business and that was something she couldn't afford to do. Not now. Especially not now. 'I was just going to call you!' she answered brightly. 'This week has been…' Her throat went hard. 'It's been a lot.'

'Tell me about it!' Nikki panted. She sounded as if she'd just run a marathon. 'Max has had the runs! Everywhere, JoJo! And I mean everywhere! I had to throw away the rug in the hall. Well, Vera did. Andi couldn't manage it. He got it halfway to the kitchen and started retching. Vera had to take over.'

And for the first time since her husband had left, Jo smiled. She'd only met Andi Lembit briefly. Arriving back from his training session, he'd kept his eyes on his phone, managing to grace her with a curt nod as he took the stairs, two at a time. He hadn't struck her as the kind of man who had the time, or the inclination, to scoop up dog poo, Max being Nikki's very fluffy Pomeranian. Vera she didn't know, but she liked the sound of her.

'My husband,' Nikki sighed, 'can be a real wimp at times.'

Jo nodded. The moment was so unexpectedly authentic, it called for something authentic back. But what should she say? Better a wimp for a husband than one who leaves?

'I went through the catering catalogues last night.'

He'd rung. She hadn't answered. He'd texted.

We need to talk through some practicalities.

He'd texted again.

Please respond.

She hadn't.

'I was hoping you could stop by and pick them up,' Nikki said.

How could she be married one day, and not the next? It felt unreal. Her heart, if it was still there, had been encased in double-glazing.

'There's something I'd like to show you.'

Jo put her hand on her chest. Her heart was still there, beating away.

'JoJo? Are you still there?'

'I'm still here,' she startled. Was she? She wasn't sure. Waking up to silence, going to bed in silence, had been lonely. And the emptiness of her house, always one step ahead, was an unwelcome stranger. How was she supposed to get used to being alone? After twenty-five years? Just over half her life.

'There wasn't anything I liked, so I came up with my own design!'

'Design?' She had no idea what Nikki was talking about.

'For the cake? I'd love to run it by you.'

'Yes.' A rod went through her spine, snapping her upright. 'Absolutely,' she said cheerily. 'When suits?'

'Is this morning OK? About eleven?'

Leaning forward she flipped her diary open. Something was happening this morning, she was sure of it. Whatever it was was outside, knocking to be let in. And now that Nikki was talking she could almost see it, past the single plate in the dishwasher, the space where his coat had hung, she could almost see the shape of it, feel the urgency with which it willed itself into her consciousness. 'I think,' she said, grabbing her reading glasses, 'I think I've got…' There it was! She was needed at the hospital. Dr Dandicott had called yesterday. Her mother's physical injuries were healing nicely, he'd said, but the scan had shown signs of vascular damage. *We can assume she's been having problems with her memory for a while.* He'd left a pause. She remembered now. A gap in which she might answer. And despite a clear image of the post-it notes and the unopened post at Bobbi's bungalow, she hadn't. *It's time to discuss future care arrangements,* he'd eventually said, in a noticeably flatter voice. *Bobbi will have to undergo assessments before she can be discharged. It would be helpful if you could attend.* It hadn't sounded like a request.

'I can't do eleven. How about early afternoon. One o'clock?' she said, closing her diary. She could call in on Nikki on the way back from the hospital.

'Sounds great, Jo,' Nikki said. 'I'm really excited!'

And with the timing agreed, she ended the call, eased back in her chair and looked at her phone. *Celebrate good times.* Really?

9

'It's good to see you up and about, Mum,' Jo said, as she sat down. They were in Dr Dandicott's office, a small white room, with standard accessories: a plant, a painting, a photo. And although Bobbi had walked to the office, and was indeed up and about, Jo's voice was overly cheerful, masking, she hoped, the shock. Because it was clear. Like a photograph left in the sun, her mother was fading. It hadn't been as obvious on her previous visit after the operation. It was now. The dull yellow of her eyes, the curve of her spine, the lakes of liver spots across her hand as it trembled to hold a kettle.

Jo had arrived just as the first part of the assessment was ending. In a small mocked-up kitchen, a physiotherapist had been guiding her mother through the process of making a cup of tea, and shocked, Jo had held back. Going about the simple tasks of filling the kettle, finding a cup, unscrewing the cap from a milk carton, her mother was hesitant and frail. The pause between remembering and not remembering what came next, blurred her. Softening her, like water softens clay, so her feet were hesitant, her knees bent, her whole body tipped forward in anticipation of the fall, her eyes unsettled, roaming.

'You seem much better than last week.'

Turning, Bobbi looked at her in surprise. 'You were here?'

'Of course,' she said and smiled, as if she popped by every week.

'They need to fix the pavement.' Her mother's right hand rested in her lap, her left arm supported in a sling. 'It's not safe.'

'How is your arm?' she said, keeping her eyes on the sling. The bruises on her mother's face had blossomed a deep purple, tide marks of yellow lapping the edges. She could barely look, even though it was exactly what she should be doing. Making eye contact, offering reassurance.

'Bones heal,' Bobbi said. 'There was no need for you to have come. I'm not losing my mind, you know.'

Briefly, Jo closed her eyes. What could she say? That she hadn't wanted to come? That she probably wouldn't have come but was made to feel that she *should* come? That she had other things to worry about...

'I asked Jo because having family present can make things a little more comfortable.' Dr Dandicott's smile was as neutral as it was professional. He leaned forward, managing to look at both of them at the same time.

Family! Jo felt the reaction in her eyebrows, the angle of the rising arches. She wanted to turn to see how Bobbi had responded, but she was so wrong-footed, she didn't. She stayed silent, nodding a silent acquiescence at the doctor, aware that beside her, Bobbi did the same. She felt like a child, next to a child, in front of a teacher.

10

The next assessment began with Dr Dandicott asking Bobbi to read a short piece of photocopied text, taken from *Country Life* magazine. Jo read too, leaning over her mother's shoulder. The article was about how an unseasonably warm winter had led to snowdrops blooming before the New Year. Bobbi took a long time to read, and when she had finished, she looked up and said, 'I never knew that.' Smiling, Dr Dandicott took the piece of paper and put it to one side. He pulled out another clean sheet, and asked her to draw a clock. She forgot the nine and the twelve.

He asked her to list as many things as she could beginning with the letter P. And as they sat in a deepening silence, plants and prams, poppies and pineapples passing before Jo's eyes, photos *on the wall,* a painting *on the wall* for heaven's sake... Bobbi's lips moved, only twice; first for pen, and then for potato.

She couldn't remember what she had had for breakfast, or even if she had had breakfast.

Now they were on to the calendar.

'Can you tell me what month it is?' Dr Dandicott said.

'September.'

The silence in the room widened into a chasm as the clock ticked the seconds past. It was a sensible clock, Jo thought as she looked at it. The minute hand, clear. How could Bobbi have missed two hours? Have drawn a ten-hour clock? Two a day, gone. How many since Toby had left? Blinking hard, she turned away to look at the painting. Sailing boats in a squall. And then the shelf behind the doctor's head, where a spider plant hung in a brown wicker pot. The plant needed watering. Several of its leaves had curled brown edges. Next to the plant was a framed photograph. The doctor and presumably his wife, with their children. And suddenly the fabric of her chair was uncomfortably warm. She was looking at nothing more than a happy, normal, family photograph. The kind of family who really would have been able to provide reassurance to each other. But it wasn't her family, and it wasn't her. Her hand curled, fingernails digging into her palm. Lowering her chin, she looked sideways at her mother.

'March.' Bobbi tapped a finger on the desk. 'It's *March*. I am not losing my mind.'

Jo closed her eyes, sunlight filtering through her lids, fringing them orange. It was almost as if Bobbi was answering incorrectly on purpose. It was May, and that was fortunate. Apparently, like burglaries, hospital admissions followed a seasonal curve and with the arrival of sunnier days, they'd been able to keep Bobbi in longer than usual. A nurse had told her this when she'd arrived. *My husband is a policeman,* she'd added. *That's how I know.* And my husband has just left me, she'd wanted to reply. For a younger woman, who is having his baby. She hadn't. She'd bitten her lip and nodded and said nothing.

'OK, Bobbi. I know you're tired,' the doctor said.

'I am not tired,' Bobbi snapped. 'I just want to go home! It's September. When can I go home?'

Jo's foot jerked up.

Over the top of his small round glasses, Dr Dandciott smiled. 'We're nearly there.' He pulled a piece of paper towards him and looked down at it. She recognised it as the text he'd asked Bobbi to read earlier. Turning the paper face down, he said, 'Now, can you tell me what you remember from this article we read a little while ago?'

Bobbi didn't speak. She was looking at the paper, her head making small movements side to side, a reluctant, unspoken negative.

'Anything at all?' The doctor smiled encouragingly.

Still, Bobbi didn't speak.

Jo leaned forward. 'It was about snowdrops,' she said. 'Remember, Mum? You said it was interesting.' If there was one thing she knew her mother enjoyed it was gardening. But her voice was a jangling note of artificial cheer in an otherwise quiet room, and she sat back, arms crossed. Over the course of the assessment, as Dr Dandicott's office had shrunk, her incredulity had grown. It was hard to believe that her mother wasn't pretending. That she really couldn't remember anything about this article she had so recently read, that she really had forgotten to include space for midnight, the turning of each new day.

Bobbi looked at her, lips pressed tight together. 'If you say so.'

'It's not if *I* say so! You said so yourself! You read it and said—'

'It's OK.' Dr Dancicott leaned forward. 'We've done enough for today anyway.'

'Then when can I go home?' Bobbi said.

11

Moments after Dr Dandicott had shut the door of his office, his hand was still on the handle, as if the shutting process wasn't complete without this meditative pause.

Jo dipped her head. It wouldn't be polite to nudge him out of the moment. She didn't want to, anyway. She was as wary as he looked of the conversation she knew was coming. Bobbi had been escorted back to the ward. No one answering her question as to when she could go home.

'So.' Dr Dandicott let go of the handle, walked to his desk and sat down, the smile at his lips never failing.

'So,' she said, smiling back.

'So,' he said, and he looked down at the papers in front of him and for the briefest moment his smile failed.

Jo waited. She felt supernaturally calm. After the loneliness of her house, it was a relief just to have another person in the room, to be able to study the face in front of her. And Dr Dandicott had such a kind, intelligent face, she felt she could look at it for a long time. How many of these tests, she found herself thinking, did he conduct every week? She glanced up, and as she did, she felt a surge of warm shame. He was taking a moment to compose himself. No matter how many times he had witnessed this, it had moved him. Dry-eyed, she lifted her chin. Her hands felt heavy on her lap. Apart from that, she felt nothing.

'These conversations are always difficult,' he said as, finally, he looked up.

She wanted to help, to put him at ease. When she'd arrived he'd taken her to one side and warned her that it would be difficult to witness. Dementia, he'd said quietly, robbed people of their loved ones in the cruellest way. And although she'd hoped he hadn't seen, she hadn't been able to stop herself bristling at that word: *robbed.* It spoke of an active violence, something that had happened *to* her mother. But you can't steal what was never there. No robbery had taken place. Desertion, not robbery. 'It's OK,' she said now. 'It's sad, but I don't have a very close relationship with my mother... we're not... close.'

Dr Dandicott nodded. He spoke slowly. 'Before today, were you aware of the extent of your mother's memory loss?'

She felt the thrust of her chin as she shook her head. 'No,' she said. 'No, I wasn't.'

'May I ask you a question? And please.' The doctor lifted his palm from the desk, like a small animal raising its head. 'This is a question. Not an accusation. I'm trying to ascertain a timescale. When was the last time you saw your mother?'

'Umm.' Jo frowned. 'Probably around three years ago.' She watched as he took his glasses off and leaned back in his chair. 'Yes... around then.' And looking down at her hands she willed herself not to say any more. For so many years, watching other women prepare for family visits, or listening to their relief as overseas contracts came to an end, and they talked only of moving back home, she'd offered up explanations to anyone who'd ever asked. Book-ended every enquiry about her own family with euphemisms. *My father's dead, and my mother and I don't have the best relationship. It's just me, and it's never been easy, so...* Only with Toby had she gotten anywhere near the truth. Toby, whose family were warm and uncomplicated, who had accepted their simple register office wedding, because she hadn't been able to bear the comparison a bigger event would have shone on the inadequacies of her own situation. But she was older now, and weary of rushing in, making excuses, for things she had no control over. And besides, it was only a question, the doctor had said. Only a question. 'Quite a while,' she said quietly.

Dr Dandicott nodded. 'OK. Well, there's no easy way to say this, so I'll keep it simple. Your mother has dementia, Jo. My recommendation is that she doesn't continue to live alone. It's only going to get worse.'

'Of course.' The dullness in her voice made it sound detached, as if someone else were speaking. Her mother was losing her mind and she had lost her marriage. She felt swamped, as if she were at the bottom of an ocean, so deep no one could see her. Or ever would again.

'Under the circumstances,' he said, 'a care home is probably going to be the best option. We can extend her discharge date another week, but after that we will need to have something in place.'

Jo shifted her weight. Her mouth was dry as she pushed back in her chair and crossed her arms. *Under the circumstances,* she knew, meant her, and her lack of care. But it also meant, no, there was not going to be anyone at home to care for a woman who had walked out on her family decades ago. It also meant three years of almost no contact, and so many more before that, and all those ever-ready, conversation ending euphemisms. The *we don't talk much* and the *it's not easy.* 'As I mentioned, the relationship with my mother is difficult. I've spent many years abroad. Of course, if things were different...' Her voice trailed off.

'I understand.' Dr Dandicott smiled. 'I was referring to her memory loss, Jo. Under *those* circumstances it would be difficult, even for the closest of families.' He frowned and a sea of tiny lines knitted his forehead. 'There is a very good home called Ashdown House. Unfortunately, they don't have any vacancies at the moment, but we can get Bobbi on a waiting list. And if that isn't an option, there's always care at home.' Frowning deeper, he looked at her. 'It's a costly business. Unless she has considerable savings, going into a residential home will probably entail your mother selling her house.'

'Her house!' Less than ten minutes ago, her mother had left Dr Dandicott's office demanding to know when she could go back there. Now the doctor was talking about selling it. 'How much,' she said, light-headed. 'How much does it all cost?' She didn't have a clue.

'That depends. She'll have to undergo a financial assessment, which will take a little time. But immediate care at home? You're probably looking at a thousand or so.'

'A month?'

'A week.'

The figure drifted off. Noughts dissolving into air as she looked past the doctor and out of the window. Far away and high up, the silver belly of an aeroplane caught the sun, winking down like a sky-bound lighthouse. She squinted at it, at the clean blue sky and the vapour that trailed behind and thought of all the times in the past when she and Toby had been there. Flying away together, to another new destination.

'Can I get you some water?' The voice was so close it

startled her. When she turned, Dr Dandicott was standing by her chair.

'Yes please.' And maybe it was his kind face. Or because he was a doctor. Or because he had his back to her now, water splashing from the cooler as he poured. Or because the only other person in the world to whom she'd actually confessed the whole shameful truth had also now walked out on her... All of these things, as she heard herself saying, 'My mother left when I was eight years old. I came home from school one day, and she wasn't there. I remember sitting in a chair by the window waiting for her to come back.' And again the doctor was at her side, offering her the flimsy paper cone of water. Grasping it with both hands, Jo watched as he sat down. 'I'm sorry,' she whispered. 'It's a shock.'

'I understand.' His smile was genuine and warm.

A shock and a shame so raw, it didn't bear touching. Because what she hadn't said was, *I remember sitting in a chair by the window waiting for her to come back, hoping that she wouldn't.* She looked down at the water, remembering the way the water in the glass had wobbled as the woman in the bed opposite her mother had lifted it. 'Do you really think she needs full-time care?' she said. 'She won't agree to it. I know she won't.'

The doctor nodded, his glasses dangling as he held them between his hands. 'We don't want to believe it when it happens. None of us does. But yes, in my opinion it's no longer safe for your mother to live alone.'

'We just watched her make a cup of tea.' She could hear the plaintive tone in her voice, a child, pleading one last chance. But she had just watched her mother make a cup of tea, and frail as she was, long as it had taken, Bobbi had completed the task. Everything was happening so fast.

'With no tea.'

Jo stared at him.

'Your mother forgot to add the tea bag, Jo. Harmless I agree. But what if we were talking about a pan left to boil? Or a door left unlocked?'

She shook her head. 'I… I don't know.'

'And there are other issues. I'm not saying that back home, amongst familiar surroundings, the situation won't improve. We're still not sure how much of this is down to the head injury. But the way things stand today, your mother's short-term memory is so impaired she can't be relied upon to keep herself safe. And she certainly needs help with bathing. If the condition worsens, she'll need help with her food, making sure it's cut small enough. Choking can be a hazard in patients with dementia. They forget they're chewing. These are things that we have to take into consideration.'

The words that she wanted to say were queued up, ready. All she needed to do was open her mouth and say them. But she couldn't. Because Dr Dandicott was looking at her, his face so open and honest, it disarmed her. *What would happen* – that's what she'd been going to say – *what would happen if I just stood up and walked out on my mother, like she walked out on me?* She didn't say anything. She shifted her weight. She re-crossed her arms.

'I understand there will be hurdles,' the doctor said gently. 'And she may not be ready for this.'

A lump formed in her throat. *She* wasn't ready for this, let alone her mother. What the doctor was suggesting terrified her. Since her father died, keeping a cordial but distant relationship from Bobbi had been the only thing that had worked. The further away, Singapore… New York, the easier it had been. Distance had allowed her to bury a sack of stuff labelled *Bobbi* that she'd never understood, and preferred not to dwell on. Now, she was expected to wade back into her mother's life – and take over? 'I just don't understand,' she said. Post-it notes to help keep track were one thing. But not knowing the month? 'It's happened so quickly. How can she not remember how to make a cup of tea?' But before she'd even finished talking, she could hear the lie. Post-it notes on a desk or a fridge were one thing. Taped onto every surface, they were quite another. For Bobbi, it hadn't been quick at all.

The doctor leaned back in his chair. 'Dementia is a disease, Jo. It's like driving through patchy fog. One minute the view is clear, the next you can't see a thing. Besides, I don't think this has happened quickly. The scan we took clearly showed earlier damage. It could even be related to your mother's psychotic episode. And I don't think the medication will have helped. Anti-psychotic drugs can make even the smallest of tasks seem like a mountain to climb. She was on them for quite some time. Too long, in my opinion.'

The words whistled past, bullets so clean and so fast she could barely catch them. 'Psychotic episode?'

Opposite, Dr Dandicott looked at her. 'You were unaware?'

Her face must have told him. Between her thumb and her palm she felt the blunt edge of cardboard and a cool wetness as the paper cone crumpled. Psychotic. Had she heard right?

'I'm sorry,' he said. 'I assumed you knew.' He placed his palms on the table as he leaned forward.

'You mean as her daughter?' The words sneaked out, defensive as a snake. She felt the threat of tears and it confused her. 'I've been abroad a lot,' she whispered. 'As I said, we're not close.'

Dr Dandicott's face darkened. 'The episode I'm referring to was in 1982.'

Jo stared.

'I'm sorry. I can see it's a shock. But I have a duty to share information with you that I believe will support your mother's care.'

'1982?'

The doctor nodded. Leaning back in his chair, he linked his hands together, made a steeple of them. 'She was admitted to Broadfields psychiatric hospital, Jo. In Norwich. The diagnosis was psychotic depression. She was there for a couple of months.'

'When? You said 1982? When in 1982?' The questions rattled off like bullets. Hard and fast. She watched as Dr Dandicott leaned across to pick up a piece of paper. Her head was hot, her hands cold. Her arms floated. 'November,' she said, answering her own question with one final salvo.

'November,' he echoed, and the paper in his hands trembled.

'That was when she left.' Jo pushed back in her chair, her hands balled to fists. Her father had taken her to the bonfire display in town. She remembered the heat of the flames, vibrant orange against a black night, the crackle of sweet toffee and the sour tang of apple, two tastes in one bite. Her father had bought her a toffee apple and November was when her mother had left. 'What does that mean?' she managed. 'What is psyc—' The word stuck.

With infinite care, Dr Dandicott laid the paper down. 'It can mean many things,' he said. 'Although, for everyone, it involves some sort of break from reality. Seeing and hearing things that are not there. Hallucinations, voices.' And turning to her his face was open, his eyes soft. 'Almost you might say, a return to the magical thinking of a child.'

'My mother heard voices?' Her voice was hollow as a reed, her thoughts clouds, wispy things that she couldn't find the beginning or end of. An image of a child in an armchair, pulling white school socks tight over her knees, the dance of those orange flames, and something else that was less clear, that she couldn't picture but felt she must.

Dr Dandicott cleared his throat. 'If I may I say something?'

'Go ahead,' she whispered.

'Sitting on this side of the desk, Jo, I have been party to more family secrets than I care to remember. These things are delicate. You're perhaps wondering why you were never told?'

His words were permission. They released tears she hadn't felt waiting. *Wondering why you were never told.* He may as well have reached his hand to her heart and wrung it out.

The doctor pulled a tissue from a box that was so conveniently placed it made Jo think of what he'd just said. *More family secrets than I care to remember.*

'I'm sorry,' he said, as he handed it to her. 'Mental illness is still a subject most people prefer not to discuss.'

'I was eight years old.'

Dr Dandicott nodded. 'And I'm sure that whatever decisions your parents made, they were made with your best interests at heart.'

But the doctor's voice was suddenly distant, because she was trying to remember something she'd said. So similar and so recent. And here, in this hospital... *I would have been ... seven years old...*

'Excuse me.' Her heart raced and her hands felt clumsy

as she bent for her handbag and unzipped it. The nurse. That photograph, with its neatly written date. The baby her mother kept secreted in the folds of her purse. She took out the photograph. 'This,' she said as she held the photo up, 'was in Bobbi's purse. When she fell, they gave me the contents of her handbag. *Look,*' she urged as she handed it over. 'Look at the date on the back.'

'April 1982.' Dr Dandicott pressed his lips together as he read.

'Was it hers? Was this my mother's baby?'

'I don't know.'

'But it would be in her medical records?'

'Yes.'

'Can I see them? Have you seen them?'

He shook his head.

'But you're a doctor!' She tipped forward on her seat. 'Surely you can...'

Handing the photo back, Dr Dandicott cut her off with a small, but firm, shake of the head. 'I only requested the information we've discussed today, Jo. And I have to say I wasn't expecting what was sent.'

Slowly, Jo turned it over. There it was, there was the date. April 1982.

'Is there anyone else in the family it might be a photo of?'

'I have a cousin in Canada, but he never had children.' And as she looked up, ice ran down her back. The expression on the doctor's face mirrored what she was thinking herself. 'Do you think something happened to it? And that's why Bobbi...' Jo stopped talking, the whisper of her mother's words loud in her ears. *I am not losing my mind.* Bobbi had sat beside her and said those very words. She'd been adamant.

Dr Dandicott nodded. 'It will have been very difficult for her.'

Jo looked at him. He'd known her mother for barely two weeks, and here he was, his sympathy for Bobbi utterly sincere. But she hadn't known. Not as an adult, not as a teenager and certainly not as a child sitting in a blue-and-green checked armchair, hoping her mother wouldn't come home.

'And yes,' he continued quietly, 'to answer your question, Jo, I do suspect that there may have been a loss. Post-partum psychosis is a phenomenon we know a lot more about now than we did then.'

Jo nodded. From the corner of her vision she was aware of movement and when she turned she saw that a dried leaf of the spider plant had fallen. It lay now on the shelf, the crinkled edge curling upward. 'I'll never know,' she heard herself saying. 'Bobbi doesn't even know what month it is. I'll never know, will I?'

Dr Dandicott leaned forward. 'She's still there,' he urged. 'The mother you knew is still there.'

She smiled, but it didn't reach her eyes. How could she explain? How could she say, I have never known my mother. I don't know anything about her. Her favourite colour. Her favourite flower. Winter or summer? Snow or rain? How could she say that she had never made her mother laugh? That she didn't know what made her mother laugh... That she had carried, every day of her life, the shame of being the kind of child a mother could leave. The sound of a chair scraping the floor cut her reverie. Dr Dandicott was on his feet again, his smile warm.

'Your mother,' he said, 'may not have a grasp on some things, but other parts of her brain, other memories, will be perfectly clear. She was telling us the other day about the street she grew up on. Where she used to work. She was a window-dresser apparently.'

'I wouldn't know,' she said. 'She's never talked to me about that part of her life.'

The doctor nodded. 'I think,' he said, 'that sometimes it helps to understand there is no natural order.'

'I don't follow you.'

'Talking or listening, Jo. It doesn't matter what comes first.'

12

It was a loose slab I think. The pavement crashed into me, that's what I remember it felt like, I heard the crack and I thought it was my nose and my hair felt warm and sticky, there was grit in my cheek like my knees. It felt like my knees when I fell over in the playground at school. I can remember blood and grit, but I never felt the bone snap and it didn't hurt. The grit in my knees did hurt. I could go back and look and see if I can find the slab. I know my mind isn't working the way it should, it feels as if there's a kind of gap between what I think and what I do, I think my foot will step onto the pavement, I think it has stepped onto the pavement, and then I find it hasn't. They're saying it's dementia, a young woman came to see me with some leaflets and she said I should start a diary, it will help me remember if I write things down and I was going to tell her that I don't have anything to write down, I don't go anywhere, I go to town to do my shopping and on Thursdays I meet my old volunteering friends for coffee, and then I had the funniest feeling because I felt sure someone had told me the same thing before. Someone had told me it would help me if I kept a diary, I can't remember anything else, but there's a feeling of comfort when I think about that like having a warm rug on my knees, isn't that strange. Mostly it's only feelings I remember, lots of places and names have just gone. When it's very bad I don't remember anything and it's like thick fog when you're walking in winter. One minute I can see clearly and I know where I am and who I'm with, I know the number of the bus I catch and the name of the road I live on and then I don't. It's happening more and more I think. Sometimes when I'm at home I don't recognise where I am and I open the back door and go outside and all I know is that I feel safe there so I sit down and wait and the fog lifts. I can't explain it better than that and I don't want to because when they say dementia what they mean is that I am losing my mind and those words scare me because I know I just know I've been told them before. It must be getting worse because everything takes longer. I have to put a chair in the doorway when I have the oven on and so I know if it's there I need to stay in the kitchen. If I try and read I can't keep up with the story. When I go back to a book it doesn't make sense and it's the same with the television and sometimes I turn the sound off and just watch. They talk too fast. A strange thing is happening though. For everything I forget there is something new I remember. Yesterday I think it was I watched a line of birds outside on the telephone line, through the window. Starlings, they were, and then I remembered another time when I watched starlings, the day we moved into the cottage, and it was so quiet. He asked me what I was thinking and that's what I said. I remember the conversation as clear as day. He said we needed the peace and quiet. He said 'we' a lot, and I stood and watched the starlings as I counted telephone poles. I was imagining all the people talking to each other and all those conversations travelling on those wires and I knew I was going to be lonely. There were only two cottages and a barn and a field of cabbages for company. I wanted to learn to drive but he said there was a bus stop not very far away. He was handsome then with his aviator sunglasses, like Robert Redford, his open-necked shirt and his leather jacket. It's funny to remember so much, and not know why I didn't ask him. Why did you buy this house before I even saw it? Why do you keep saying 'we'? Maybe if I am losing parts of my mind I'll find other parts, and then I'll know, but I wish I had asked. Joanne was here. I thought I had dreamed it, but she came.

13

Dressed in a yellow velour tracksuit, hair scraped into a gravity defying ponytail, Nikki held up a piece of A4 paper. On it she'd sketched a square, covered in doodles of boots and bows and an over-fussy scrawl, that read: *Boots or Bows, soon well know!* 'Tada!' She beamed. 'What do you think?'

Jo smiled. Her head was throbbing, and the sketch before her was simple and silly.

'Oh, and the icing is a mix of blue and pink! Every other letter. So... *what do you think?*'

She was thinking about that child in the armchair, and of where Bobbi would have been as that child sat and waited. And she was thinking about another baby, a life that existed only as a photograph. And then she was thinking about the telephone calls she'd made on the drive over. The care agencies she'd been recommended, where the eye-watering price of round-the-clock care had shocked her into silence. It had almost been a relief to hear there was no one available anyway. Not at such short notice. 'JoJo?'

'It's great! Really good.' She should have made an excuse with Nikki. Gone home, shut the door, sunk into a bath. Stopped this world that she didn't recognise, and gotten off.

'Isn't it!' Nikki clapped her hands. 'I just came up with the idea. Boots for a boy! Bows for a girl!'

'Morning.' A woman, similar in age to herself, twice her size, appeared in the doorway. She was holding a ball of golden fluff. She had short peroxide hair and a downturned mouth. The kind of face that looked as if it could never be surprised again, that was set in pre-determined resignation to what life had to offer. She was dressed in white drainpipe jeans a size too small, and a Metallica t-shirt.

'This is Vera,' Nikki said.

Jo nodded. Vera who'd dragged the rug out.

'Oh, and I wanted to double check. You're absolutely sure about the smoke?'

'Smoke?'

'That it's edible? Because things go wrong, don't they? I mean, I read about a boy whose face got dyed pink.' As she talked Nikki stared at her coffee maker, eyeing it as if it were the Enigma machine. 'They couldn't wash it off,' she said, turning back to Jo. 'The dye. I mean, I know we're not supposed to be worried about boys being pink any more, but you don't know Andie's family.'

'Nikki.'

'And everyone should be standing well back...'

'Don't worry.'

'But you can't control kids, can you?'

'*Nikki.*' Her smile was as wide as it was painful. 'The smoke from the smoke gun is made with edible cornflour,' she said. 'As is the confetti. If anyone is in the wrong place, at the wrong time, they can lick it off!'

'Thank you!' Nikki whimpered. 'Thank you, JoJo. You think of everything, that's why I hired you. My friend Tanya didn't have edible confetti at her baby reveal, and her Goldendoodle was shitting pink flakes for weeks.' She turned back to the coffee machine. 'I'm scared of using the wrong nozzle.'

'I'm not cleaning up shitty flakes, whatever the colour.' Vera dumped the dog into Nikki's arms. 'He needs training,' she muttered. 'And I need a cigarette.' Pulling a pack of Camel from her jeans pocket, she opened the kitchen door and lit up, tipping her chin to the sky as she exhaled, leaning on the frame. 'Don't worry,' she said. 'I blow it all outside.'

Jo watched. Nikki's husband probably earned more in a day than Vera did in a year. It was strange to see how timid Nikki was around her.

Nikki cradled the dog. 'Andi,' she whispered, 'would be furious if something happened to Max. Sometimes I think he loves the dog more than me. I just...' And to Jo's horror, huge glassy tears formed in her eyes. 'I just hope...' she sniffed, 'that he's going to love the baby.'

'Of course he will,' she said. And then again, 'Of *course* he will.'

'Are you sure?'

'I know he will.' She was here to plan a party, not give life advice. And who, given the current circumstances, would take advice from her anyway? She really wanted to get home. Sink a glass of wine, and forget her husband had walked out, her mother couldn't remember what month it was. Her mortgage was now unsustainable, her mother's care unaffordable.

Nikki bent to put Max down. 'Thank you,' she said as

she straightened up. 'I'm being silly, I know. Every parent loves their child, don't they?'

'In some countries,' Vera muttered, 'if it's the wrong sex, they throw them away.'

'Of course they don't!' Nikki laughed.

'Of course they do! Sometimes they just throw them away!'

'*Vera!*' Nikki put a protective hand over her stomach. 'I can't understand that. All babies are precious.'

'All babies are a lot of work.' Vera shrugged. 'They make a lot more poo than a dog.'

'Well, I could never do that. Imagine giving your child away.' Nikki turned to Jo. 'Can you imagine doing that, Jo? I mean I know you don't have children, but if you did?'

And Jo tried to smile, she really did, but her mouth would not form the shape. She was here to discuss cakes. Nothing else. Not parents giving children away. Not parents who might not love their children... Aware that her face had frozen, she opened her mouth to speak; nothing came out. Nothing that could get past the rock-hard lump in her throat, the vein in her temple she could feel pulsating.

'I'm not judging!' Nikki panicked. 'Please don't think I am, Jo. Not everyone wants children. I think it's great if a woman makes that decision. Vera hasn't got children either, although—'

'Don't worry,' she said, because she had to put Nikki out of her discomfiture and end the moment. She was also aware of Vera, looking at her.

Nikki blinked, her cheeks flushing with embarrassment. 'I'm sorry...'

'Please don't worry.'

'I didn't mean...'

'*It's fine.*' How many times had she done that? Cut off an embarrassed apology? She'd lost count. She always seemed to be the only person who wasn't uncomfortable with the fact that she didn't have children. But she had no regrets, and right now it was the last thing on her mind. 'We tried,' she said, aiming for a relaxed tone. 'It just didn't happen. Anyway last week my husband left me for someone who it obviously has happened with.'

The blood left Nikki's face.

From the doorway, Vera made a sound like a snake.

'Jo... I'm so sorry.'

'It's alright.' Jo nodded. It wasn't easy to watch someone else's discomfort, but she couldn't have stopped the second half of that sentence even if she'd known it was coming. Which she hadn't. Was it always going to be there? Was it always going to slip out, a last sly punch? They had tried... and they had decided... or at least she'd thought they had. 'It's alright,' she said, as she frowned and set about being busy, taking papers from her bag. There was another part of the sentence that bothered her, that she wanted to forget because it was making it real all over again: *my husband left me.* Because if there was ever a day when she needed someone to come home to, it was today. But this was the confirmation. The first time she'd said the words aloud. She looked up and smiled. 'I'm alright. Really. I mean, I thought he had accept—' But the word was sliced off by a sob that folded her like paper under someone's hand. And then another.

'Fucking hell!' Nikki said.

'Fucking men!' Vera muttered.

Nikki was at her side, arm around her shoulders. 'Jo, I'm so sorry. You should have said. The last thing you need is me and my cake ideas.'

'That's true!' And before anyone could respond, Vera had stubbed out her cigarette and yanked her t-shirt down. 'I'll make coffee,' she said, already at the machine, grinding beans, twisting nozzles, taming it like a cowboy with a rope.

Long silent minutes passed, every one of them increasingly embarrassing. Nikki's hand on her back was so small, but now she'd started, she couldn't stop crying. Every time she thought she had it under control, it started again. And it wasn't for Toby, she knew that. She wasn't crying for him. She was crying for that little girl in the armchair. Why hadn't she been told? Why hadn't anyone told her?

It was only when Vera nudged a cup in front of her that Jo looked up. Nikki had gone. She'd slipped her hand away and left without Jo even noticing. 'Thank you,' she murmured, her hand reaching for the cup.

'Not yet.' Nikki was back. Unscrewing a bottle of whisky, launching a shot of it into the coffee.

Jo's hand went up in a half-hearted attempt to cover the cup.

'You need it,' Nikki said, adding more.

Vera nodded. She was pouring herself a coffee. Nikki dropped a shot in.

'I always need it,' Vera muttered. Her eyes narrowed. 'Is that—'

'Andi's single malt. Yes.' Nikki held the bottle up. 'Last night he said he was too tired to even look at my sketch. That's the third time I've asked him. I'm so sorry,' she said, opening a drawer and dropping the paper out of sight. 'I had no idea.'

'Why would you?' Jo smiled. She took a long sip of coffee and it was warm and intensely rich, twenty years of fermented barley lining her insides like velvet peat. Her head hummed. She felt as if she were floating. She felt as if talk of psychosis and dementia belonged to a dream she had had. She felt as if she was among friends. 'The same day my husband left,' she murmured, 'my mother fell. She's in hospital at the moment. She's...' The floaty feeling evaporated, and unsure of how to continue, she stopped talking.

'The same day?' Vera said.

'I had to go and collect a few things from her house.' Jo looked down at her cup, deflated, as she remembered Bobbi's bungalow. 'It wasn't good. I don't think she's coping very well.' *Coping?* Barely a couple of hours had passed since she'd watched her mother attempt to remember what month it was. 'Anyway!' Nailing a smile in place, she looked up. 'Now, I have to find a nursing home, but there are no places. Not right now at least, and I can't even get care at home. Not immediately... which is what I need. They're planning on discharging her next week. It's difficult. We aren't close. She... I...' *Shut up, Jo! Shut up!* Bright half-moons formed across her palm as she dug her nails in, forcing herself to stop talking.

'Oh, Jo.' Nikki tipped her head to one side.

Jo shrugged. She took a large swig of her coffee. It tasted wonderful. It slipped the latch and opened the door and out came the words. 'Would you like to know what my husband said? Before he left?'

Nikki nodded.

Vera leaned in.

'He said, *we're* having a baby. *We.* Two weeks ago, he was planning on cycling the Swiss Alps. Now it's *we're* having a baby!'

'Men,' Vera muttered, 'have to get in on everything.'

The doorbell rang, cascading chimes that echoed through the spacious hallway and made Jo's ears tingle. No one spoke, and no one moved.

'I'll get it,' Nikki said. And as she left, Vera came around to the kitchen side of the island, topped up Jo's cup with coffee and whisky, and hefted herself onto the stool. 'What are you going to do?' she said, unbuttoning her jeans.

'I don't know.' Dazed, Jo looked at her. Vera was Nikki's cleaner. It wasn't right to be sitting drinking whisky with her while Nikki answered the door. Then again... she took a sip of coffee... Nikki had offered... She took another sip, and Vera was the type of woman she felt she could sit and drink whisky with all day.

'She can't go home?'

'Not without full-time care, which isn't available right now.'

'I can help.' Vera slapped her palm onto the counter. 'I'll come. Until you can get something in place, I'll do it.'

'No!' In horror, Jo's jaw fell slack, visions of all the wives and girlfriends of Andi's colleagues, all those prospective clients melting away. No one would touch her, if she was poaching Vera. Which she wasn't! It hadn't been her suggestion. 'No,' she managed again. 'Vera, that's very kind of you but...'

'Listen.' Vera leaned across, her voice low and conspiratorial. 'I need a break from that idiot husband of hers. And it will do Nikki good. She might even learn to use her coffee machine.'

'*No, Vera. I—*'

But Vera was sliding off the stool and buttoning her jeans, as if it was decided. She smiled, a flash of gold revealing an expensive-looking filling. 'I did this work back in Estonia. I know what to do. Don't worry about Nikki. When do you want me to start? Monday?'

But before she could answer, Nikki returned.

'I'm going to help Jo with her mother,' Vera said. She was at the sink now, rinsing her cup. 'From Monday, yes?'

'I...' She couldn't answer. First her husband, then her mother, now her business? Cold panic ran through her veins.

And stranded in the middle of her vast kitchen, Nikki's face registered both surprise and fear, but not, Jo saw, anything like the annoyance she might have expected. 'Are *you* OK with that?' she said as she turned to Jo.

No, she wasn't OK with it. And yes, it would solve at least one of her immediate problems. She managed to shake her head and nod, at the same time.

'Who was at the door?' Vera said.

'My tarot card reader.'

'Exactly,' Vera grunted. 'You can manage a week, Nikki.' And picking up her spray cleaner, she left.

Jo sat, newly sober. Whatever Nikki was thinking about being bulldozed like this, she was hiding it well. The situation was astonishing. Vera had acted as if she were the employer, and Nikki the employee. On the one hand, she was desperate to secure care for Bobbi, on the other she was desperate to stay in Nikki's good books. 'Vera just asked me to think about it,' she said, hands in the air. 'It wasn't my idea, Nikki. She's your cleaner. The last thing I'd—'

'Vera's my sister, Jo. She's been telling me what to do since I was born!' Nikki's face lit up with a wide, uncomplicated smile. 'You'd better get used to it! She can be bossy. Anyway...' She paused, her smile fading as she added. 'I think she should go. She hasn't been happy lately. She doesn't get on with Andi.'

'Oh.' Jo looked towards the door, where Vera had gone. Not getting on well with Andi was something she could easily imagine... and sympathise with. But... *sisters?* Nikki and Vera were so different.

'Anyway,' Nikki shrugged. 'It seems to me that you need the help more than I do right now.'

Her throat was tight with emotion. She blinked, embarrassed to realise she was tearing up again. She was supposed to be the grown up here, Nikki the child, the believer in unicorns. 'Yes,' she managed. 'I think I do.'

14

There was no sound of taps running in the kitchen downstairs, no soft babble of sports commentary from the radio, no footsteps back and forth. Her hands had wrinkled to prunes, and her knees were rubber. The silence of her house was so complete that she could hear the soap bubbles as they creaked and popped on her stomach. She pushed the soles of her feet flat against the bathtub and raised a leg out of the water toward the open window. It was a strange feeling, the coolness of evening air against the warmth of the water. But at least it was a feeling.

The drive home had been another deep ravine of calm. Inside, she'd dumped her bag, poured a glass of Chardonnay and run the bath. An hour ago? She didn't know, she was losing hours as fast as her mother was. Slipping into the warm, scented water had been like slipping into another dimension, so much that easing herself up now to reach for her wine was an effort she wasn't sure she could complete. But she did and as she did, a clumping sound had her turning to the open doorway. The noise had come from downstairs. Knees to chest, she sat very still. A loud ringing silence was all that answered.

She slipped back into the water, cold wine on her tongue. Her mother had lost a baby and had a breakdown and left. Her husband was having a baby and he too, had left. It was almost comical. Except it wasn't. It wasn't in the slightest bit funny.

The thumping sound came again, and this time she could feel the change of air, a fresher front drifting up the stairs that raised goosebumps along her arms. The front door of the house was open, she was sure of it. Wine sloshed as she put the glass down and clambered out. Dripping water, she grabbed a towel and dashed onto the landing.

Toby stood on the top step, keys in hand.

'You could have rung the bell!' she shouted, and the towel flapped as she struggled to cover herself.

'I still have a key, Jo.'

He looked confused. He had, she thought as she stared at him, the temerity to actually look confused. Water ran down her neck and as she took a corner of towel to blot it, the other corner fell, exposing her again. 'What do you want?' she said, turning away.

'Jo. It's just me.'

But it wasn't just him. Not any more. A week ago she would have walked past him, naked as the day she was born. And he would have done the same. Her throat went hard with grief, her eyes scalding hot. She was angry, and she was embarrassed. He had left her for someone else and the rules meant that she had to turn away, that he should have knocked, that it wasn't *just him* any more and it never would be again. Her shoulders were rigid with hurt.

'I'm sorry.' Toby muttered, stepping back. 'I've been ringing you. I assumed you'd be at work.'

'Maybe I didn't feel like answering.'

He stood aside as she went into the bedroom and shut the door. 'I've been at the hospital,' she said through the closed door, pulling on a pair of leggings and a t-shirt. The top had no support and catching sight of herself in the mirror, she yanked it off, put on a bra and pulled it back on. 'Why are you here?' she snapped, opening the door.

'I came to pick up some things. Clothing and stuff.' He looked like a boy caught stealing sweets.

The corners of Jo's mouth turned down. 'You'd better come in then.'

15

Downstairs in the kitchen she topped up her glass and stood listening to his footsteps criss-crossing the bedroom, traversing the landing, into the bathroom... for his *stuff*. If she could, she would have taken her keys, gotten in the car and driven away. But she'd already had a full glass and anyway, where would she go? And who would she go to? Who would she empty the contents of this day onto? It was, she considered as she watched her reflection in the window, one of the reasons why she hadn't yet told Diane. What was the point? Especially when she hadn't worked out how to deal with today herself. She raised her glass to her reflection, in a lone *salu*. 'Cheers, Jo,' she said grimly.

'I'm sorry about earlier.' Toby's voice broke her reverie.

'Do you have everything?' He was standing in the doorway holding a large canvas bag.

'For now. Is it OK if I come back tomorrow?'

She shrugged. 'It's your house, Toby.'

'You know what I mean.' There was a note of patience in

his voice, patronising patience, as if he was talking to a child. *It really is past your bedtime. You know what I mean.*

'Are you asking my permission?' she prodded, and when he didn't answer, added, 'Well you have it, just be prepared that I might change my mind. Like you changed yours.'

'Don't.'

'Why not?'

'Because…' He let the bag drop. 'I didn't want to hurt you, Jo.'

'No? Well. You have.'

Neither of them spoke. Toby stood looking at the ground, and Jo stood looking out of the window. Half of her wanted him to go, to leave her alone to her wine and her empty house. The other half wanted him to take his shoes off and sit down, to tell her he was back, it wasn't real, she wasn't alone. 'I was at the hospital earlier,' she said, still looking out of the window.

'How is your mother?' His voice was quiet.

Jo turned. 'Not good. They're saying it's dementia. She doesn't know what month it is.'

'I'm sorry, Jo. That's hard.'

Teeth clenched, jaw set, she managed a tight nod. She wouldn't cry, not in front of him. But no one knew her like he did. So many years, more than half her life, she'd slept alongside him, woken up to him. Monday through Sunday, over and again. It wasn't fair that he was leaving her, that he'd sliced off this part of his life as easy as if he were slicing fruit. But who else was there? 'I found out something today.' Her voice was a whisper. 'When I was a child, my mother was admitted into a psychiatric hospital.'

'Admitted?' Toby paused. 'A psychiatric hospital? Admitted into a psychiatric hospital?' For a long moment, he didn't speak and then in a voice laced with kindness, he said,

'We're still friends, Jo. We'll always be friends. Do you want to talk about it?'

'Yes,' she said, looking down at her wine glass. 'I do.'

He went to the cupboard and took his own glass and Jo watched as he filled it, put the bottle down and sat on the stool opposite.

Tears fell. It was exactly what she'd wanted him to do. She took a tea towel and wiped her face.

'Are you OK?' And now he was on his feet, moving towards her.

'I'm OK,' she said, as she edged back. He couldn't touch her. She couldn't allow him to hold her, and then watch him leave again. She couldn't do that. She put her glass down and turned to her handbag. 'Don't ask me who it is,' she said as she handed the photo over. 'Because I don't know. But Bobbi had a breakdown about six months after it was born.' She didn't add, that's why she left. She didn't say, *that's where she was when I was just a child, sitting at home, hoping she wouldn't be coming back.*

Toby stared at the photo.

'The doctor thinks it was maybe Bobbi's baby, and that it died. He said she had a postpartum psychosis.'

'I don't know what to say, JoJo—'

'Please,' she whispered, dipping her head and pinching her nose. 'Please don't call me that.' And now she was glad she hadn't said everything.

Slowly, Toby put the photo down. 'OK,' he said quietly, and paused. 'Is there a way you can find out?'

'Find out what? If I had a brother, or sister? She can't remember what she had for breakfast, Toby. How am I going to ask her about things that happened over forty years ago?'

'Is it that bad?'

'Yes,' she sighed. 'Yes, it's that bad. I can't ask her about anything. The day you left, I'd been at her bungalow, and I know they're right. She has dementia. I can't ask her.'

Toby lowered his chin. 'I didn't time it that way.'

'No.' Turning from him, she moved to the window. It was hard to fathom the language they had fallen into so naturally. *The day you left. I didn't want to hurt you.* The past tense, to describe what had until so recently been a continuous present. Past-perfect, actually, because the action was completed and done. He *had* left. 'It's too late,' she said to the window, and she was talking about her mother, and her marriage. It was all too late. Behind, she heard the gentle clank as Toby put his glass down on the marble countertop. The marble countertop they had chosen together, in the house they had chosen together, a forever home that had lasted five minutes, that she wouldn't be able to afford to stay in.

'Perhaps this could be an opportunity to try and get to know her?'

It was the words he used! The man who had been her husband, but had decided he wasn't, sitting here in a house he'd left, but still let himself into, telling her what her opportunities were. She turned to face him. 'You've never understood, Toby.'

He didn't answer immediately and when he did, his voice was quiet. 'Well,' he said, 'I guess you've made your mind up.'

'What is that supposed to mean?'

Shaking his head, Toby sighed. 'It doesn't matter.'

Jo looked at him. He'd walked out of their marriage without so much as a backward glance, let alone an explanation. And now suddenly, here it was. The crack. The small shaft of light she was hellbent on forcing her way through. 'It does matter. Tell me what you mean.'

'Alright.' He paused. 'Alright, I'll say it. The fact that Bobbi has dementia makes no difference. You decided years ago that your relationship with your mother was beyond repair.'

'It was.'

He didn't speak.

'It was, Toby!'

'You're so defensive about it. You always have been. Maybe... just maybe, you could have kept trying. Maybe you could now, but you won't. You're too stubborn, Jo. Once you make a decision, you won't change your mind.'

'*Stubborn.*' Jo nodded, a slow warm anger rising. 'I had a very hard childhood, Toby. You know that! And I chose to focus on the positive. Most people would find that admirable. Most people wouldn't call that stubborn. It's OK to go around changing your mind, if you have options. *I didn't!*' But the tender hurt was tearing itself free. She *had* focused on the positive; what else was she supposed to have done?

'I know,' he said. 'I know.' His shoulders had rounded and he looked exhausted as he raised a hand and waved it at the kitchen, at the string of fairy lights across the window. 'There's a party for every occasion. A few twinkling lights. Cupcakes.'

A few twink... Jo put her hand to her chest, her heart pumping. 'There bloody well is a party for every occasion and I'm making a living from it, Toby! Which is a good job, all things considered!'

Hands in his pockets, Toby looked at her. 'Don't you ever get tired of it, Jo?'

'*Of what?*'

'All the parties. The pretence.'

'Who,' she gasped, 'is pretending?'

'You are, Jo. *You* are. The birthday parties every year. It could never be a quiet thing. And now you're doing it for a living. It's like every party you organise for other people is compensation for every party you never had. You told me about your eighteenth. About the card she sent that was late. The second-class stamp. And I was there on our wedding day, remember? You, me and the two women we dragged from the florist shop to be witnesses. I can't even remember their names. I'm not sure I ever knew. It was so quick, even my parents couldn't make it.'

'And you were OK with that,' she whispered.

'At the time.' He stared at the floor. 'At the time.'

'Angie and Louise.'

Toby looked up.

'It was Angie's shop. She'd only been open a month.'

'Right. Angie and Louise. You probably know more about them than your...' But he didn't finish. He thrust his hands deep in his pockets, his head shaking as he picked up his glass and took a long sip.

Jo didn't speak. All the confessions she'd ever made to him about her childhood that he'd so casually hurled back had left her unstable. 'People like parties,' she whispered. '*I* like parties.'

Toby raised his head. 'People like celebrating *nothing*, Jo, with cupcakes to match. It's all just to cover up the fact that their lives are empty. Maybe...' He paused, his eyes glassy with unshed tears. 'Maybe that's why I left.'

Her hand was still on her chest, but her lungs felt as if they had seized. She couldn't get them to open and fill and every gasp passed empty. So that was why. He'd left because he thought their lives were empty.

'That's not fair...' She scratched the sound out. 'If it's

about... If it's because... *We* decided, Toby. We decided that if it didn't happen, it didn't happen. You said—'

'No. *You* said it, Jo. *You decided. You* said that. Not me. I never said that.' He stared across the kitchen. 'If we could have just talked about it.'

'We were happy,' Jo whispered. It was a plea. 'You were happy, Toby. We decided it was for the best.'

'No.' Toby shook his head. 'I wasn't happy, Jo. I haven't been happy for a long time.' He lifted his hand and waved it at the kitchen. 'Fairy lights don't make people happy. They never have.'

16

Bobbi worried her free hand at her cheek, her head shaking as she said, once again, 'I don't want a stranger in my house. I don't want it.'

Leaning back in her chair, Jo took a deep breath and looked at Dr Dandicott. The conversation was going around in circles, she was exhausted with it. With everything. Two days ago she'd arrived at her mother's bungalow, a takeaway coffee in one hand, mop and bucket in the other. A brush, rubber gloves, bin-liners, crates of cleaning products, a portable speaker, strings of fairy lights and her solar butterflies in the car. The butterflies were already in Bobbi's garden. She could barely tolerate her own loneliness, let alone theirs.

Forty-eight hours of rubbing grime from light-switches and door-handles, scraping away dried dirt from window sills and floors, vacuuming, sweeping. She'd been shopping. Bought a new kettle and toaster, a new doormat and bright new place mats. She'd had handrails installed by the front and back entrances. And as she had worked, his words had replayed over and over... *You're too stubborn, Jo... You're too stubborn...*

The second time he had left had been worse than the first. The silence had been louder, the bed bigger, the bathroom cabinet so much emptier. She'd sat in an armchair in the gloom of twilight watching the empty driveway. And as she sat, the child she had once been had kept company. Was this it, she thought? Was this her destiny? To always be the one left behind? And when she'd worn herself out with questions that couldn't be answered, she'd gone to her too-big bed, nursing grievances like a child nurses a toy.

But the next morning, she had woken to a kaleidoscopic display of colour as the sun picked up and threw back the reds, blues and greens of the butterfly wings. Putting her hands behind her head and watching the display, she thought two things at once. First, she hadn't known. She'd bought the butterflies as solar lights, and she hadn't known they would reflect in sunlight. And second, Toby was very wrong. Sometimes a little light was exactly what was needed.

By the time she'd made coffee, the idea had set. She would accept Vera's offer of help. For this first week at least, Vera could take the daytime shift and she would move in with her mother and be there for the evenings. In this way, and at least until her mother's finances were sorted, she was looking at a lot less than a thousand pounds a week. An awful lot less.

She'd spent an hour on the phone with someone from the Alzheimer's Society who had pointed the way to a hundred different tricks that would, she promised, make life easier for both of them. It had been the emphasis the woman had put on *both of them* that had worried Jo. As if she knew something

Jo didn't. In place of the post-it notes, laminated photos of each cupboard's contents were now taped in place. The bathroom taps had red and blue stickers, and there was a tray on the hall table with compartments clearly marked: *Post; Keys.* A note on the new toaster: *7 for toast.* The address and telephone number of the house printed out and sellotaped to the hall mirror. *It will help her to remain independent,* she'd been advised. *And stick to simple questions. Yes and no answers.*

17

'I'll be fine,' Bobbi said again. The third, or fourth time? Jo had stopped counting. 'It's not necessary.'

She let her eyes close, dry and heavy.

It was unnecessary. She'd never heard of anything so unnecessary. Jo had her own life. She didn't want a stranger in her house. Had anyone considered that? And so on and so on...

Her mother simply would not accept the common factor. She fell because the pavement was uneven, she forgot to put a teabag in the cup because the physiotherapist was talking too much, she hadn't missed midnight on the clock, there just hadn't been enough space. This last explanation had left Jo open mouthed. Father Time, the irrefutable dimension under which they all existed had apparently bent himself out of shape while no one was looking, had done away completely with the need for midnight. It wasn't her mother who was wrong. It was time itself.

Everything was ready at the bungalow, everything was in place. Everything except Bobbi.

'Think of it as a compromise.' Dr Dandicott smiled. 'It

will take some adjustment. Someone there through the day. But you'll be home again.'

Jo opened her eyes. She could have hugged him.

'These conversations are difficult,' the doctor continued. Pulling a tissue from the box on his desk, he handed it to Bobbi. 'But this way,' he said, 'you will be home.'

Jo could barely look. She kept her chin lowered and her eyes down, as beside her Bobbi folded the tissue and dabbed, folded and dabbed. Beyond a vague awareness that Bobbi might resist these new arrangements, she had tried not to think about how she might react: that instant weekly care bill had trumped everything. Feelings – neither her own, nor her mother's – had come into it. Not much. Right now, this was the only solution. Correction. As far as the rest of the world went, this was the only acceptable solution. Because she could have closed her eyes, and covered her ears, and turned her back and left her mother to sink or swim alone. And so many of her thoughts were still bound up in that *what would happen if I just...?* She hadn't found an answer yet. Not one she could live with. And it had her wondering how Bobbi had been able to. Because she'd never explained herself and she had done exactly that: left her only child to work it out by herself. Why hadn't Bobbi ever told her about the hospital? About the baby? Listening now to her mother's subdued sobs, Jo felt uncomfortable. She shifted her weight and re-crossed her legs. A part of her wanted to reach a hand out to Bobbi. Just not a big enough part.

There was a soft rap on the door and almost immediately it opened. A woman wearing the pale blue tunic of a nurse leaned into the room. 'So sorry to disturb,' she said, looking at the doctor. 'I just need your signature for a discharge. It won't take a moment.'

Dr Dandicott nodded. 'I won't be long,' he said and tucking his glasses into his coat pocket, he left.

Jo didn't speak. And Bobbi didn't speak. And for the longest minute in the world, they sat alongside each other, the second hand of the clock the only sound.

'Mum,' she tried. Because someone had to say something. 'I know—'

But she was cut off by Bobbi turning in her chair. 'I'm best off on my own, Joanne. I know where everything is. If I put something down, it'll still be there.'

Jo sighed. They'd been through this. 'It's not just that, though, is it?' she said. 'You heard the doctor earlier. It can be dangerous. What if you leave the gas on?'

'I'll buy a numbers-face.'

'A numbers-face? What do you mean?'

'A thing...' Bobbi brought her hand to her face, tracing the line of her brow as she said 'A thing for measuring... a...'

'A timer?' She watched as her mother turned away, neither confirming nor denying that this was what she meant. 'I want to help,' she said quietly.

Bobbi shook her head. 'I've lived on my own for a long time, Joanne. It's better that way.' Staring across the room, her eyes glazed. 'It's for the best.'

A shiver of *déjà vu* crept along her arms, pushing up goosebumps. Once upon a time, she was sure, there had been a similar scene, where her mother had said similar words. *I'm better off on my own.* What she didn't know, what she couldn't remember, was if she had asked, or if Bobbi had just told her. She would have been young, still a child. And it would have been on one of those difficult weekend visits. Either way, that had been the only explanation. *It's for the best.*

'I know that's what you think,' Jo said, and her words

were sharp and quick with resentment, the adult she was now doggedly giving voice to that child. 'But you heard Dr Dandicott. He'll only approve the discharge with this care plan in place. You either need care at home, or we'll have to find a placement. A care home. It's already been decided.'

Bobbi turned. Her face, already pale, paled again. 'Who?' she said. 'Who has decided this?'

'The doctor.' Jo paused. She swallowed. 'And me.'

'You?'

Helplessly she glanced at the partially open door, but there was no sign of Dr Dandicott to help her along, to hold her hand.

Bobbi sat there, the dry skin on her good hand whispering as she rubbed her thumb across her fingertips. The knuckles were white, bulging and bent out of shape with the swan-necked deformities of arthritis. 'You would do that?' she said. 'You would decide for me? Put me in a home?'

'If it came to that.' But her mother's stare was a blowtorch, and she could feel her edges melting.

'I have a home.'

'I know.' It was an effort to keep her voice steady, to smooth the irritation out. She was tired and she wasn't a child any more, and this time her mother didn't get to decide. 'But until we can come to other arrangements, I'll be in the spare room and, as we have already explained, Vera will come during the day.'

'I have a home,' Bobbi whispered. 'And I won't go into an institution, Joanne. *Ever.*'

The soft syllables of that unforgiving word settled between them like cold snow: *institution.* Jo felt the chill. There were two people in this room, but only one of them understood what institution meant. And it wasn't her. As she had held the tangy sweetness of toffee apple on her tongue, it had been her mother who was learning what it meant to live in a place where someone else decided when and what you ate, when and where you slept, how you spent your time. Painstakingly slow, she unfolded her fingers and inched her hand towards Bobbi. 'I promise,' she said as her fingertips brushed her mother's, 'that any decisions made will be in your best interests.'

Bobbi didn't move.

Feeling the lightness of static between her mother's hand and her own, Jo took a deep breath. 'And perhaps,' she said, 'to make things easier in the future, we can set up something more formal. I'd be able to help you. Make decisions that are getting difficult. Like banking or—'

Before she could finish, Bobbi had snatched her hand back. 'That's what he said.' Her voice was strong and clear. 'That it was in my best interests... But I won't be put in an institution, Joanne. I won't let it happen again. And if you think you can force me, if you think you can decide for me, like he did, you're wrong.'

18

Standing in the spare bedroom, Jo dropped her bag onto the single bed and looked across at the wardrobe where as a child she would unpack her weekend bag. Bobbi's words haunted the room. *If you think you can force me... like he did...* It didn't seem possible that her father could have ever forced anyone to do anything. He hadn't even blinked when she'd come home after the first term at university and told him she wanted to change course. *It's your choice.* That's what he'd said. That's all he had said. It was the drink that had rendered him indifferent, she'd known it then and she knew it now and she simply couldn't remember a time when she would ever have described him as forceful. She unzipped her bag and looked at the contents, but it was too much. The bag, and her past.

Bobbi's bag was still by the front door.

'I'll take this through to your room,' Jo said as she went into the kitchen, but her mother didn't answer. She was staring at the cupboards, her head following the photographs like a cat follows a bird. Bowls and cups, for the crockery cupboard. Saucepans. Tumblers. And watching, Jo felt a sense of pride that she'd taken the time to follow the advice so thoroughly. They looked good, they looked clear.

In her mother's bedroom, she went over to the chest of drawers, pausing as she opened the top drawer. Along with the photograph, she still had the envelope with the lock of hair. She hadn't put either of them back, and as the nurse had handed Bobbi her handbag, Jo had watched as her mother had looked through. Would she even know what was missing? And if so, would she ask? And then how would Jo answer? Start the conversation she'd already had countless times in her head. *Who is it, Mum?* She reached her arms up and let the nightie in her hands unfold, shook it out and re-folded it. That imagined scene felt as impossible as catching the freed dust motes that swirled up to the ceiling.

As she closed the drawer, she heard Bobbi's voice, shrill and angry at someone... or something. She rushed through to the kitchen, where her mother was tearing at one of the laminated photographs, the fingers of her free hand scrabbling as she pulled at the plastic. 'I won't have,' she was saying. 'I won't have it!'

'Mum.' Moving across, Jo reached up and pressed the sellotape back in place. 'Don't.' Gently, she eased Bobbi's hand aside. 'It's just a memory aid. To help you remember where everything is.'

'What have you done?' And moving faster than Jo could have anticipated, Bobbi was at the next cupboard, scrabbling and reaching, shaking her head. 'I won't have these everywhere.' She turned to another cupboard and opened it, the crumpled photo in her hand. 'Where has the bin gone? Where have you put the bin?'

'The bin—' Jo's hands went cold. 'The bin is here, Mum,' she said, opening the cupboard underneath the sink. 'The bin is *here,* where it's always been.' And she stood and watched as her mother stuffed the photo into the bin.

With the slam of the cupboard door, a new silence crept in. Bobbi one end of the kitchen, Jo facing her at the other. She could still go home. Back to an empty house, where no one was waiting for her, leave Bobbi alone to not remember to lock the door, or turn the gas ring off, or add cold to a scalding-hot bath.

'I forgot,' Bobbi said, and she looked down at the bin as if she'd never seen it before. 'I'm tired. I forgot.'

'I know,' Jo covered her eyes with her hands. Me too, she wanted to say. I'm exhausted too, Mum.

19

Later, with Bobbi lying down for a rest, Jo went into the garden, to get some fresh air, to find some space to wonder again at what she was doing. It didn't seem real, this arrangement. And it certainly didn't seem plausible. Not like it had in the neat sterile atmosphere of the doctor's room. She'd escaped, hadn't she. Emerging like a chrysalis from the loneliness of her childhood. Spreading wings, to fly to the furthest corner of the globe for years at a time. Standing by the back fence, arms crossed, she breathed in deep and deliberate. Duty – and what else was it? – found everyone in the end.

Across the lawn, behind the tangle of brambles and bindweed, a lilac tree stretched unruly arms of feathery purple. Daises and dandelions had seeded the grass, weaving their white and gold like embroidery upon cloth. Nettles abounded; the hydrangea had grown spindly. Only the border of lavender, with the beginnings of purple spikes, seemed to have maintained a degree of cultivation. She lifted her face to the sun, the floral, slightly camphorous scent of lavender filling her nostrils. She could cut some. A bunch of lavender for the table. Dr Dandicott had said there was no natural order in which things happened. Maybe the lavender could start the talking, and she could listen.

But the stalks were woody, and it took her a long five minutes to saw through them with the only thing she could find, a blunt pair of scissors. By the time she'd tugged and yanked a generous handful, sweat had broken out all along her spine. She stood up, and as she did an alarm ripped the air, so sudden and so urgent it made her arms go weak. She couldn't work out where it was coming from, turning confused half-circles, until, tilting her head towards the kitchen door, it became clear. She rushed towards it, the alarm growing ever louder, ever more urgent. As she pushed the door open, black smoke billowed out and the alarm screamed a crescendo.

'*Mum!*'

Bobbi was standing in front of the toaster, pressing the lever down, again and again, carbonised toast popping up, again and again. Down, up, down, up. It was like watching a child with a toy.

In two strides she was across the kitchen, flinging the stalks onto the table and grabbing her mother's arm. 'What are you doing?'

Again, Bobbi pressed the lever down.

'It's done, Mum!' Again, she yanked her mother's arm away. '*It's done!*'

'It doesn't work. I can't get it to work.'

'*It's done!*'

The shouting – *her* shouting – broke the trance. Bobbi turned, her eyes pulsing fear. 'Make it stop,' she said, and covered her ear with her good hand. 'Make it stop.'

'I will... I...' She dragged a chair across the room and clambered on, stretching for the alarm. 'Don't touch the toaster!' But Bobbi had backed as far from the toaster as she could.

Jo's hands fumbled and the sweat freckling at her back had turned into a stream. It pooled under her arms, and dripped from her hairline. Even her knees were sweating, and still the bloody alarm would not twist off! With every second that passed, and every screech, her arms doubled in weight. They ached and cramped and she couldn't think straight and she couldn't get the battery free.

'*Make it stop*,' Bobbi cried.

'*I'm trying!*' she cried back.

She gave it one last twist. The cover came off and as she popped the battery free, her nail split down to the skin. She stood, finger in her mouth, dampening the sting. At this height she had a clear view of the street. Two boys walked past, school uniforms on, gold-striped ties, their heads down as they studied their phones. She took a deep breath, her heart slowing, a cold drip running down her calf. 'I *said*,' she snapped, as she thrust the chair back in place, 'that *I* would make a sandwich. What on earth were you doing? Plus!' She turned and pointed at the toaster. 'It says *seven for toast!* What were you doing?'

'You left.'

'I just went to the garden! I told you that!'

'To the garden?'

'I told you!'

'I thought you had left,' Bobbi said. 'I was hungry.'

'You can't do that!' She paused, pushing damp hair from her forehead as she looked at Bobbi, so small in the corner. 'Your memory isn't...' Her words dried up. The headlamps of her mother's stare were so intense she had to turn away. What was she going to say anyway? List all the things Bobbi couldn't do any more? She had no idea of what her mother was still capable of, and more to the point, neither did her mother.

20

Long difficult hours later, with Bobbi asleep, Jo lay in the single bed of the spare room, staring at the ceiling. She was thinking of her own house. The moonlit expanse of a bed no one was sleeping in, the clean polished surface of a table no one sat at. They'd only bought it a year ago. A place, after years of globe-trotting, to call home. A place she would grow her business from. And she had. But worlds fell apart as quickly as they were built. That day she had sat in Nikki Lembit's drive, victorious, happy, about to buy champagne was a lifetime away. Through her open window she could hear the small night-time chatter of voices passing on the street outside. She rolled onto her side and covered her face with her hands. She was nearly forty-nine years old, sleeping in a single bed, in the spare room of her mother's house. It wasn't where she had ever imagined herself to be. It wasn't where she wanted to be. The future had gone dark. Tears ran down her cheek into the pillow, cold. And through the smallest gap in the curtains, soft reds, blues and greens of the solar butterflies shone their light.

21

When she said we it was just like he used to, he made decisions for me. She said in your best interests like he did. I don't want to argue with Joanne, but she doesn't understand that I'll never let it happen again. I remember the ceiling, domed like a church. There were no pictures on the walls, there was no lock on the bathroom. I remember an arched window, looking out at the world outside. They took my clothes and they told me when to go to bed and when to eat and there was nowhere to go to be alone. There was noise and crying all night. No one understands. If it hasn't happened to you, how can you understand how it feels to lose everything like that, to have to earn the reward just of going outside into the sunshine.

She's asleep across the hallway, in her old room that I chose for her. When she came to visit, I thought she would like to lie in bed and look at the garden. I knew how she loved the cottage The open spaces didn't scare her like they scared me. Perhaps she was too young to be scared. Two years old when we moved there and growing up brave. A cabbage field wasn't going to change that, but I hated it. The land was so flat and the skies were so big. I never knew what loneliness was until I lived there. Some days, in fact most days, it was just me and the land and the sky. Here, there's a streetlamp outside my bedroom window, and the bus runs all hours. Tonight I'll fall asleep to the sounds of traffic and it makes me feel safe, knowing I can open the door and there will be people. Why did he move us so far away from everything? Why wouldn't he let me learn to drive? Why did I stay? Marrying him was the biggest mistake of my life. I used to think about that a lot. And then I didn't, and now I'm beginning to think about it again. In the leaflets they've given me about dementia what I keep reading is dementia is like losing yourself. That's what I keep reading. As if that's something I should be scared of. But I'm not afraid because I feel that already happened a long time ago.

I can't hear her breathing. When she was a child, I would stand outside the bedroom door and listen to the sound of her breathing. I have a feeling it was because I needed to check she was still there. That doesn't sound right. When I read it back, it doesn't sound right at all, but it's the way I remember my life now, in feelings not words, and in pictures not names. She's tired, I can see it in her eyes. I burnt the toast. But there's something else. She won't tell me. She's never been able to tell me things, and I've never found a way of telling her. I know there are twelve numbers on the clock, and if I had had more time, I would have remembered where they all went. I know that if the lavender is in bloom, it is May. It will always be May. I don't know why I said September. I've written it down now, and put the note on my bedside table.

22

Coffee in one hand, toast in the other, Jo stood at the living room window, watching as Vera got out of her car and hitched her jeans up. She was showered, dressed and ready to go. She didn't need to be. She didn't have any appointments in the diary. No new venues to scout, no menu-tasting with Jules, her caterer. But her phone was charged, her handbag waiting by the front door. She couldn't have stayed even if she had wanted to. 'Vera's here,' she called, swallowing the last mouthful of toast with coffee still so hot it burnt her mouth. Bobbi didn't respond. She was in the kitchen eating the cereal Jo had laid out, a prickly *good morning* the only conversation between them. She was, Jo knew, still utterly resistant to the arrangements. 'I'll let her in,' she called. A quick introduction. That was all that was needed. She'd written out a list of instructions longer than her arm. As she opened the front door, she noticed the greasy thumbprint she left. She'd been in too much of a hurry to even wipe her hands.

'Are you're sure you feel you can cope?'

Vera, whom she had steered along the hall, and into the

living room, was flushed. Her cheeks a high pink, as if just the walk from the car had winded her. How, Jo thought as she watched Vera collapse into a chair, was she going to cope with Bobbi all day?

'Of course.' Vera waved a hand of dismissal. 'I've worked with many elderly people. More than you, I should think.'

'Well, I won't disagree with that.' Lowering herself onto the arm of the settee, Jo smiled. Vera was as direct and accurate as an armed missile. 'My experience is zero.' My patience even less, she didn't say. 'I had no idea you and Nikki were sisters.' She had time for a little small talk. Right now, Vera was invaluable.

'You didn't know?'

'No.'

Vera shrugged. 'No one believes it. They look at Nikki and they look at me... I can't understand how they find it so difficult.'

'I can't either!' Jo laughed, the first time she had in days. 'Why are you...' Her voice trailed off. She'd started a question without thinking about the answer.

'Why am I cleaning for her?' Vera finished.

'It's none of my business.'

'But you want to know?'

Another laugh. 'Of course I do!'

And another shrug. 'Nikki got rich,' Vera said. 'Well, that idiot she married got rich because he can kick a ball.' Leaning back, she undid the button of her jeans. 'Sorry. I shouldn't have worn these. I have to lose some weight. Everything cuts me in half.'

'Me too.' Jo smiled. With every moment, she was liking Vera more and more.

'He got the transfer here, and Nikki asked me to come. I said yes. But...' Vera lifted a finger. 'I said yes before I shared a house with *him*. If I'd known what a selfish, *silly* man he is…' The corners of her mouth turned down. 'Trust me, Jo. You are doing me a *big* favour. It was this, or a one-way ticket home and Nikki knew that. At least this way, I'm still in the same country.'

'I see.' She did see. If Vera was happy, then Nikki was happy. And if Nikki was happy, she would keep throwing parties, with lots of friends, and Jo could keep paying her mortgage. *Start* paying her mortgage. 'Well, you saved my life this week,' she said, and she meant it. 'It's going to be very easy. Bobbi isn't helpless, but her memory is bad and of course with her arm, she is very restricted in what she can do. I'll be home for dinner in the evenings, so you don't have to cook.'

'No cooking?' Vera's face fell.

'Well… I mean you can if you want to.'

'I want to. Andi doesn't like me to cook.'

'Then go ahead.' Breaking into a wide smile, Jo shrugged. 'Bobbi likes to eat, so I'm sure it will work out fine.' Her mother's appetite was the one thing that didn't seem to be failing. Last night, as Bobbi had devoured a huge plate of fish and chips, Jo had watched, astonished, marvelling at the way the body seemed to remember when the mind forgot. If Vera cooked, it would be one less obligation. And that was the right word, because her own appetite had packed up and left. Which was no bad thing. 'Oh, and she will need help with a bath,' she said standing up. 'The discharge nurse wants her to keep a daily routine, and she can't shower at the moment because of her arm. I hope you're comfortable with that?' This last part of her very brief job description she delivered without eye contact, picking at an invisible thread on her blouse. Bathing someone, or at least helping them to bathe, seemed such a big thing to ask.

Still, it was easier than Jo attempting to do it herself. How could she help Bobbi like that, when they could barely touch fingertips? The task required a professional. Or a different kind of daughter. Or a different kind of mother.

'Of course.'

The swiftness of Vera's response had her looking back up.

'Well then,' she said, and her laugh was too high, because in the face of this formidable woman she was beginning to feel silly. She buttoned up her jacket. If Vera had done this kind of work before, of course she wouldn't flinch. 'You're better equipped to deal with my mother than I am,' she said lightly.

'I agree.'

Vera hadn't even bothered with a veneer of politeness, and now Jo felt as uncomfortable as she had with Dr Dandicott. As if the whole world knew how woefully inadequate she was. And she wanted to shout it from the rooftops. It isn't my fault, this situation I find myself in! She stood up. 'I'm afraid I have an appointment I need to get to. Shall I introduce you? Give you a quick tour?'

Vera too, stood.

'Oh, and no toast.'

'No toast?'

'Under no circumstances is my mother allowed to make toast.'

23

Everything she needed for the next week she had brought with her to Bobbi's bungalow. Nipping back to her own house, for a box of supplies, or a file, wasn't something she'd anticipated being able to face. Forward thinking she was thankful for now. She had her laptop and charger in her bag. She could find a sunny corner in a quiet coffee shop and get on with her life.

But forty minutes and half a sneaked bag of chocolate animal biscuits later, she'd completed the few brief jobs that needed immediate attention. She'd opened the sample envelope from China, only to find a banner that read *Happy 18nd Birthday*. And she'd fired off an email to the care home Dr Dandicott had recommended. Now she was slouched back in her chair, scrolling through the memories Facebook had picked out.

On this day five years ago.

It was a photo of her and Toby, on the beach in Malaysia. He had his arm wrapped around her shoulders. He didn't look unhappy.

She stretched her arms to her table-edge and looked out

of the window. People passing to and fro. Talking to other people. Busy. But apart from preliminary bookings for an engagement party, the kind of low-budget rinse and repeat event she'd been doing for years, there was nothing urgent in her diary and the day rose up now, sudden and empty as a hidden canyon. She'd been so focused, so intent on getting away from the bungalow, she didn't have a clue how to fill the hours.

She picked her phone up, her hand on autopilot, tapping on his name as it had countless other times.

Hi, it's me. What are you up do? Nothing much. Same here. Just thought I'd ring.

There he was in the middle of her screen. Toby. Husband. Three options: Message. Call. Video

Twenty-five years together and she couldn't do any of them.

She opened up favourites again, hesitating just a moment before she swiped right. Diane had her grand-daughter on a Monday, it wouldn't be fair. She swiped anyway.

'Hello stranger,' Diane answered.

'Sorry, been hectic.'

'Sourcing unicorns?'

'Fancy a coffee?' she said, and it was all she could do to keep the sob out of her voice.

24

The café Diane had suggested was loud, with a soft-play area in the corner. Jo ordered her coffee and took a seat as far away as possible from the towers of brightly coloured balls, the screeching yells, the blockade of prams and buggies. By the time Diane arrived she was onto her second cup.

'I'm too old for this!' Diane said as she hefted the pram through the door. Her hair was plastered to her face, and the buttons on her coat were done up wrong. Frowning, she yanked it off and collapsed into the seat opposite. 'Tell me, what in God's name do they need this for?' Reaching forward she grabbed a fabric book, clipped onto the pram. It crackled like dry leaves. 'Women in the Gobi desert manage with a bloody sling!'

Jo smiled.

'I offered her my old Silver Cross,' Diane said. As she talked she stood up again and lifted Esme, her granddaughter, out of the pram. 'Would your mummy have it?' she cooed, rubbing her nose against Esme, who giggled. 'No she wouldn't! It was good enough for her, but not for you. Oh no, nothing's good enough for you!' Esme giggled again.

And still, Jo smiled.

'Oh, I'm sorry Jo – can we move?'

'Move?'

Turning, Diane nodded along the length of the café, back towards the play area. 'If we sit over there, Esme can play and I can keep an eye on her.'

'Of course,' she said. 'Of course.'

'Soooo...?' Licking cappuccino froth from her teaspoon, Diane stretched the word. 'How is Nikki Lembit?'

'Fine.'

'And the unicorns?'

'Actually,' she said, her smile tight now, 'Nikki is lovely. And she has a sister, Vera, who believe it or not is working for me.'

'Oh, how did that happen? *Esme!*' Diane turned away. 'Grandma needs to wipe your nose!'

Déjà vu surging again, Jo waited. She was beginning to wish she hadn't called. That she'd waited the moment out and found something else to do. That moment when the need to talk had been overwhelming. Diane didn't have the time, and this wasn't the place. 'My mum fell over,' she said loudly. She had to be loud. They were sitting in the middle of a building site! The constant banging of espresso shots measured, the violent blasting of milk heated. A building site, that doubled as a playground. 'She's been diagnosed with dementia, and they wouldn't release her unless there was sufficient care in place.' Jo sighed. She was talking to Diane's left shoulder. 'I couldn't get an emergency placement, so Vera has stepped in to help. She's doing days. I'm doing nights until we can come up with a more permanent solution. A home, I suppose... Do you have any idea how much care costs these days?' she added, loudly. Very loudly.

Tissue in hand, Diane turned. 'I'd say around a thousand a week, Jo.'

'Yes.' Chastened, Jo put her cup down. Diane had heard. Everyone in the café had probably heard.

'Simon's dad is getting very frail,' Diane said, folding the tissue and managing to pull Esme back at the same time. 'Since his mum died, his dad has sort of given up. We're trying to decide the same thing. He says he can cope, but it's obvious he can't. It's an incredibly difficult conversation to have. You have to be so delicate. I don't envy you, Jo.'

'Envy me?'

'Having that talk with your mum. Unless she wants to go?'

Avoiding Diane's eye, Jo picked up her cup. She didn't know where to start. Not with Daine, nor for that matter with Bobbi when the time came. There had been nothing delicate about Bobbi's refusal, *if you think you can force me...*

'This is awful.' Diane leaned forward. 'Simon had to help lift him off the toilet not long ago. He couldn't get back to his feet. We've had rails put in now.'

'You didn't say.'

'What's there to say?' Diane shrugged. 'It's not the cheeriest of subjects.' She bent forward and sniffed the seat of Esme's trousers. 'I don't want that,' she said, looking sideways at Jo. 'I don't want my children having to do that for me.'

'Me neither.' Jo shook her head. 'I mean, if I had children, I wouldn't want them pulling me off a toilet.'

'Go and play.' Diane patted Esme's bottom.

'Do you need to change her?'

'She can wait. What her mother doesn't know won't hurt. So? Your mum is back at home now?'

Jo nodded.

'And you're staying with her? What does Toby—'

'She can't be on her own,' Jo said, cutting off a question she didn't want to hear asked.

'Oh, that's hard. Does she still know you?'

'At the moment.' Jo nodded. 'But I suppose the day will come when she doesn't.' She was thinking of Dr Dandicott. What he'd said, right at the beginning. *Rivers don't flow back out of the sea.*

'I'm sorry, Jo.' Diane put her head to one side. 'I know you weren't close. Even so that's really hard.'

Jo nodded. She was looking past Diane's shoulder to the gaggle of children beyond. The easy way they toddled over to mothers, or maybe grandmothers, to have noses wiped, tears kissed away, troubles – all their troubles – soothed. *Not close* was about as far as she had got with her friends. They hadn't asked too much, and she hadn't offered too much. There had been so many other things to discuss. Careers, mortgages, travel, children for them, a little for her too, when it had still been an option. It felt strange now, to discover there no longer were so many. To be reaching this signpost. What would come after? she found herself wondering. What would they be talking about after their parents had gone? What would be left to say about life?

'And this Vera?' Diane smiled. 'You're miles away.'

'I know. Sorry.' She took a sip of her coffee, everything she wanted to say slipping away like water. 'Vera is there now,' she said. 'It's her first day, actually.'

'Is your mum OK with the arrangement?'

'It's fine.' Jo waved a hand. 'Vera's done this kind of work before, and I left plenty of instructions.'

'Knowing you, I'm sure you did.'

Jo dropped her head to one side, her smile on the tight side. 'I'm not sure how to take that, Di.' She'd kept her voice light, but it wasn't, she was sure, a compliment. Not entirely.

'You're thorough.' Diane smiled. 'Let's just call it thorough.'

Thorough. Holding her cup at her lips, Jo nodded. This was the first time she had seen Diane since everything had happened. The first time she had even felt ready to talk. *Thorough?* The word tripped her. She was thinking of the greased-in grime she'd scraped from the kitchen tiles. The stickers she'd bought for the taps. Yes, she'd been thorough. Thorough with the bungalow and thorough with Vera's instructions and there was nothing wrong with that. 'It took ages!' she said testily. 'I spent two days cleaning her bungalow! I had to throw away the kettle and the toaster. It was easier just to start new. There was a bit more to do than just toilet rails,' she added, unable to hide the testiness.

'OK.' Diane said, her nod slow.

'I think I spent a whole afternoon on the phone to the dementia people. There's a photo on every kitchen cupboard now. To show what's inside. All laminated!'

'Every cupboard?'

'Yes.' Shifting her weight in the chair, Jo crossed her legs. 'Not that my mother is happy about it. The first thing she did was try and tear them down. Then she set the smoke alarm off trying to make toast.'

'In the *new* toaster?'

The emphasis Diane had placed on *new* was unmistakable. Jo sipped her coffee. It was cold and bitter. *It doesn't work. I can't get it to work.* That's what Bobbi had said yesterday. She'd barely heard.

Titling her head, Diane smiled. 'It must be hard though, don't you think?'

'What?'

'Accepting that you need the help? That you're always going to need it and it's not just forgetfulness.'

Jo shrugged. 'Well, that's one thing she won't do! She won't accept it. My mother can be very stubborn, Di. I mean, she says she fell over because the pavement was uneven. And she forgot to draw midnight on the clock because she didn't have enough time. Which is funny, if you think about it.'

Diane smiled. 'You should take her to the memory café at the community centre.'

'Memory café?'

'They do it every Sunday morning, so family can come along. My niece, Violet, is involved. It's a branch of the Alzheimer's Society. They have live music. Sometimes they even set the café up especially with props, stuff from years ago. Memory tools, I think she called it.'

'Does it work?'

Diane laughed. 'What do you mean?'

'Just... I'm just wondering if it helps,' she said and putting her cup down, she reached for her handbag. 'When Bobbi was in hospital I found...' But once again she was talking to Diane's shoulder as she turned to check on Esme. 'Anyway.' She let the envelope slip back into her bag. 'Anyway,' she murmured again. 'I'd be terrified.' Diane turned back.

'Sorry?'

'I'd be terrified, Jo. Knowing that one day I could be looking at my daughter and not know who she is.' Diane shook her head. Her hand, Jo noticed, trembled a little as she picked up her coffee. 'I can't even begin to imagine how alone you must feel when you get to that point. When you know it's coming and there's nothing you can do to stop it. It must be very scary to lose your identity like that, don't you think?'

Pressing her hands against her cup, Jo looked down at it. 'I... I hadn't thought of it like that.' There was so much she'd wanted to say when she'd called Diane. Now she just wanted to sit and feel the warmth of the coffee. Was Bobbi lonely? She hadn't even considered it.

'Anyho-o-w...' Diane leaned back in her chair. 'On to cheerier subjects! Have you made up your mind about your birthday? What did Toby say about the Vegas theme?'

But before Jo could answer, a loud shriek pierced the air.

'*Esme!*' Diane jumped to her feet. '*No biting!*' She waved a hand at Jo. 'Hold that thought, I'll be right back. While I'm up, I'll change her.'

'Oh, don't worry.' Jo smiled. 'I need to be going anyway.' She reached for her jacket, more than willing to hold the thought, to put it in cold storage for a thousand years. She was thinking about the word Diane had used. *Identity.* What would happen when the day came that Bobbi didn't know who she was? When the river had completed its journey? If her mother didn't know her, could she still claim to be a daughter? She'd never been a mother. Could she even claim to be a wife any more? So who would she be then? Even the weightiest of anchors could be lifted. Who and where would she be, when the last of hers had gone? She glanced up. Diane was disappearing into the depths of the café. Yes, she thought as she watched Esme's tiny fist, clutching at her grandmother's sleeve, it must be lonely. To be set adrift so completely, must be unbearably lonely. Bobbi and she had more in common than she could have imagined.

25

The disquiet Diane had stirred up would not settle. By mid-afternoon she had given up on both Renée and sunny corners and driven back to the bungalow. She could answer emails there. Perhaps even in the same room as Bobbi. She could do that. As she stepped out of the car, she heard voices, a swell of music. The living-room window was partially open, laughter coming from the TV.

Bobbi was in the living room.

'Hello, Mum,' she said, then. 'Hello, *Mum*!' because whatever Bobbi was watching was loud. She sat down on the arm of the settee.

Bobbi turned. 'You're back?'

'I'm back.'

'Are you leaving again?'

'No.' Jo frowned. 'Where would I be going?'

But Bobbi didn't answer. She turned to her show,

'Never mind.' And for a few dazed, tired moments, Jo too watched as a portly couple sat fully clothed on a double bed.

They were discussing how comfortable it would be to sleep in. 'Has everything been OK? With Vera?'

'Vera is in the kitchen.' Bobbi didn't take her eyes off the TV.

'OK.' She'd guessed where Vera was by the smell of cooking that had hit her the moment she'd opened the front door. It was wonderful, a rich aroma of tomatoes and garlic. 'OK,' she said again, and her stomach turned over as she realised that for the first time in days, she actually felt hungry. 'Have you had a nice day?'

Bobbi nodded.

'OK.' She looked down at her car keys. She was trying to talk, and she was ready to listen, but it felt as awkward and forced as ever. Two birds, pecking at winter ice. 'Mum,' she blurted. 'Yesterday, at the hospital, I was a little frustrated, and I'm sorry. I won't force...' As she stopped talking, Bobbi finally took her eyes off the screen and turned to her. 'I won't force you to do anything you don't want to. I really won't.'

A moment passed. Neither of them spoke, and then slowly Bobbi turned back to the TV.

Jo tipped her head forward, pinching at the bridge of her nose. Winter ice, and no sign of any spring thaw. 'I'm getting a drink,' she said as she hefted herself to her feet.

'Vera makes a nice soup. We had ham and pea for lunch.'

'Oh.' Halfway out of the room, Jo waited. It felt like the finest of breaks, a hairline fracture in the ice that might spread.

'And the photographs are a good idea, Joanne.' Bobbi nodded. 'It was...' She paused, her hand wavering, tracing the air, as if it were tracing the flight path of a fragile winged thing, trying, and failing, to pin it down. 'It was... I can't think... I didn't expect them to be there.'

'A surprise?'

'That's right.' Now Bobbi turned. 'Surprised,' she said. 'I was surprised.'

Jo nodded.

'There's a lot,' Bobbi said. 'I didn't know I had so many things.'

'Oh.' Her legs felt heavy. She'd caught it. The winged creature her mother couldn't. Opened her palm and held it out. And now they could both see.

'That's all,' Bobbi said. 'That's all it was.'

'OK,' she said and watched as Bobbi turned back to the screen.

'Hello!' Vera was at the hob, stirring a pan. 'I didn't expect you so early.'

'I didn't expect myself so early,' Jo said, peering over Vera's shoulder. 'What is it?'

'Verivorst. Blood sausage.' Vera grinned as she turned a sausage over. 'Nikki dropped them over. I'll take some back for this evening. I haven't made it since I came here. Andi has to have protein this, no fat that.' She shrugged. 'Tastes of nothing.'

Jo's smile faltered. 'Well, it smells delicious.' It did, she was just wishing Vera hadn't told her what it was. 'Where did you get the secateurs from?' she said, moving aside a vase of cut lavender, and a pair of secateurs. 'I could have done with them at the weekend.'

'The shed. I had a tidy up while I was there.'

'Was it bad? I haven't looked yet.'

'No. Some of the tools need a good clean-up and there's an old box in the corner that looks as if it could be thrown out.'

Jo nodded. Leaning back against the counter, she pulled free a stalk of lavender, holding the delicate grey-purple spear under her nose. It was such a strangely reassuring scent. There was, she thought as she looked around, a lot of laminate, holding a lot of photographs. Every cupboard and every drawer. Even the cupboard above the oven had a plastic A4 sheet attached. *Baking tins.* When had Bobbi last baked? She'd need steps just to reach it. And seeing anew the bright colours and the glare, she began to understand how it would have been a surprise for Bobbi. And she began to consider how she might have felt if someone had come along and stuck them all over her kitchen. Yes, she had followed the advice. But she'd also used a loudspeaker to make a very private announcement: HERE LIVES SOMEONE WHO CAN'T REMEMBER. HERE LIVES SOMEONE WHO IS HELPLESS.

Carefully she threaded the lavender stalk back into the vase. 'How was everything?' she said, as she went to her handbag and took out a packet of chocolate animals.

'Everything was fine, Jo. Your mother and I spent a long time in the garden this morning, and she ate a good lunch. But she won't let me help her with the bath.' Vera tapped the excess sauce off the spoon and laid it down. 'I'm a stranger,' she said as she turned to Jo. 'This morning, she forgot my name. When I woke her after her nap, she got worried because she thought I was a man.'

'A man?' Jo put her hand to her mouth, catching elephant crumbs.

'It's the hair.'

'Oh.' Smiling, she turned to the sink to brush biscuit from her hands. When she turned back, Vera was looking at her.

'She's not ready to let me see her naked, Jo. If you do it while I'm still here, I can help.'

'*Me?*'

'Yes.'

Jo's stomach dropped. 'You mean bathe her? Now? Today?'

'Yes.'

'I'm not sure I...' She couldn't bathe her mother. She just couldn't. Sliding onto a chair, she reached a hand out to the biscuits, but Vera was there first.

'If I'm cooking, you can't spoil your appetite with this rubbish.'

'Sorry.' She wasn't sure why she was apologising, only that it felt like the easier option. Nikki had said Vera was bossy. Had said Jo better get used to it. Covering her face with her hands, she rubbed at her eyes. How was this going to work? Even for a week, how would it work? She was disappointed and frustrated and deeply uncomfortable. Vera had been so calm earlier, and yet she hadn't been able to fulfill a basic duty. Because her mother had to wash. Someone had to help her wash. And really, what was the point of all the work she'd put into making the bungalow safe when the woman whom she was paying to care for Bobbi couldn't get her washed?

As if she had said the words out loud, Vera turned. 'Rome wasn't built in a day, Jo.'

Dropping her hands, Jo opened her eyes. 'No. No of course not.'

'She's writing things down. She told me that the hospital suggested it. Did you know? Bobbi's trying to help herself, and when she gets used to me, it will be OK, but today she preferred to be left alone.' Turning back to the pan, Vera stirred, silent and slow.

'I didn't know,' Jo said. She looked at her hands. 'I'm sorry.' And this time she knew exactly what she was apologising for. She'd managed a scant ten-minute introduction before she'd left Bobbi with a stranger and then she'd run away. Only it was worse. A stranger she fully expected her mother to stand naked in front of. She was warm with shame. She wouldn't do that to herself. She wouldn't do it to a friend. How could she have done it to her mother? 'Should Bobbi eat first?' she said, her voice quiet.

'Bobbi has been eating all day. Let's get this done.'

'And you'll still be here? If I need help?'

'I'll still be here.' Vera turned. 'And after, you need to eat something grown-up. Some good blood sausage to make you strong.'

'I do.' Jo nodded, tears pricking her eyes. Never, she thought as she blotted them away, had she imagined that the offer of blood sausage could be an act so kind it would make her cry.

26

But twenty minutes later and the urge to flee was as strong as it had ever been.

The stand-off had been going on for that long. The bath was ready, filled with lavender-scented bubbles that again felt strangely familiar. And she'd persuaded Bobbi from the TV to the bedroom, an achievement in itself. But that was it. She'd gotten no further. 'Just a quick dip,' she pleaded now as Bobbi sat on the edge of the bed. Her stomach cartwheeled hunger. She was out of ideas, and patience. 'In and out, Mum, and then we can eat?'

'No.' Bobbi's thumb worked back and forth. She was back at her rubbing, the dry skin whispering.

Exasperated, Jo looked to where Vera stood in the kitchen doorway. 'Help,' she mouthed.

'She's uncomfortable,' Vera mouthed back.

She didn't answer. 'I'll be right back,' she said to Bobbi, frustration rising as she hurried out. Closing the kitchen door, she turned to Vera. 'I know she's uncomfortable! That's obvious, Vera! So am I. But what am I supposed to do? Pick her up and drop her in?'

'No. But you could tell her that.'

'Tell her what? That if she doesn't get in voluntarily, I'll throw her in? Threaten her?'

Surprise widened Vera's eyes, made her shoulders rise. 'That you're uncomfortable too,' she said. 'That's what I meant.'

'Oh.' Jo's mouth held the shape as she looked at Vera, and Vera looked back at her.

'That's all I meant..'

'OK.' She still had a hand on the door handle. 'Of course.'

'I'll be in the garden. Taking a cigarette.' And with a final stir of the Verivorst, Vera left.

Jo let go of the handle. How had she reached that conclusion? How did she come to think that Vera was suggesting she threaten her mother? She dipped her head and stared at the floor. She was still staring at it when Vera popped her head back around the door and said, 'You can do this, Jo. You have to do this.'

Shoulders sagging, Jo nodded. The aroma of the Verivorst had deepened. Now she was light-headed with hunger. She went to the pan and gave the sauce a half-hearted stir. Wasn't that what her life seemed to have become now? A long list of things she had to do.

27

Back in the bedroom, Bobbi hadn't moved. She had her face turned away, but Jo could see how her jaw wobbled. Slowly she moved across, the mattress sagging as she sat down. Bobbi didn't turn and Jo didn't speak, and the only sound was the whispery rub as her mother rubbed her thumb and fingertips together, thick as rope, dry as autumn leaves. 'OK,' she breathed. Vera was right of course. She did have to do this, and she might as well just get on with it.

As she looked up, ready to try again, she caught sight of the reflection in the mirrored wardrobe opposite. There they were, middle-aged daughter and elderly mother, and behind those wardrobe doors were hangers and hangers of Bobbi's clothing. How many times had she seen her mother naked? Never. Just as very few people had ever seen her naked. And now she was thinking of a place where the kind of privacy she took for granted would not be possible. Where you might well be stripped and forced to bathe in front of strangers. Places, perhaps, like a psychiatric hospital. And she couldn't believe her thoughtlessness, the blithe assumptions that had had her expecting her mother to let someone she had never met before lead her naked to the bathroom.

'If it helps,' she whispered, 'I'm finding this very hard too. I—' But her voice choked. She felt stripped herself, her utter lack of consideration on full display. She brought her hand to her mouth to stop the tears that threatened, aware, as moments passed, of a new sound in the room. Silence. The whispering had stopped. The dry rub of skin. Bobbi's hand was still in her lap. 'Keep your dressing gown on,' she said, her voice hoarse. 'I'll help you into the bath and you keep your robe on. It doesn't matter if gets wet. It doesn't matter at all. When you're comfortable we can take it off.'

After that, if it wasn't easy, she couldn't have said it was hard either. Throughout the process of undressing, of climbing into the bath, she had held a towel high, ready to offer help if Bobbi asked. Which she didn't. 'Is the water warm enough?' she said now, her arms still aching from holding the towel.

Facing away, her free hand on the edge of the bath, Bobbi nodded.

'OK.' Jo ran her hand through her hair. 'Why don't you have a soak for a few minutes. I'll leave the door half open and you can shout if you need me.'

'Thank you,' Bobbi nodded, her voice small, but clear.

She didn't move. This close, closer than she had ever been, she could see how the skin across her mother's shoulders was pale and speckled as an egg, the vertebrae like the buried bones of an ancient creature. She could take a brush and sweep away the papery surface, reveal the bones, the scaffolding that had held her mother upright all these years. Not a brush. A sponge. She could take a sponge and... 'Shall I rinse your back,' she heard herself saying, 'before I go?'

And again, Bobbi nodded.

She got onto her knees and took the sponge, the water warm as arms. And the rhythm that snared her, as she dipped and squeezed, was hypnotic, and scents of lavender warped her senses, like heat warps air. Trance-like she held the sponge up, water trickling through her fingers. From the kitchen, music was now playing. It felt good, these sounds of a house, lived in. The moment felt possible. As if between them, they had pecked away enough ice. 'Mum,' she said, but the sponge, light as air before, was suddenly heavy. 'Mum.' She couldn't get any further. She couldn't start the conversation that led to talk of psychosis. To a photograph of a lost baby. Where was the beginning? In the midst of now, when her mother was losing her mind, how could she ask about then, when she had lost the whole of her mind?

The song that had been playing ended. Another began. 'Close to You', by the Carpenters. Jo turned her head to listen. She could feel her mind crimping, the soft insistent scratch of something outside, wanting to be inside. But as quickly as it had appeared, the feeling slipped away. She turned back to her mother. There was more soaping and rinsing to be done, but not at the spine. Stretching the sponge forward, she said, 'Call if you need me.'

Bobbi didn't answer, and she didn't take the sponge. She'd turned her head toward the open window, the knuckles of her hand white as her grip on the bath tightened.

Jo too turned, towards the unmistakable scent of cigarette smoke drifting in.

'Who is smoking?'

'It's Vera,' she said. 'She was in the garden.'

'No.' Bobbi shook her head. 'It's him. Has he come back?'

'Vera is a woman, Mum. She just has very short hair.' As she spoke, Jo kept her voice calm. She did not want to spoil the feeling of a moment ago. The sense of possibility that had existed. Left alone, it might come back of its own accord.

'Are you getting in my water, Joanne?'

'Vera is...' The sponge dropped from her hands.

'Has he come back?'

And then the memory burst in, knocking her sideways, sending her hand out to clutch the edge of the bath, to hold on, to stay upright. She could see a child, sitting in a bath. And Bobbi, bending forward to wrap her long hair in a towel. The absolute clarity of the vision had her turning her head back to the window, to the faint scent. But even as she did, she knew it was the wrong direction, because now she could see tiny hands cupped to hold a pyramid of bubbles, tiny shoulders turning to look over her shoulder – not towards the window, but towards the door. Along the hallway of her father's cottage, to the open front door.

The child in the bath had been her. The doorbell had rung. It rang now in her head. Her mother had gone to answer, and there had been a man's voice, hers and his. And laughter. And that was when she had smelled the cigarette smoke. But her father had never smoked a cigarette in his life.

28

It was only as the clock had crawled to midnight that she gave up and collapsed into the armchair by the window to sit gazing out, seeing nothing.

Long after Vera had gone, hours after Bobbi was safely tucked into her bed, she'd opened every drawer in the kitchen dresser and every cupboard in the living room unit. She'd pulled out old copies of *Woman's Own* magazine and *TV Guide,* dawdled through photo albums, where her parents were forever young, forever soaked in the sepia tones of a Polaroid camera. But she hadn't found what she'd been looking for. A photograph of her father with a cigarette in his hand. It didn't matter that she knew he'd never smoked. Or that every memory she had of him was consistent in confirming this. It didn't even matter that she remembered what he'd said when he'd rung to tell her about the cancer. *Just my luck, isn't it? I've never smoked a cigarette in my bloody life.* It didn't matter, because if the last week had taught her anything, it was that she knew nothing.

There had been plenty of other smokers. Her maternal grandparents? She stretched the photo to arm's length. She hardly knew them. They'd lived in Ireland and the only occasion she remembered seeing them was a Christmas visit to Bobbi's bungalow, perhaps a year after her mother had left. A stern, stiff-lipped occasion, filled with what had felt like stern stiff-lipped people. She'd been in New York when her grandmother died, Australia when her grandfather went. There they were now, puffing away within the small square frames in which they had been immortalised. And a glamorous-looking woman whom Jo guessed would be her aunt Lillian. Her mother's only sister, who had emigrated to Canada, never to be seen again. Everyone, it seemed, had smoked. Everyone but her father.

29

My mind feels like a bookcase. What used to be on the bottom shelf is now on the top. Days that happened a long time ago I can remember as if they were yesterday. They say that, don't they, that you can't remember what you did yesterday but you can remember every detail of a day twenty or fifty or seventy years ago. It's true, I can.

I can remember that it was warm and the sky was clear, and the cabbage smell had gone. I don't need anyone to tell me because I remember. A lot of the fields round the cottage were full of ripe wheat like gold and like the carriage she rode in. It was July 29th 1981. That was the day a girl became a princess and the day I tried to give Joanne her first real party. How funny life is. She never had a real party as a child and now she has a business running them. There are a lot of things I regret and a lot of sadnesses but one of the biggest is that I never gave my daughter a birthday party because he wouldn't let me. Here is something else coming back. Her first birthday. He said there would be too much mess. I said I would leave and take her with me. So we did have a kind of tea party, just us three, and my parents. I can still see the look he gave my mother when she dropped her plate. She didn't forget either. They never visited the cottage, they stayed away, I know they did.

On that day, July 29th, we had been living at the cottage for two years. He went off and I didn't ask him where he was going because I guessed he wanted to go and drink and staying at home meant at least I could watch it all on television. I remember standing at the kitchen sink looking out at the fields thinking of everyone making cakes and putting up bunting and laying tables for street parties. People camped in London so they could have a good view, thousands of people all together. There had been a firework display the evening before as if the whole country was going to a party except me. How I wanted it, I longed to be a part of something. All these years later and I can still feel it. He had taken the car and anyway I couldn't drive and there were no buses that day. It was a holiday everywhere. I remember watching a plane cross the sky and a tractor a long way away, just moving, where the sky met the land, a yellow tractor, it was so tiny I could have framed it between my fingers. It felt as if me and whoever was on that plane and whoever was driving that tractor were the only people in the ordinary world who weren't part of what everyone else was part of, they were calling it a fairy tale. Joanne was counting people too, on the television. I had left her watching with her Holly Hobbie doll, and then she came out to find me, she was cross because it was too hard to count all the people they said had come to London and all the people they kept showing who were putting up bunting. It was too nice a day for her to be cross, and I thought there could be no harm. So I told her we would have our own street party. She said we couldn't because we didn't have anyone to invite. Then she said, we could ask him, and when I turned I saw that the tractor had grown bigger, and it was coming towards us down the edge of the nearest field, and I could see the face of the man driving it. He was going round the edges of the fields. Him, me, Joanne. The plane had gone now. Joanne waved and I didn't stop her, and he waved back.

Sometimes, I see things that are not there. I smell things that are not real. It doesn't frighten me. I understand that it's not real. I understand that when I smelled the cigarette this evening, he came back to me only in my memory, and that's why I know I'm not losing my mind. It's the opposite. I feel as if I'm finding it. He said he had a little more to do, he was checking the wheat in the fields, and then he would love to join our street party. He laughed and shouted would there be lemonade and Joanne shouted back yes! She jumped around and shouted, yes! She spread a blanket on the front grass and arranged her toys at each corner. Holly Hobbie, with her blue cap and her yellow plaits. I remember. I really do remember. A Tiny Tears doll, a yellow carriage pulled by a brown horse and her teddy bear. She put a plate of grass for her teddy. We made ham sandwiches. I ran a bath, because I had seen it in his eyes, and he had seen it in mine. Joanne came into my bathwater, because she wanted to wear her best dress. Me too. I wore my favourite sundress. It had blue flowers, and it was pinched in at the waist. I knew what I was doing, the decision I was making. I didn't realise what would come out of that decision. I just wanted to stop feeling lonely. I left her playing with the horse and carriage. I left her collecting daisies for her Holly Hobbie doll.

I am seventy-eight years old. My skin is puckered and ugly. I don't recognise my feet, they are splayed as a duck's and when I look at my face it's like looking at the face of a stranger the way my jaw has fallen, my eyes folding in on themselves. That doesn't stop me remembering how I used to be, how I was that day. I thought I was old then! If there is one thing I wish, it is that I wish I had known how young I still was. I wish I had known how powerful I could have been. It was me that took his hand, it was me that undressed him and the smell of dust and earth on his skin is still there. These things won't die until I do. My hair was long. I remember he put one hand on my stomach and one hand in my hair and pulled it back and I forgot I was lonely and that I had a daughter. When I remembered Joanne, she had gone. I walked around to the front garden with him, and the blanket was still on the grass and Tiny Tears and the horse and her teddy bear were still there, but she and Holly Hobbie had gone. I went so cold with fear, I can still feel it now.

Her father brought her home hours later. We had walked the fields, searched every ditch. I'd run through nettles and pushed back brambles. My legs stung, my arms bled, the ragwort pollen was like yellow pepper scratching and burning my eyes and my nose. I didn't know I could be so scared and still live. She said she had taken Holly Hobbie for a walk. She had got lost but she wasn't frightened she said because she came to a big road and she knew cars would be going past and someone would see her. That's what she was doing when he found her. What he must have felt seeing his daughter walking along beside that main road. He had been drinking of course. She told him that Mummy had gone for a rest with the man from our street party.

I never saw that man again. He slipped away as the car pulled into the drive.

30

For days the smell of smoke had lingered. Vera was scrupulous about only smoking in the garden, but still the trace remained. Imagination manifested into reality. And although Jo was prepared to accept this – because what else could explain it? – what she wouldn't accept was that she had imagined it all. She hadn't. Deep within the hidden recesses of memory, a key had turned, allowing a shaft of light onto something that had really happened, she was almost certain. But the fragile sense of possibility that had bloomed as she bathed her mother, the idea of asking her, had receded as seemingly far away as ever. It had been a busy time. Most evenings, Bobbi was in bed by the time Jo returned, and busy with breakfast before she left. Then as the week came to an end, unable to get Renée to understand a simple request, at a dead end in a brief search of death certificates from 1982, and disgusted with herself over another ten minutes spent stalking Toby's FB page, she remembered Diane's suggestion, and typed *memory café* into Google. After that the afternoon was lost.

Hours had trickled by as she trawled through videos and

interviews as inexplicable as they were compelling. Film of late-stage dementia sufferers, lost to their loved ones as completely as if they were polished bone on the ocean floor, now singing word-perfect to old remembered tunes. She'd watched as richly filled buckets of memory had been hauled up from the blackest depths. As a teapot offered to a woman so bent and weak she could hardly hold it had prompted a story of a travelling fair. By the time she'd closed her laptop, the barista was sweeping the floor and the café was empty. She'd forgotten about Renée, forgotten about Toby and made up her mind. The cigarette smoke had been real. It was exactly why she was now pulling into the car park of the community centre on a sunny Sunday morning, ready to attend the memory café that Diane had told her about.

'So,' she said, turning the engine off.

In the passenger seat, Bobbi leaned forward, every movement a muted display of resistance.

'It's only an hour,' Jo heard herself saying, *again*. 'And there's music. That can really help.' How many times had she said that in the last day?

'I don't need help,' Bobbi said. 'I can manage.'

And how many times had she heard that? She unclipped her seatbelt. 'Let's not go through this again, Mum. You said you'd try it.' Her voice was overly cheery, but her mother had agreed. Then again, she hadn't been given a lot of choice.

Bobbi didn't speak.

'OK.' Jo nodded. 'OK.' She took her bag and got out to pay the parking, and by the time she'd downloaded the app, and registered the car, and registered her payment method and given her date of birth... Bobbi still hadn't moved. *Stubborn,* Toby had said. Well, now she knew where that came from. 'Are you coming?' she said as she moved around to the passenger side and opened the door. 'Mum?'

There was no response. Jo tipped her head to the sky, filling her lungs and letting the air out in a slow controlled breath. 'Everyone,' she said, pacing the word, 'is trying to help you, Mum. Vera is. *I* am.'

'I don't need help,' Bobbi said quietly. 'I don't need someone with me all day. I don't need Vera and—'

'*You do!*' Jo's voice splintered with frustration. It had been difficult enough getting her mother into the car in the first place. Now, she wouldn't get out? 'Dr Dandicott wasn't even going to let you go home. Remember?'

Again, Bobbi chose silence.

'We're all trying to help you!' she seethed. 'But you have to help yourself! It's the only way. If you don't want to end up in a home, it's the only way.' And turning, she took a step away from the car, hands on her hips as she stared across the car park. A memory café wasn't the only way for Bobbi. What she had meant was, this might be the only way for her. To find out who that baby was. To find out who was smoking the cigarette.

The soft thud of a door closing behind made her turn. Bobbi was out of the car, fiddling with the buttons of her cardigan and avoiding, it was clear, Jo's eye.

She understood. If anyone had threatened her in a similar way, she wouldn't want to look at them either.

31

WELCOME TO THE DEMENTIA CAFE!

They were standing at the entrance to a large, airy room, and the wording was so large, such a bright orange, had it been lit in neon it couldn't have been more visible. Aware of Bobbi behind, Jo stood her ground. This way she was at least partially blocking the sign. It made her laminates in the kitchen look as discreet as love-notes. Sound spilled from the room in front of them. The chatter of many voices, clinking teaspoons, scraping chairs.

'Hello?' A voice said, cutting through the noise. 'Can I help you?' A young woman had appeared. She had a blue streak in her hair and a tattoo of a horse on her pale shoulder. 'Are you here for the café?'

Jo nodded.

'We like to make it easy.' As she spoke, the woman looked first at the sign, then at Jo. 'For people to find us.'

'Of course.' Jo smiled.

'One in twenty!' the woman said as she held out a hand of introduction. 'I'm Violet.'

'One in twenty?' Jo stretched her hand forward.

'One in twenty of us will get a diagnosis of dementia at some point in our lives!' Violet beamed. 'We're on a mission to banish the shame! We're not hiding!'

'I see.' Bemused, Jo took a tiny step sideways, to reveal Bobbi. Who, she knew, *was* hiding. Who was staring at the sign, an unreadable expression on her face... although it wouldn't have been hard to guess. 'This is my mother. She's recently been—' But she was cut off by Violet's large fleshy palm, raised and held a few inches from her face.

'We don't do diagnoses,' she said cheerily. 'Everyone comes as they are. There's only one rule. You have to join in!'

'Join in?'

'With the singing!' Violet turned to Bobbi. 'It's t*he Purple Irises today*. They're no spring chickens themselves, but they're a lovely bunch and it's all voluntary. I believe it's a Carpenters mix. We're going back to the seventies, with a bit of cake and tea. Now let me take your names.' And turning to a small table situated next to the noticeboard, she took a black marker pen and a roll of stickers.

'Somewhere nice and clear,' she said, as she held the sticker up. 'It makes things easier for everyone. Most of our guests won't even remember they've been.'

Jo took her curling name-tag. It looked like she felt: reluctant. She patted it onto the lapel of her jacket, careful it didn't overlap her blouse. It was like school, or a health and safety training course. And again, as if the woman had direct access to her thoughts, Violet looked at her and said, 'It sounds impossible, but the point about these cafés is that joy and dementia get to be in the same room together. You'll see! And if they don't remember they've been, they will remember the good feelings they had. That's all that matters. Isn't it?'

She smiled. People brought their loves ones here, for *their* benefit, for *good feelings.* She felt like a fraud, but it didn't stop her, stepping aside and lifting her arm, encouraging her mother all the way.

Inside, the room was as busy as she had feared. Long tables, some people in wheelchairs, others not. Quite a few looking not much older than herself, quite a few looking much older. Everyone seemed to be talking. Even the teaspoons. At the far end, on a raised stage, a group of ladies in varying shades of purple had gathered.

'Maybe take a seat in a quieter spot,' Violet said, 'as it's your first time?'

Jo nodded. She was already there, steering Bobbi towards the table furthest from the stage, because despite what Violet had said, she had no intention of joining in a sing-song.

She found her mother a seat next to a smart-looking man, dressed in a grey suit and highly polished black shoes. He nodded courteously, his hands sprouting bulbous white knuckles as he clutched his walking stick.

'I'll get us a cup of tea,' she said. 'And something to eat.' She was rewarded with the smallest of nods from Bobbi. Food, she thought as she made her way to the buffet table, or at least the suggestion of it, never failed to provoke a response.

But the spread was unappealing. Shop-bought biscuits, sandwiches already curling at the edges, pallid fairy cakes. Everything served on cheap white paper. She cut a slice of Victoria sponge for Bobbi and stood looking at the table. Yesterday she'd had a final meeting with Jules, who had shown her some examples of the cupcakes she'd designed for Nikki's party. Exquisite. That had been the only word to describe them. Delicate swirls, in pastel blue and pink, tiny perfect handprints, elegant question marks. Looking at them she had felt joy. They were works of art, and they had lifted her spirits and she couldn't help but wonder now what this table would look like if there were a few cupcakes of that calibre on offer.

Violet appeared. She reached for a sandwich and popped it whole into her mouth. 'Does your mother have a favourite song?' she said, her hand covering the chewing process. 'We can put in a request. Ask *the Irises* to sing it?'

And this time she was ready. 'Oh, don't worry.' She smiled. 'We'll just see how it goes today.' And she turned away, before it was too late. Before Violet could read her face and see how obvious it was. She didn't have a clue. If Bobbi had a favourite song, a favourite film... She didn't know.

Back at the table Bobbi had taken a flower from the vase and was trying to smell it. 'It's plastic,' Jo said, as she sat down and looked around the room. On the next table a wheelchair-bound woman covered in a blanket had slumped so her chin rested on her chest. At a table close to the window a small man, shrunk in his chair, stared out, a teddy bear in his hands. She picked up her tea. It was lukewarm, and weak as water. Joy and dementia in the same room? She wasn't hopeful. She wasn't hopeful about anything. 'We'll just give it a try,' she murmured. 'We'll just try.'

How wrong she was! *Joy overflowed. Not least because the Purple Irises* were irresistibly fun. Dressed in damson, aubergine, violet. In glittery lilac cardigans that strained over substantial bosoms. In feathery fascinators of cerise, lavender and lilac that bobbed on their heads like a nervous flotilla, shaking and trembling, folding completely on the odd high note. Belting out tunes, drawing their audience in with the familiarity of the lyrics and the sheer zest of their mid-life energy. As if they knew, she thought, as her heart swelled and tears formed. As if within the secret heart of each purple-hued bosom, these women understood how short time was, how quickly they could become the audience – wheelchair bound, memory fogged, groping their way along the last lyrics of their life. One in twenty... one in twenty.

Everyone was captivated. Including the man in the suit, who swayed as he sang along always a word or two late. The woman in the wheelchair, who raised a feeble hand, waving it like a flag to a melody her mind had not forgotten. Bobbi, whose expression of grim acceptance had melted as she sat, quietly singing lyrics Jo doubted she had sung in decades. 'It's fun, isn't it?' Jo whispered as another song came to an end. And to her astonishment, Bobbi turned and smiled.

'Are you enjoying it?' She felt like a child, desperate for approval. Which was exactly what she was.

Bobbi nodded. 'I am,' she said and reached across and patted Jo's hand. 'Thank you.'

The touch was so unexpected, it burned. She pressed her lips together and looked at the hand her mother had just patted and forgot why they were here. Why she had pushed and persuaded, cajoled and bullied her mother into coming. Joy and dementia. In the same room.

'I'm afraid,' a voice said loudly, cutting through her thoughts, 'that we only have time for one more.' The tallest of the Irises had stepped forward.

'Boo,' Violet called, from the buffet table.

The tall woman smiled. 'Well, we'll finish with a good one. "Close to You".' She turned and pressed play on the sound system.

Bobbi leaned in. 'I used to sing this to you.'

'Did you?' Tears sprung, so hot and so fast she had to dig

her nails into her palm to stop them. She was looking at Bobbi, willing her to look back, but her mother had turned to watch the Irises again, was swaying, lip-synching the lyrics of a song that had always folded Jo in two. A punch of inexplicable emotion that she had convinced herself was down to the melancholic melody, the mournful tone of the vocals. But Bobbi had just said, *I used to sing this to you.* And now something new was remembered... Heads dipped close together as they did what? Set the table? Folded laundry? Walked along the lane? Maybe one, maybe all of these things. The song had risen up, presenting itself as a backdrop to days the size and shape of a clam shell, days that had contained everything she needed, days so long gone she had forgotten they ever existed. Her throat burned. She couldn't swallow. The emotion was hard as cement, turning her to stone and she hadn't for a moment imagined memory could be so brutal.

And now the whole room seemed to be moving as the song neared its crescendo and everyone sang, everyone joined the avalanche of goodwill, of hope, of a fruitless desire to claw back something that could not be clawed back. And she was helpless in the pathway, unable to run, bound to be swept along. Not singing, unable to sing. Shoulders rounded, forehead in her hand, she sat waiting for the ending because it had to end, *everything* had to end.

It did. And the silence that bloomed was rich and sacred.

She folded her arms, pressed them tight to her chest. If she had dared to look up, she would have seen the pause, the space in which they lived again, the wheelchair bound, the feeble of mind, the hopelessly fragile... She would have seen how their youth and strength had returned, how for a fleeting moment they had re-joined the dots that made them who they were.

I was an engineer ...

I was a teacher ...

I cycled the country, pitched my tent in fields ...

She would have seen the smiles as a grey-haired son remembered a long-dead mother, a wife saw again the way her husband had carried his jacket, a mother could trace in the middle-aged face next to her the perfect perfect profile of her newborn child. Dots that spell the story of a life. That once again allow us to love who we love. She would have seen what remains. What always remains.

But she could not lift her head, and behind the Irises, a column of sunlight fell from ceiling to floor, a thousand million dust motes swirling upward. Vanishing. The Irises breathed out; their fascinators bowed.

Slowly, she turned to her mother. And now she didn't wait. Now, she took her handbag and reached inside for the photograph. And all the time her heart thumped, and her hands worked independently of her head, as if they were only a cog in a much larger, unstoppable sequence. 'I found this,' she heard herself saying as she turned and placed it, so carefully, onto the table between them. 'The day you went into hospital, they gave me your handbag. And I found this photograph. It was in your purse, Mum.'

'You found it?'

'Yes.'

Bobbi stared at the photo. So long that the egg-hope Jo carried broke free and began to stretch eagle wings. She would be ready. Whatever was coming, whatever her mother had to say, she would be ready. She would be here to support her mother. To be a daughter.

'A baby?'

'Yes.' Her voice was barely a whisper. 'I think that's your handwriting on the back.'

Frowning, Bobbi turned the photograph over. 'No.'

'It was in your handbag.'

'No.'

'Well then! How did you find that?' Violet stood in front of them, a fairy cake half-eaten in her hand. 'I saw you both! Singing along. It's always fun when *the Irises* come.' She beamed. 'It's just amazing. I mean, some of our regulars are so far gone they don't know their own families, but they remember the words! Odd the way a human brain works, isn't it?' And giving a full moment's pause to consider the oddity of the human brain, she popped the rest of the fairy cake in her mouth, turned and left.

32

Because the woman in the queue at Starbucks had been unable to make up her mind between a chocolate or a blueberry muffin, Jo missed the window-seat by moments. Disproportionately resentful, she found a table further in and watched the couple who had beaten her to her favourite spot settle themselves down. The only other option for open access internet was the library, but with pre-school story time, it was the noisiest place in town. Driving back to her house and her home office wasn't something she wanted to face. And it was impossible to concentrate at the bungalow. Bobbi kept the TV loud, Vera kept cooking.

They were well into the second week now. One of the care agencies had called on Monday morning to say they had someone available. Jo had declined. After the wobbles of the first day, it was clear that the set-up was working. Vera's patience with Bobbi was astonishing. The little routine she went through every morning, *Hello Bobbi, it's me, Vera. I've come to take care of you today.* The ways in which she got Bobbi involved in the kitchen, stirring a pot, allowing her to feel useful. The bulk of her shoulders, next to Bobbi's fragile frame, steering her to the right room. Already, it was hard to imagine anyone else in the role. And she too had become accustomed to Vera's presence. Coming home, her company for the cross-over time in the evenings was something Jo didn't want to let go. Vera was happy, Nikki was happy and bookings for Party Girl were steady. But despite Dr Dandicott's cautious optimism about familiar surroundings helping her mother, it was clear to Jo that Bobbi's memory was not improving. In fact, it seemed to be getting worse. Two nights ago, she'd woken to a blinding light as her mother, mistaking Jo's bedroom for the bathroom, had turned the lights on, was standing in the doorway as bewildered as Alice having stepped through the looking glass. Sitting up, Jo had suddenly understood how little time she had left. But she was lost.

No, her mother had said. *It was in your handbag: No... I think that's your writing: No.*

If she couldn't ask Bobbi, who could she ask?

She slipped her jacket off and opened her laptop. Lindsey from Ashdown House had answered her earlier enquiry with an offer of an appointment to view the home, but not unfortunately of a place. Although, she had added, circumstances for our residents can change quite quickly. Jo's smile was wry. There was, she had to agree, a substantial difference in the circumstances of being alive one day, and dead the next. Difficult, Diane had said about the conversation she would have to have with Bobbi. *Delicate.* Jo glanced up at the queue of people waiting to order, her eyes fixed. There wasn't a conversation she could remember with her mother that hadn't been difficult. It was hardly unchartered waters for either of them. Sighing, she fired off a response, accepting the appointment, and opened the next mail. From

Toby. *Something for you to sign* in the subject line. Blowing froth from the top of her coffee, she scanned the lines.

Hi, hope things are going well. Can you sign this please?

She clicked on the attachment, a D8 form from HM Revenue and Customs. A D8 form being an:

Application for a divorce, or dissolution.

Heart pounding, her eyes raced ahead. Skimming.

Section 1:2 Are you applying as a sole applicant or joint applicants?

Toby had ticked the box that read:

A joint application – We are applying together

Section 2 About you

He'd filled in his details.

Section 3 About the respondent or applicant 2

He'd filled in her details.

Her head went hot. *He'd filled in her details. Her* name, *her* middle name. Address, email, phone number. Everything. The only thing left, was, as he had written, her signature. *Can you sign this please?* Coffee in hand, she sat back, her free hand covering the perfect o-shape of her mouth.

'It's a joint form,' she said the moment he answered. 'A *joint* form, Toby.'

The coffee was now in a paper cup, she was back in her car, rain teeming down as she stared at the console. *Husband* it read. Because in her phone, he was still her husband.

'You've read it.' He sounded strained. At least he had the decency to sound strained. 'I'm sorry. I really meant to ring to say it was coming. I got tied up.'

'You filled out my details?'

'I know...' His voice trailed off. 'Don't take it like that, Jo. I'm just trying to make this as easy as possible.'

'For yourself.' Mouth turned down, Jo sat. She wasn't going to help him. Whatever he had to say, whatever excuse he was digesting, he could spit up by himself. Her mouth pinched. She was black with anger, back in that conversation, the one where he was saying, *You're too stubborn…* the one where he was saying, *Once you make a decision, you won't change your mind.*

'I appreciate it's a shock.'

A shock, she mouthed. 'Is that the best you can do, Toby?'

'Look, it wasn't my intention… It's just that we would like things done… finished before the baby arrives.'

'*Things?*' Her voice made a rope of the *S,* curling it into a weapon. '*Things* like our marriage, I suppose? Ending our marriage.'

'Jo—'

'What other *things* would you like finished, Toby.' But she knew. She knew what was coming.

'The house,' he said quietly. 'I would…' His voice crumbled.

She turned away in disgust, staring out of the window. He could drown in his discomfiture.

'I'd like to get the house sold.'

Jo didn't speak.

'Or you could buy me out?'

'And how am I going to do that?'

He didn't answer. Of course he didn't.

'I just thought—'

And suddenly she didn't care what he thought. This man whom she had spent such a big part of her life with. Whom she had believed she would spend the rest of her life with. She didn't care and she didn't want to hear. 'I'll sign the form,' she said, 'and you might as well put the house on the market.'

33

'How's it going?'

As soon as Diane answered, Jo knew she shouldn't have rung. 'Where are you?' Diane sounded like she was in the middle of an airport.

'At the airport. Rachel's gone into labour. I'm about to catch a plane to Chicago.'

'Oh, Di. That's too early, isn't it?'

'Well, it's a couple of weeks before anyone expected, yes. I was going to ring,' Diane said. 'Are you OK?'

'Fine!' she said, matching Diane's bright tone. The first lie.

'Still at the bungalow?'

'I'm still at the bungalow.'

'Any news from the care agency?'

'Not really.' The second lie.

'So you still have Vera?'

'Yep.'

'What does Toby think? Isn't he missing you?'

In the background the metallic swell of a flight

announcement rose up. *Will all passengers...* Jo heard. All passengers? That would have been her once. Not so long ago, she would have been one of those *all passengers.*

'Hang on!' Diane's voice was excitable. 'That's my flight they're calling. I'm going to have to go, Jo. I'll give you a call as soon as I can.'

'Of course.' She made a fist of her hand and held it to her mouth. 'Go,' she choked. 'You can't miss the plane.'

'Jo?' Diane paused. 'Are you really OK?'

'Fine,' she blinked. 'I'm fine.' The third lie.

And there she was. No office to work from, no favourite window-seat. No husband to come home to, no best friend to talk to. Shocked. Sad. Angry. Confused. Rain teemed down the windscreen, and the taste of coffee was sour on her tongue. She leaned her head back against the headrest and watched as the world went about its business, lonelier than she had ever felt it possible to be. 'Reneé,' she whispered to her virtual assistant, as she picked up her phone. 'Are you there?'

Hello, Jo. What can I help you with today?

Reneé's typed response scrolled across *the screen.*

'I'm feeling sad,' Jo said.

It's OK to feel sad, Renée responded. *Allow yourself to experience emotions without judgment.*

'OK.' Jo gulped. 'I can try and do that.' And she threw her elbows wide as she placed her hands over her eyes and sobbed. 'I have no one else to talk to, Reneé! My friend is too busy, my husband has just filed for divorce. What am I supposed to do? Can you tell me what I'm supposed to do?'

The Bourne-Holmes Stress scale indicates that divorce is the second highest stressor for humans, second only to the death of a spouse. It's natural to feel a range of emotions such as shock, sadness, anger, confusion.

Jo stared at her phone. If Reneé had conducted a full body scan she couldn't have come up with a more accurate description of the maelstrom of emotion she was experiencing. 'What should I do?' she said.

Understand the legal process. Familiarise yourself with the divorce process in your area. Consider consulting a lawyer to understand your rights.

Jo nodded. 'And my mother?' she said, with a small, wry smile. 'Can you tell me what to do about my mother's dementia?'

Dealing with dementia, whether it's your own diagnosis or that of a loved one, can be overwhelming. Here are some steps and strategies to help manage the condition.
Understand dementia
Learn about the specific type of dementia e.g. Alzheimer's disease...

'Thank you.' She smiled again. Reneé was great with

facts, less accomplished at backtracking the myriad pathways of a human brain, all those paths not taken, all those taken far too often. *Facts.* And again, Jo stared at her phone. '1982,' she said. 'Tell me about 1982.'

Here are some notable events and facts about 1982. Margaret Thatcher was serving as Prime Minster. She was known for her conservative policies. NASA's Space Shuttle Columbia completed its third mission...

She sat up. What other facts did she have? She had 1982. She had a hospital. 'Broadfields Hospital, Norwich, United Kingdom,' she said. 'Renée, tell me about Broadfields Hospital, Norwich, United Kingdom.'

Broadfields Hospital opened in 1814 as the Norfolk County Asylum. It joined the newly established National Health Service in 1948, and this is when it was renamed. After the introduction of Care in the Community the hospital went into decline and closed in April 1998...

'Stop!' She almost yelled it. Opening her door, she threw the contents of her coffee into the drain, closed the door again and leaned very close to the console. 'How do I find out what doctors worked at the unit?' she said, and her heart was beating so loudly it echoed in the car.

Finding out which doctors worked at a specific hospital can be challenging but there are several avenues you can explore.

1. Hospital Records
2. Hospital Staff or Alumni Groups...

And this time she didn't interrupt. This time she sat and listened all the way through as Renée listed the many and various options she had. 'Thank you,' she whispered as the list came to an end. 'Thank you, Renée.'

34

Three had passed away, one hadn't proved traceable and one had refused to see her. In the end, there had been only a single name left. That of an Elizabeth Morris, attending psychiatrist at Broadfields Hospital, in the early eighties. Over the course of a week and several emails, in which she had explained the situation, Dr Morris had eventually agreed to meet her. Because, she thought as she rang the doorbell, it was as Toby had said, she was stubborn. And once she made up her mind...

'Dr Morris?' The door had opened to reveal a tall elderly woman with frizzy grey hair and red-framed glasses.

'Jo?'

Shaking the hand held out to her, Jo felt the dry shock of fear. She was, she realised, scared. She hadn't expected to be, she hadn't even considered the possibility of it, but the person in front of her was living proof of Bobbi's psychosis. Her period of insanity. Solid and real in a way that emails and medical notes could never be.

'Come on in.' Elizabeth Morris held her arm up, the

copious drape of her rainbow cardigan falling like coloured mist.

'Would you like some tea, before we start?'

'That would be nice.'

'Back in a jiffy then. Make yourself comfortable.'

'Thank you.' But making herself comfortable didn't seem possible. The room she had been led through to was stuffed full. With two maroon sofas that sucked up light. Alcoves straining with books and photographs, snow-globes and teapots. A patterned rug in front of the fireplace, and at the windows swathes of netting. It had to be the most claustrophobic room she'd ever been in. Doctors in their white coats came to mind. Dr Dandicott specifically, with his neat head and his blank white room. Was this house crammed with things really the house of a doctor? Even a retired one?

She found space at the far end of the window sofa, and sat, handbag clutched to chest. On the adjoining cushion, a TV guide lay open, pages struck through with yellow highlighter. Jo peered. *Say Yes to the Dress* had been highlighted. And *Married at First Glance. Say Yes to the Dress?* Didn't psychiatrists go through years of training? Longer than other doctors. Longer than vets?

'So!' Dr Morris reappeared. She was carrying a large tray with cups and a teapot shaped like a pig. Snout for a mouth, tail for a handle. She placed the tray on top of a pile of magazines, and poured.

'It's very good of you to see me like this, Dr Morris,' Jo said, her smile as tight as it was small. She was thinking that the tray would topple over. She was also thinking that this was all a mistake. A teapot in the shape of a pig?

'Lizzie. Please call me Lizzie. I haven't been called Dr Morris in years. And I didn't much care for it when I was.'

And settling herself between cushions, Lizzie peered over the top of her glasses. 'So. This is about your mother?'

'My mother. Yes.' Lizzie, she could see now, had an open face, with kind eyes and a huge forehead that spoke of a copious brain. 'Roberta Carter,' she said, feeling calmer. 'She was under your care at Broadfields Hospital back in 1982.'

'Still referred to, even then, as the lunatic asylum.'

'I'm sorry?'

Lizzie smiled. 'That's how it was when I started. Carbolic soap and ECT. On occasion, without consent.'

'ECT?'

'Electric shock therapy.'

She felt the blood drain from her face. Electric shock therapy belonged in films about the First World War. 'That was still going on?'

'In some places, unfortunately, yes. Not where your mother was. But her admission form was signed by, I'm presuming, your father, so she might well have been admitted without her consent. That was still happening. The Mental Health Act didn't come into force until a year later.'

I won't be put in an institution, Joanne. Jo swallowed, her throat rock hard. There couldn't be any *might well* about it. Bobbi had been very clear. *If you think you can force me,* she had said, *like he did.* Which could only mean one thing. Her mother had not consented. Pressing her hands together, she lowered her head, her voice soft as she said, 'I think she was. I think it was without her consent.'

It was the best she could do. It was the furthest she was willing to go. Her father had had many faults, none more troubling than his drinking. But he always made supper. He kept the house warm, her school uniform clean. Most of all, he was the one who had stayed.

Lizzie nodded, and for a moment neither of them spoke.

'So.' Smiling, Lizzie took a strainer and poured two cups of tea.

Leaf tea, Jo thought as she watched. For some reason, that made sense.

'You said in your email, that you didn't know anything about it?'

'No.' Jo shook her head. 'I didn't know my mother had ever been admitted. I didn't know she'd had this baby, who would have been my brother, or sister. I didn't know anything. I mean, I was a child at the time but...' And without warning, her voice dried. She bought her hand to her mouth and coughed, and tried again. 'I... My father never...' But again, she hit a wall. Hearing her thoughts was like ripping a scab off a wound. It hurt, and she wanted to know. She understood that now. She wanted to know why she hadn't been told. Why he'd never explained. 'Do you remember her?' she said, her voice sudden and blunt.

Fingers entwined on her lap, Lizzie dropped her head to one side. 'I was a practising psychiatrist for over thirty-five years, Jo. I've attended to so many patients I can't possibly remember them all. But I will say this. That you weren't told, even in later years, was normal. People were ashamed. They still are.'

Disappointment soaked. The idea that this was going to be a dead end crushed her. 'I understand,' she said trying to keep her voice light. She wanted to stand up and run away. A great lump of emotion was pushing its way up her throat and she needed to be alone in the car when it came. She'd exposed herself more than she could ever remember doing. Let drop the armour she'd worn since she was a child, pulling up knee socks, looking out of the window. If she'd been told, if her father, someone, anyone, had explained, it might have helped. Because she had been hurt. Very badly. She still was. It had never gone. How could it, when the child hadn't either?

'Have some tea,' Lizzie said.

Jo forced herself to pick up her cup. More pig-shaped crockery.

Lizzie picked up her own cup. 'I fill my house with things that amuse me and give me pleasure,' she said as she nodded at Jo's cup. 'My late husband was a saint for putting up with it, but he worked in insurance, so he didn't have the same need of whimsicals that I did.'

Whimsicals. The word stayed in her ears as she glanced up at the snow-globes.

'In my profession,' Lizzie said, 'self-care is not only important, it's necessary, Jo. There's a danger in becoming too close to your patients. Especially those you think you can help, and then... well you realise that maybe you can't. That maybe no one can. The damage, usually done so early in life, is sometimes just too great.'

Her mouth turned up, but the smile went no further. She was thinking of herself, and she was thinking of damage. The defensive child she had become, the prickly teenager, the fortified, self-justifying woman she had grown into and still was. Stubborn, according to Toby. *Thorough,* Diane had said, and it hadn't been a compliment. Her hand shook as she put her cup down. What were fairy lights, if not whimsical? What were solar butterflies? Hadn't she done the same as Lizzie? Hadn't she filled her own house and life with things that amused her? That banished the darkness?

'Jo?'

'Thank you for taking the time,' she said, swallowing down what she couldn't face, reaching for her handbag,

'But I haven't done anything.'

'I shouldn't have come. I understand. It was wrong to expect you to remember.' She stood up.

'Sit down.' Lizzie waved her hand, indicating the sofa. 'You came to talk about your mother. We haven't done that yet.'

'But you said you didn't remember.'

'I think you decided I said that. I didn't say that.'

And sinking back into her seat, Jo didn't answer. The words Lizzie had used were almost exactly the same as those Toby had used. *You decided.*

'After your email, I went away and looked through some of my old records and I was able to find your mother, but... I don't want to raise your hopes. It's basic information. The detail would have been in the patient's session notes, but I'm afraid I didn't keep those. I'm sure you can understand.'

Jo nodded, her eyes again drifting up to the snow-globes. Yes, she understood. Voices as fragile and unreal as the snow in those globes, haunting the house? She wouldn't have kept them either.

- Name: *Roberta Carter.*
- Age: *Thirty-six.*
- Sex: *Female.*
- Reason for admittance: *Patient reported missing on the evening of November 4th. Discovered by police at 3.20am on the B134. She was disorientated, unable to give her name or address. Dressed in nightclothes. No shoes.*
- Is the patient at risk for trying to commit suicide?

. . .

Jo's face paled. She looked up from the papers Lizzie had handed her, to see the doctor shaking her head. She looked down and read. *No.*

- Does the patient pose a danger to others around them? *No.*
- History of present illness: *Patient has been observed on several occasions talking to herself. When questioned she refuses to confirm or deny this. Husband has reported that this is occurring more frequently and the incidents appear to be becoming more aggressive in nature.*

'So she did hear voices?'

'She heard one voice.' Lizzie nodded. 'Yes.'

She dipped her head and read on. Is the patient dirty or clean? How are they dressed? Is the patient agitated or angry? Cooperative? Pleasant? Does the patient know their name, where they are, and the date? Are they angry, anxious, apathetic, euphoric, irritable?

But apart from cuts and callouses to her feet, her mother had been clean, she had been calm and cooperative. She knew her name, she knew what day it was and where she was. She wasn't angry, but she was anxious. This, the admissions nurse had noted, was most noticeable in the company of the patient's husband, Simon Carter, who had, as Lizzie had guessed, signed the admission papers.

Within the first hour Bobbi had been injected with 4mg of a drug called risperidone, and prescribed 25mg of clozapine, morning and night. 150mg of trazodone, taken orally. 'What are they?' she said. 'What do they do?'

'The drugs?'

Jo nodded. In her hand, the first page of her mother's admission paper trembled. She laid it on her lap, her palm keeping it in place. As if to soothe.

'Risperidone and clozapine are anti-psychotics. We would have been trying to see what combination worked. They help restore balance in the brain. Trazodone is an anti-depressant. I'm sorry to say it, Jo, but economically, medication was the often the only option. It still is. Your mother would have been under the care of a psychiatrist on the outside of course, but for how long and how often that continued, I don't know. I do know that she would have been on medication when she left and, for quite some time after. Anti-psychotics can take months to really take effect. Some patients are on them for a long time.'

'Dr Dandicott said she was on them for years.'

Resting her chin on her hands, Lizzie nodded. 'Health services rely too heavily on drugs as the only source of intervention. It doesn't surprise me.'

'There would have been side effects?'

Lizzie nodded. 'You were so young, you probably don't remember. I can't imagine that while your mother was taking them, she had tremendous reserves of energy. Anti-psychotic drugs can eliminate ambition, imagination, even memory. They can render a person somewhat detached, if that's the right word?'

'Yes,' she heard herself whisper. 'That's the right word.'

She had been young, but Lizzie was wrong. She remembered. She remembered clearly. All through the difficult childhood visits she'd made to Bobbi at the bungalow, and later, far less frequently, as a student, most definitely as an adult – for all these sporadic interactions she'd had with her mother, detached was absolutely the right word to describe Bobbi. And herself. She looked down and the neat lines of the form blurred. It was the right word for herself as well, because by staying so far away, for so long, what else had she done, other than detach herself? Her arm felt heavy as she lifted the paper to read the next page. She was looking at a summarised paragraph that detailed medications and dosages. A signature on the release page that wasn't that of her father. A Mrs Maureen O'Hanlon, her maternal grandmother. Jo couldn't remember exactly. In her memory it went like this: one day her mother was there, in the cottage, and then she wasn't. Then, she was living in a bungalow in town. Did she go to Ireland with her mother? And then return to England? There was so much she didn't know. 'Is that it?' she said.

'I'm afraid so. I said there wasn't much.'

Lizzie had handed her just two pages. Two pages, to document all those weeks Bobbi had spent haunting a no-man's land between sanity and madness. *'Responded well to diary sessions,'* she read. It was the final sentence. 'A diary?'

Lizzie nodded. 'It was quite a new practice at the time. It helped us, and them, evaluate the experiences.'

'Of hearing voices?'

'Yes. They wrote down what they heard. As you can see, your mother responded well.'

'Do you have it?' The question was so blunt, it was rude, but she hadn't been able to stop herself.

'No.' The answer came back, equally fast.

'Of course. I'm sorry.' She put the papers together, lining up the corners neatly. There wasn't anything here that would help. But she didn't want to hand them back either. It was, she felt, as close as she had come to her mother in a long time. If ever. 'Can I keep these? I just... I'd like to keep them.'

'Of course. You know...' Lizzie smiled. 'Maybe all is not lost, Jo?'

Jo smiled back. How could something be lost, she was thinking, when it had never been found in the first place?

'Because if your mother responded so well to the diary while in hospital, there's no reason to think that she wouldn't have continued with it at home.' Lizzie's smile was full of warmth and compassion. 'It's certainly what we would have recommended, and if she did carry on with it, and if you could find it, you might find the answers you're looking for.'

35

She went straight to Bobbi's room. To the chest of drawers where she had found that lock of hair. Any trepidation once felt at entering her mother's private space long gone. Lizzie had said, *might.* She might find. That was enough. In the first two, she found nothing but clothing. In the bottom drawer, tucked away at the back and wrapped in tissue a collection of postcards. Singapore, New York, Malaysia.

Hi Mum,

Settling in nicely. Weather is stormy / hot / freezing...

Take care,

Jo

The few short lines she'd managed to scribble had been almost interchangeable: still Bobbi had kept them all. She re-wrapped the cards and put them back. Careful to place them exactly where she had found them.

The wardrobe was next. Hanger after hanger of clothing Bobbi couldn't have worn for decades. Material that still carried the ethereal floral of her perfume. Pulling the sleeve of a jacket close, Jo laid her cheek against the fabric and closed her eyes. Breathing in the scent on old clothing was like wallowing in photo albums. As pointless as trying to ride the coat-tails of a wind that had long since blown itself out. Opening her eyes, she let the fabric drop and pushed the remaining hangers aside, looking to the empty space she had created. There was nothing. Just the rough wood of an unfinished interior. A tap at the window startled. Heart pounding, she turned to the sound. It was Vera, and behind her Jo could see the slope of Bobbi's shoulder, her straw hat as she sat, taking in the sun.

'Everything OK?' Vera mouthed through the glass.

'Fine,' she mouthed back. *Everything OK?* It was what her father would say as they ate, at a table that had once sat three. *Everything OK, JoJo? Fine, Dad.* Her smile was tight as she waved Vera away, her cheeks warm with embarrassment. Would Vera think she was snooping, wonder what she was looking for, rifling through Bobbi's wardrobe? Slowly she slid the door closed, her palm leaving an imprint on the smooth glass. She was looking for the child who should have been allowed to answer differently, that's what she was doing. The child who should have been told.

36

It was dark by the time she was able to continue. Vera and Bobbi had come inside soon after. And unwilling to come up with an explanation as to why she would be going through her mother's wardrobe, Jo had hidden herself away in her room under the pretense of work.

She stood now in the moonlight of the living room, chewing at the skin of her nail. Vera had left. Bobbi was sleeping. Where might her mother put a diary? That she had kept one was something Jo had convinced herself of. And Vera had said, Bobbi was writing things down. If she was doing it now, wouldn't she have done so then? It made sense. She made it make sense.

And perhaps it was the contrast with Lizzie's house that enabled her to see anew how sparse her mother's living room actually was. Where the shelves in Lizzie's home were stuffed, her mothers were bare. Where Lizzie had deep forgiving sofas, her mother had kept her chairs unforgivingly upright. There wasn't a single cushion to soften the fall. On the mantlepiece the domed pendulum clock, in the corner the television, across the room the wall cabinet in which she had found the photo albums. At the window hung blue curtains that had been there for decades. If Lizzie's house had struggled to contain the detritus of an engaged and enquiring mind, her mother's home seemed only to reflect a mind that had closed itself off to the world. She couldn't see where there was even the possibility of hiding a diary. She walked to the large front window. A car pulled out of the avenue opposite, the headlights moving across the wall like curious eyes. Jo stood. Wherever the diary might be, it wasn't in this room.

37

The loft too was bare, the torch from her mobile phone more than adequate to show that there was nothing but a rolled-up carpet. Hoisting the ladder back into place, she wiped dust from her hands and went into the kitchen. As she stood, hands on hips, a dark flapping from the garden caught her eye. Vera had left some towels on the line. The least she could do was bring them in. She opened the door and went out, surprised by the warmth of the evening. It was only as she turned to go back inside that she saw the shed and remembered what Vera had said... *an old box in the corner.*

It took a long moment for her eyes to adjust as she held her phone high and peered into the gloom. In a corner a spider's web shivered. The handle of a spade lay dark against the back wall. The bench was strewn with nails, a net bag of papery brown bulbs that had waited through how many springs for their chance to bloom. As she turned away, the rectangle of light from her phone moved across the dusty floor, coming to rest upon a rusting lawnmower, and next to it, a cardboard box pushed tight into the far corner. It had been closed and sealed with wide black tape. The kind of tape that is hard to undo.

Her mouth went dry. She wheeled around, looking for something to cut through the tape and found a trowel, blunt and dirty, but just enough to force a tear.

The cardboard scratched her as she forced her fingers through. A layer of tissue paper had been placed on top. She moved it aside and the first thing she found was a white shawl and a pair of tiny shoes. Fingers curling over the edge of the cardboard, Jo sat back on her heels. If the diary existed, this would be where she would find it, with a shawl that had sat against a baby's skin, shoes that were never worn. Slowly she closed the lid. It felt like grave-robbing. It almost was. She lifted the box, turned sideways and edged through the partially open door back into the moonlight.

38

The first thing she took out was a school report, dated 1979. The name at the top read Joanne Carter.

For the longest moment Jo stood very still, her hands hardly able to bear the weight of what she was holding. This was her. She laid it to one side. The next thing she pulled out was a hand-made Mother's Day card.

To Mummy, I love you lots and lots, JoJo xxx

She didn't stop. She couldn't have stopped. If the box had been a nest of snakes, she'd have stuck her hand back in. The shoes were next, and now that she could see them in the light it was clear these weren't baby shoes. The right shoe was scuffed, they had been worn. The t-bar leather strap faded and scratched. She took out a pile of papers, childish stick-figure drawings, each of them with her signature in the bottom right-hand corner... *JoJo aged 5, JoJo aged 6.* A small patchwork handbag, with a pocket in the front. Memory surging, Jo pulled a doll from the pocket. Holly Hobbie, with her blue cap and her yellow plaits. A plastic brush and a Tiny Tears Baby Doll, a plastic yellow carriage, pulled by a plastic brown horse.

Item after item she removed and laid on the kitchen table. Drawn by Jo, created by Jo, played with by Jo. Her childhood in a box, stuffed away in the dark, among dust and dirt and dried up insects? It didn't make sense.

The last thing she put her hands on felt like a book. She pulled it out, her heart pounding as she read the simple inscription across the front cover: Page-a-Day-Diary 1982. So impatient was she, so focused, she nearly missed the photograph that lay underneath, and it was almost as an afterthought that she picked it up.

It was a photograph of Bobbi, standing in the back garden of her father's cottage. Jo was there too. Aged no more than seven, with her back to the camera, watering the flowers. Bobbi stood sideways on, a stance that seemed to suggest the camera had caught her by surprise. The dress she wore was thin, and with the sun behind her, almost transparent. Easily it revealed a truth the billowing material had so clearly been designed to hide: the round swell of a heavily pregnant belly. But it wasn't the dress Jo was captured by, it was the expression on her mother's face. Her head was turned towards the camera, and that expression could only have been described as fear. It was not the radiant look of a woman smiling back at the man whose child she was carrying. Because who else could have taken the photograph, other than her father?

... most noticeable in the company of the patient's husband, Simon Carter.

The sound of a voice on the street outside floated in through the open window breaking open her thoughts. Jo looked up, and, if anyone had asked, she would have sworn, she would have staked her life upon it... someone was smoking. Close enough for sense to bypass reason, skim across logic and push open, once again, the deepest vaults of memory.

39

The tea was cold. The new day had already passed its first hour and still Jo sat in the armchair by the front-room window, the diary closed on her lap as she stared across the room. It had taken her barely ten minutes to read it through, beginning to end. The promises it might have held, over before they had even begun.

January 15th and one line: *New home.*

The next few weeks were blank.

February 12th: *Stopped medicine.*

From February 19th, day after day had been filled with the spidery scrawl of what looked like a child's hand...

WHERE DID YOU GO?

March 1st

WEREN'T HERE WHERE DID YOU GO?

March 5th

NEED YOU YOU DIDN'T COME BACK
WHERE DID YOU GO

Then on the same page, a neater hand appeared, a hand she recognised as Bobbi's.

I'm here. Mummy is always going to be here. I won't go away again. I promise.

March 7th had been covered with both sets of handwriting.

PIE.CHICKEN PIE. CHICKEN PIE
GOOD MUMMY'S CHICKEN PIE GOOD.

Will you be quiet?

GOOD AND QUIET GOOD AND QUIET
GOOD AND QUIET GOOD AND QUIET

March 12th:

FEELS NICE FFELS NICE WHEN
HE'S GONE. I LIKE CUDDLES YOU
FEELS NICE

I can stay until he comes back

STAY NOW YOU CAN'T GO STAY
FEELS GOOD MUMMY

I will stay until he comes back

LIKE THIS CUDDLE YOU I LIKE THIS

March 16th

TELL HIMGO TELL HIM GO AWAY TELL HIM YOU DON'T WANT HIM TELL HIM

I will tell him.

TELL HIM WE WILL GO. TELL HIM WE WILL LEAVE.

Stop. Stop saying this

TELL HIM

Jo re-read the lines, her focus so intense she didn't notice her teeth grinding, until she'd clamped down hard, drawing blood, an unmistakable metallic taste on her tongue. Who was the *he* that her mother didn't want? That the other voice wanted to leave? Her father? The laughing voice at the door, the smoker? Hand nursing her cheek, she read on.

On March 23rd the voice had refused to eat vegetables.

NO CARROTTS NO CARROTTS WON'T WON'T

On March 25th it had run in and out of rooms. Playing hide and seek.

FOUND YOU.LOVE MUMMY. LOVE YOU. FOUND YOU.

Mummy loves you too.

After that there were only blank pages. What had she missed? Or was that all there was? Cuddles. Food. Hide and seek. She held the diary up and flicked through the pages, and it was here she saw the pages she had missed.

May 5th DON'T THINK BECAUSE YOU ARE BIGGER THAN ME THAT YOU CAN KEEP DOING THIS.

This entry had been written in neat blocky capital letters, as if the writer was trying to assert an authority.

The scrawl underneath was barely legible, zig-zagging across the full width of the page, much bolder, less childish.

DON'T LEAVE ME AGAIN MUM DON'T LEAVE MUMS DON'T GO MUMS DON'T

Jo ran her fingertip over the word *mum.*

I NEVER LEFT YOU. I HAD NO CHOICE

~~No no no NO NO NO NO~~

~~NNNNNNOoooOOOoo~~

The long and angry line had been scoured into the page so forcefully it had ripped the paper.

SHE TOOK YOU SHE TOOK YOU AWAY

Jo's hand sneaked up to her mouth, covering it like a gag. Who was *she*?

SHE NEEDED ME. SHE NEEDS ME. SHE IS REAL SHE CAME TO SEE ME. I KNOW SHE IS REAL.

The next line was nothing but an upward stroke of an *I* that had ended in an explosion of scrawl.

She turned the next page, but it was blank. The page after that was a tornado of scrawl. The page after that was blank, and the next page.

Then on May 13th in a controlled, neat hand.

I'm taking my medicine again. It makes me sleepy. And I'm putting you away. You have to leave me alone now. You won't be able to find me. Everything's gone. Your toys and your drawings. And this is going in too. This is going in and then I'm going to hide the box.

These pages were discoloured, the ink smudged. Someone had wept tears over the words. The final entry consisted of four words.

I'm sorry. He made me choose.

Slowly, Jo closed the diary. The *she* was her. It had to be. And she had needed her mother, very much. She had missed her mother. She just hadn't ever allowed herself to feel that.

Everything's fine, Dad. How else could she have answered? Cocooned in shadow, Jo sat, the truth she had spent her whole life running from beating loud in the silent room.

There was no comfort. The words her mother had

written were markings on paper, steered by a mind in turmoil. They could never have replaced the warmth of touch. Not then, or now, and if she'd only known. If she'd ever been told, ever understood how weighted Bobbi's arms had been. Her veins loopy with trazodone. Ambition, imagination, energy, all the necessary components of a vibrant life, stunted.

She leaned her head back and looked out of the window. It hadn't been easy reading. Then again it hadn't been hard. Within the bubble of her madness, Bobbi had been more loving, more demonstrative, more of a mother, than she'd ever seemed to manage outside of it. But the fear had been evident.

She made a steeple of her hands, chin on thumbs as she leaned forward. Something was once again scratching at her mind, wanting to be let in. And suddenly she could see it. The collection of Dinky cars her father had kept. The orange VW van that had always been her favourite. How she'd loved to take it out and open the tiny doors. How once, her father had appeared behind her, silent as a shadow, taken the van from her hands and put it back in its place. *Exactly* in its place. His face unreadable as he'd closed the cabinet door.

Turning, she picked up the photograph of her mother and once again, studied it closely. She could see it so clearly now. The fear that had stalked her mother had had nothing to do with her psychosis. Nor, she was sure, had it been the man who had laughed, the man who smoked. She sat, the image of her father taking the van from her hand replacing it... so clear now. From outside, the long slow hiss of air-brakes punctured her thoughts. Jo turned to the window. A bus had pulled up to the stop. It was so close. The pavement, and then the bus stop. So close she could drop everything, fling the door open and be gone before anyone could see or stop her. And now, finally, she understood why Bobbi had chosen to come and live here. Her mother hadn't been scared of the voice she had heard, she'd been terrified of her husband. Because the baby had not been his.

40

Showered, dressed, fuelled by coffee but still barely awake, Jo pulled down the sun visor and looked in the mirror, stuck a finger in her mouth and pulled it open. Her tongue traced the sore. She could see actual teeth marks, little tombstones where she'd continued chomping and chewing in her sleep. *If* she'd slept. She had no idea when she'd drifted off, but it wasn't much before three. She'd woken to a stiff neck and this stinging cheek. The box was back in the shed. The diary in her handbag. It didn't feel safe to leave it in the bungalow, and it didn't belong in the shed and she didn't know what to do with it, because she didn't know what to do. Thankfully she had an early appointment, and a day that would keep her mind occupied. She turned the engine and pressed the open-window button, filling her lungs with morning air, the sweetness of fresh cut grass sweeping away thoughts she did not have the tools to dismantle. At least the axis of the earth kept turning, at least summer was coming. Always the best season for parties.

Her diary was full. A couple of weddings, one anniversary. A couple of small Year Six leaving parties for a couple of aspiringly affluent mums. A garden party for the local branch of *Women & Business.* And now, at last, an enquiry from one of Nikki's friends to plan her engagement party, with a budget of fifteen thousand pounds! *More or less,* the email had ended. *More or less!* She took out her lipstick and pulled down the sun visor again. Everything she had hoped for professionally; nothing she could have dreamed of personally.

Toby.

Her hand stopped moving, frozen as she held the lipstick to her mouth and looked at herself in the mirror. This was the first morning. The first time she had woken up and not thought about him. She clicked the lipstick closed and put the car into drive, aware for the first time ever of the tilt, the way the world really did keep turning.

41

Her first appointment was Nikki. One last run-through before the party.

'Amy will arrive around eleven.' As she followed Nikki, Jo looked left to right, up and down. The house was pristine. Polished and clean and organised. 'Then Tom and Jules will be here by twelve...' Nikki's voice drifted off. Jo was distracted, staring across at the shiny whiteboard someone had attached to the kitchen wall. *Cleaning rota. Monday: bathrooms.* How many bathrooms did Nikki have, she wondered, if a full day was required.

'What about you?'

'Sorry?'

'What time will you be here?' Nikki cradled Max in her arms. So that was two sets of baleful brown eyes looking at her.

'Oh, I'll be here by twelve as well. That's a full two hours beforehand. It's going to be fine. Don't worry.'

'And you'll stay?'

'To the end!'

'You promise? I've never thrown a party this big before. I don't know the other women.'

'I promise,' Jo said. The party was only a couple of days away, but Nikki couldn't have looked less excited. She was, Jo realised, nervous. 'I'll be here to hold your hand all the way through.' It was the least she could have said. Having taken Vera.

'Vera said something about you not being able to make it. She said your mum is supposed to be going to a memory café, but she doesn't want to.'

'*I'll be here,*' she said underlining each word. But her smile was tight as she took her file from her handbag. Nikki was right. Her mother's stubbornness was inexplicable, because despite the fact that she had enjoyed the last visit, Bobbi was point-blank refusing to go to the memory café on Sunday. She'd explained about the party, that it was Vera's sister and no, she couldn't possibly ask Vera to come in. But still Bobbi had refused. So Jo had arranged emergency care. What choice did she have? 'I'll be here,' she said again.

Nikki nodded. Neither she, nor the dog, looked convinced.

'Well!' Jo beamed, keen to get on, get going. She was tired, Nikki really didn't look happy and she really wanted to avoid all discussion of Vera... 'Everything looks lovely!' she said, and did a wholly unnecessary half turn, waving her hand at the clutter-free counter-tops and the polished kettle. 'You're managing really well! I was worried you'd be wanting Vera back.' Her smile froze, her eyes locked on Nikki's. Why say it?

'I thought you still needed her? That's what she told me.'

'Oh.' Jo's head wobbled. 'I do. I really do.' It didn't feel like a lie. Vera had made it perfectly clear where she preferred to be. Besides, she thought as she tucked her blouse into her trousers, and got busy opening her file, Nikki had disposable income enough to hire an army of help.

'What flavour would you like?'

The bleakness in Nikki's voice had Jo looking up. 'Flavour?'

Nikki had put the dog down, and was now holding a box of coffee capsules.

'I don't mind,' she smiled. 'You choose.' Her jaw was getting tight again. Nikki looked so miserable.

'There's six to choose from.'

'Then you do it.'

'Are you sure? It's so hard to decide.'

'Anything then!'

'Anything?'

'Yes,' she managed. '*Anything.*'

Nikki's face crumpled. She burst into tears. 'I know you'll think I'm silly,' she cried. 'And I know she's not far away, but Vera has always looked after me. I've never been without her. *Ever.*'

Jo let the smallest moment pass, and then she was slipping off her stool, her voice warm and reassuring. 'I'll make the coffee,' she said. 'Shall I do it?' Because what she should have said, of course, was, *You have Vera back. You must have Vera back!* But the words didn't come, and although she was riddled with guilt she could sense the creeping relief as Nikki put her hand to her nose, blinked her eyes clear and turned back to the coffee machine. Holding her breath, Jo sat down again. This was going to go one way or the other, and there was no telling which.

Steam hissed, water gurgled.

'I decided on mocha,' Nikki said, blotting her eye with one hand, handing Jo a cup with the other. 'I've tried the gingerbread, and the coconut. I can't believe it took me so long to work it out. It's simple.'

And Jo went light-headed with relief. 'It's delicious,' she said. It was. She put the cup down. Nikki would be fine. She and Vera were cut from the same cloth. By Saturday, hopefully, she would be beaming. 'There's a big age gap,' she said, 'between you and Vera?'

Nikki nodded. 'Twenty-one years. She was the eldest of my five brothers and sisters. I was a mistake. My mother was forty-four when she had me. She died when I was six.'

'I see.' Mocha bubbles tickled her lip. She ran the tip of her tongue over them as she looked up and gave Nikki a warm smile. 'I see,' she said again, because now she did. 'That's why Vera looked after you?' No wonder Nikki found it so hard. They were less like sisters, and more like mother and daughter. The opposite kind of mother and daughter to her and Bobbi.

'Here.' And opening up a gold locket she wore around her neck, Nikki leaned forward to show Jo a picture of a not-young, but definitely not-old woman, sad resignation in her eyes, a straw-coloured lock of hair glassed in alongside. 'Before she died, our mother had these made for all of us. I don't really remember her, but Vera does. She stayed at home and nursed her when she was dying and then she gave up her job to look after me. She's spent her whole life looking after people.'

Nikki closed the locket and as she did, Jo's smile was easy. 'She's beautiful,' she murmured. But she wasn't thinking of Nikki's mother, she was thinking of Bobbi. And the envelope with the lock of hair she carried. And the lost child her mother had imagined a loving and caring relationship with.

'It's funny,' Nikki said, 'when people find out we're sisters, they think Vera must be envious of me. But she's not. I know she's not.'

And again Jo's smile was easy. She believed this completely. Not once had she seen a sign of envy or jealousy from Vera.

'The thing is, Jo...' Nikki sighed. 'I'm actually envious of her.'

Jo didn't speak. She took a sip of her coffee and nodded. Nikki was young and beautiful and wealthy. About to have her first child. Vera wasn't any of those things. What on earth could she possibly be envious of?

'All my brothers and sisters got to know our mother, but Vera most of all, and I didn't. She got to know who she was as a person. Not just as a mother. I never had that.' Nikki shrugged. 'And I never will.'

The words were so perfectly timed, she felt that Nikki had read her mind. Had opened it up and fished out her thoughts, hung them to shrivel and die in their narrow inadequacy.

Again, Nikki shrugged. It was a slight movement and as she looked at Jo and smiled, her eyes were perfect glass orbs. She turned back to the coffee machine, quietly deft now with the tapping out and lever pulling.

Silenced, Jo watched. Nikki had been a young child when her mother died. She had the best excuse ever for not getting to know someone. More or less the same age, she thought as she dipped her head and sipped her coffee, as she had been when Bobbi left... To live in a town not far away. So what had Jo's excuse been?

'I'm having mocha too.' Nikki turned, cup in hands. '*NO!*' she shouted so sudden, and so shrill, that coffee spilled over Jo's cup, scalding her hand.

'*NO!*'

Across the room, a shame-faced Max crouched.

'*In your toilet.*' Nikki pointed to a large box in the corner of the kitchen. 'His toilet,' she whispered.

'Is he using it?' Jo whispered back.

But she didn't need an answer. Astonished, she watched as Max sulked across the room and stepped into his toilet.

'It's brilliant! I bought it off Amazon.'

A mechanical whirring sound started. Max darted out, gave Nikki a reproachful look and left the room.

'I'll show you how it works.'

'Oh there's no need—'

But Nikki was moving around the kitchen, obviously looking for something.

'It's really OK.' What was she looking for? Spare poo?

'This will work!' She grabbed a banana and dropped it onto the gravel at the bottom of the kennel.

The whirring sound started again, and leaning forward Jo watched in horrified fascination as the floor of the kennel opened up and the banana was scooped up, and disappeared.

'You see!' Like a child shown a trick, Nikki clapped her hands and beamed.

'I do,' Jo laughed. Nikki's enthusiasm and joy in life were infectious. First her mother, and then Vera, had done a wonderful job.

'You know, Jo.' Nikki looked down at her belly. 'I'm glad Vera's not here. I didn't want to believe it, but I needed her to leave. She's been like a mother to me my whole life, but if

I'm going to be a mother to this one, I need to learn to do without that, don't you think?'

'I...' As her voice failed, Jo's eyes filled. The truth of what Nikki was saying was undeniable. Everyone had to grow up. Everyone had to let go of the hands that had first held them. It was just that now, she felt she'd never needed those hands more.

42

It was nearly five by the time she pulled up outside her mother's bungalow. Vera had texted to say she was roasting a chicken. There hadn't been time for anything more than a sandwich, and as Jo sat in her car looking out, the thought of a dinner waiting made her stomach growl. She took out her phone and scrolled through mail one last time. A Mr Bowers from the council had mailed to confirm a time for a financial assessment. It would, he had written, be useful if Jo could familiarise herself with her mother's position beforehand. Jo leaned her head back. She didn't need familiarising with anything. Bobbi didn't have the kind of savings that could sustain the level of care she needed beyond a couple of months. The bungalow would have to be sold. More pressing was the appointment with the care home, the delicate and difficult conversation she needed to have with her mother. She didn't move. On the passenger seat her handbag, and its contents, loomed large. Difficult conversations rained on her. The diary had only made things more difficult. How could she even admit to finding such a personal item? To have read through the pages of her mother's madness. She pressed the heels of her hands against the steering wheel and lowered her head. Dr Dandicott had said there was no natural order, talking or listening. But reading her mother's diary had been to eavesdrop on her most inner thoughts, so now it had to be time. It had to be time for Jo to start talking.

43

'Hello.'

The silence that answered suggested no one was home.

'Hello!' she called. And again, no one answered.

In the kitchen the back door was wide open. On the hob, a pan boiled. Jo lifted the lid. Filthy potatoes floated in an inch of water, ribbons of dirt swirling. She bent low and peered through the oven door, relieved to see a tray of chicken. 'Vera?' There was no response. 'Mum?' Hands on hips, she stood frowning at the pan, unable to decide if she should drain the potatoes. The water was dangerously low.

'Oh, you're back.'

Jo turned.

Reaching for the rail, Bobbi came in from the garden, a bunch of lavender in her hand. She wore a large straw hat that shadowed her face but did not hide her obvious confusion.

'I'm back.'

'Are you leaving again?'

'Nooo.' The question was routine now. 'I'm not leaving again, Mum.'

'Oh.' Bobbi nodded and as she did a moment opened up, that was also, almost, routine. A moment, Jo understood, in which a test was taking place. That of her physical presence, against her mother's memory. It had been happening with increasing regularity. One day she would fail. She wouldn't be enough. Not her eyes, or her hair. Or her voice. And it wouldn't matter if she smiled, or laughed, or even tried to put her arms around her mother, Bobbi would not know her. Her identity, as a daughter, would have come to an end.

'Where's Vera?' she said, turning back to the pan. She was thinking of the loneliness Diane had spoken of.

'Vera went to get gravy granules.' Bobbi put the lavender next to the sink. 'I found this,' she said, reaching up to touch the loose straw. 'I think it's mine.' Her fingernails were black with dirt from the garden.

'I'm sure it is yours.' Jo smiled as she took her jacket off. Her mother had lived alone for most of her life. The hat was hers. She picked up a fork and poked at the potatoes. They looked awful, and she was starving. 'Where has Vera gone for the granules?' It seemed more than odd. Vera leaving, in the middle of making dinner?

'I don't know.'

Running her tongue over the sore in her cheek, Jo winced. Vera obviously wasn't in the house, and unless she was looking for gravy among the lavender, she wouldn't be in the garden either. Fighting back a sense of irritation, she took the pan off the heat. The whole point of this arrangement was that Bobbi wasn't left alone. Not even for a five-minute dash to the shop, which was where Vera must have gone.

'Did she say how long she would be?' Her voice was

tetchy and sharp, but if she hadn't come home when she had, the pan could have boiled dry. 'The pan could have burned through!' And suddenly she felt overwhelmingly sad. What had happened to her life? Her mother was slipping over the edge of a precipice before she'd even had the chance to know who she was. That wasn't fair. Toby had moved on quicker than a day, and that wasn't fair. And Vera! Where was Vera? 'What are you looking for?' she sighed, because Bobbi was now staring at the contents of an open wall cupboard.

'I don't need help,' Bobbi answered, scratching at her cheek, a silent movement that even from a distance, Jo could see left a smear of blood.

'Just tell me.' But she wasn't told, and she watched instead as Bobbi moved onto the next cupboard. 'Or use the photos!' She reached up and closed the first door. 'If you actually close the cupboards, you'll be able to see. *And don't scratch so!*' In a fit of frustration, she grabbed Bobbi's hand from her cheek.

Bobbi flinched, pulling back as if something more, something worse, was coming. A slap? A punch?

'I'm sorry,' Jo gasped... It's... there's blood, Mum! When you scratch, you draw blood.' Rubbing her forehead, she moved away to slump against the bench, hot tears filling her eyes. *Patient is not observably anxious except in the presence of her husband.*

She hadn't meant to, but she had scared her mother. As her father must have done. Had it been intentional from him? Had he wanted her to be afraid of him? There was so much she didn't know, so much she had never been aware of. Chin lowered, she watched as Bobbi turned away and began again, searching for whatever it was she wanted. Cupboard after cupboard, door after door left open. And as she watched, she was thinking of Toby, doing the same that day he'd come back to pick up some things. *Clothing and stuff.* Opening cupboard after cupboard in the beautiful house they had chosen together, the home they had created that he couldn't wait to get rid of so he could buy another home with another woman. Taking everything that was his, and nothing more. Which didn't include her. Her head felt as if it was in a vice. Squeezed from all sides. From a future that had vanished, a past that had collapsed. 'Just tell me what you're looking for,' she said. '*Please.*' If Bobbi opened one more cupboard, she'd scream.

'A vase,' Bobbi said loudly. 'I want to put the lavender in a vase. Where have you hidden all the vases?'

'I haven't hidden them, Mum.' The house was full of vases of lavender. Bobbi hadn't stopped picking it. 'You've probably used them all.'

'I kept them here.' Pointing to a corner cupboard, her mother's voice was thin as she said, 'You need to stop hiding things, Joanne.'

'I haven't hidden anything.' She went to the dresser and lifted off a vase. 'Here's one. And there's one in your bedroom, and one in the living room. We have lavender everywhere,' she said. How could Bobbi not see that?

'I don't know...' Bobbi turned and picked up the secateurs... 'why you are here, Joanne.' The words were quietly clear. 'You have your own house. Isn't it time you went back to it?'

For the longest moment, Jo didn't speak. She watched as her mother clipped away at the lavender stalks, stray wisps of straw from the sunhat trembling with each move. Any other daughter would say, *I can't go back, Mum. He's left me and I've got no one to go back to.* And any other mother would take her in her arms and say, *Come home then. Come home.*

'Do you know how long it took me to laminate those photos?' That's what she said.

Bobbi turned, held her eye for one long moment and then picked the stalks up, placing them into the dry vase one by one.

'Anyway.' *Anyway what, Jo?* She turned to the fridge, took a bottle out and poured herself a glass of wine. *You might find the answers*, Lizzie had said, but she hadn't, and it would be a miracle if Bobbi remembered to add water to that vase, let alone recall how she had once ended up walking the street at three a.m. dressed in a nightie. If she could ever bring herself to ask in the first place. Glass at her lips, she watched. Everything trembled, her mother's hands, the straw on the hat, even her own hand as she held it out and looked at it. Yes, it shook. 'Anyway,' she said, 'I know you don't want to go back to the memory café tomorrow, so I've organised someone to come in. I have a party. I did tell you before but...'

'Come in?' Bobbi turned, her eyes wide with panic. 'Where?'

'Here. Vera can't be here. It's her sister's party. My job.'

'No.' Bobbi shook her head. 'I don't want anyone here.'

Jo sighed. 'Someone has to come and sit with you, Mum.'

'I'm not a baby, Joanne.'

'You have no choice!' Grey with exhaustion, Jo turned and stretched her arms out to the dresser, head down, as she fought to control her emotion. It felt like one step forward and two back, every day. One forward, two back.

'I don't need anyone to sit with me,' Bobbi said. 'I fell over. That's all. And I got back up again.'

'It's more than that,' Jo whispered, watching as her mother placed the dry vase in the middle of the table. Her voice caught, snagging on all the grief she could not let go.

Was she talking about her mother, or herself? How was she supposed to get back up again? After so many years with him, how was she supposed to start again? At this time of her life? 'You need help, Mum,' she said. 'Your mind—'

'There is nothing wrong with my mind,' Bobbi said flatly.

And her bedroom door was loud as she closed it behind her.

44

If Vera hadn't come back, she'd have gotten in the car and driven until the fuel ran dry. But Vera did come back. Through the kitchen door, wiping the backs of her hands on her apron.

'Where have you been?' Jo snapped. 'You can't just go out shopping, Vera!'

'Who's been shopping, Jo?'

'You have! For gravy granules.'

Thrusting her hands into the waistband of her leggings, Vera yanked them up. Her eyes narrowed as she looked at Jo. 'Gravy granules?'

'Bisto! You left my mother to go and buy Bisto!' The despair of a moment ago had re-formed into a funnel of anger.

Vera shook her head. 'I make my own gravy, Jo. I'd told Bobbi I would make her gravy to go with the chicken.'

'She said you'd gone to buy granules!'

'I told her she had flatulence! That's the last conversation we had! We were in the garden. It was very bad, but at least we were in the fresh air. So she went indoors to the bathroom. I imagine that's when she decided to put the potatoes on.'

'Flatulence?'

'That's the right word, yes? At home the word is *peeretan*, but I wanted to be polite.'

'You said my mother had flatulence?'

'It's the cereal she has at breakfast.' Vera went to the hob and picking up the pan, shook her head as she looked at the contents. 'I have told her she needs to cut back. She eats a lot.'

'So you haven't been shopping?'

'I haven't been anywhere. We've been in the garden all afternoon. Bobbi likes to look at the butterflies. The solar ones.'

'You can't see them during the day,' Jo sulked. But that was wrong. The morning after Toby had left, hadn't she lain in bed and watched their reflected light dance across the walls?

Vera shrugged. 'She likes them. Sit down.' She was moving along the kitchen, closing cupboard doors. 'We were weeding. I told her I'd be going indoors soon to wash the potatoes.' Taking the pan from the hob, she threw the contents into the sink and said again, 'Sit down, Jo. Sit down before you fall down.'

She didn't need telling again. She dragged the nearest chair towards her and almost fell into it.

'You look exhausted.'

'I'm fine. I just...'

'Just?'

'I'm not sure I can go on much longer, Vera.'

Vera nodded. She turned the cold tap on and began washing the potatoes. She rinsed and re filled the pan, put it back onto boil and started laying the table. Knives and forks, plates and glasses. Like a carer. Someone who cared.

Becalmed, Jo watched. She had the strongest urge to ask Vera if she would stay and eat with them. It would be such a relief to share a meal with someone other than Bobbi. She didn't, she just sat, sipping wine, emotion draining out of her like blood.

'You don't have any brothers or sisters, to help you?' Vera said. She had bent to open the oven and as she did, a great whoosh of warm, chicken-scented air filled the room.

'No.' Inhaling the delicious scent, Jo closed her eyes. Had that baby lived, it might be here now. A sister or brother, come to visit for dinner. A shared history that could help her navigate her way through all this. And it wouldn't have mattered. In the sea of time what would it have mattered if they hadn't shared a father? There would have been so much else that connected them. Then again, if it had lived, Bobbi wouldn't have gone mad with grief and everything would have been different. 'It's just me,' she said as she opened her eyes again. 'It's always been just me.' The words were so forlorn she felt sorry for the person they referred to. It had always just been her. The only one to carry the shame of being the kind of child a mother could leave, the only one to carry the guilt of feeling relieved her mother had left, the only one left to pick her way through the minefield, she could see now, that her father had laid anew every week. *Don't you miss your mother?* Which could have meant, *What's wrong with you?* Or could equally have meant, *Remember who stayed.*

She looked up. Vera was scooping juices up and over the chicken.

'My mother left,' she said, quietly. 'When I was eight years old.'

Vera turned, gave her a look that said, *I'm listening*, and went back to the tray, her hands busy, as if she knew this was the way to keep the conversation going.

'So it's difficult. I've lived abroad for a long time, Vera.' She paused. 'I don't really know Bobbi. And she doesn't really know me.'

Opening the oven door, Vera bent to put the tray back. She straightened up and wiped her hands on a tea towel. 'This is a chance then.'

'A chance?' Jo frowned.

'For change.'

Jo didn't speak. And as she sipped her wine, Vera took peas from the freezer, rattling them into a saucepan.

'My mother had too many children. I didn't get to know her until she was dying.'

'I understand.' Jo smiled. 'Bobbi's not...' She stopped talking and looked across the hall to the closed door of her mother's bedroom. *Bobbi's not dying,* she was going to say, but wasn't that exactly what she was doing? The pause in her mother's eyes when they met again at the end of each day was incrementally expanding. Soon enough neither of them would be able to cross it. Every day something was lost. Every day, another rockfall. The quintessential essence of who Bobbi was, was leaving. Like a river flowing towards the sea. Just as Dr Dandicott had said. Rivers and oceans, she thought as she sipped her wine and watched Vera. Rivers and oceans.

45

Simple questions. With *yes* and *no* answers.

Rivers and oceans, and simple questions. *Yes* and *no* answers.

She had self-soothed with the mantra all through dinner, all through the dishes, all through making a pot of tea and carrying it through now to where Bobbi sat. She couldn't afford to leave space for ambiguity. Not like last time. There would be no more, *I think.* No more, *maybe.* Instead there would be...

Is this your baby?

Did you hear its voice, after it died?

Was it Dad's?

Were you scared of Dad?

Did he hurt you?

Why didn't anyone tell me?

There was nothing simple about it. The last question, the question that burned hottest, was nowhere near a yes or no.

She put the tray on the table. 'Mum,' she said. 'I was hoping we could talk.'

Bobbi turned.

A chance, Vera had said. Her mouth was dry. She took her handbag from where she had left it on the hall table and returning, sat down, the diary on her lap now, both hands protecting it. 'Dr Dandicott told me about the time you were ill.' Jo closed her eyes. It wasn't even a question.

'Ill?'

'I know about the baby,' she blurted. 'I know that a long time ago, you had a baby that died, and after... afterwards you were sick for a while. You were admitted into hospital.' Hands shaking, she stretched the diary out to Bobbi. 'This is a diary you kept to help yourself get better.'

Her mother's head bobbed like a cork in water, her eyes swam with confusion. She didn't move.

'Can you look at it?' Jo nodded. 'Please.' And not waiting for an answer, she stretched across and put it on the arm of her mother's chair. 'Please,' she whispered.

Long excruciating minutes passed. Minutes in which Bobbi took the diary and opened it, her lips moving as she read, her head shaking as her finger traced the lines of writing.

Jo sat, and the only sound in the room was the soft lap of paper as another page was turned.

'What is this?' Bobbi said finally, her face narrow with fear and confusion.

Jo didn't see the fear, she just heard the confusion and it spurred her on. Back at the memory café, there had only been a flat tone of denial, now there was hesitation. A space that all her mother needed was the gentlest of nudges to be pushed through. A small memory aid to help her remember. 'It's your diary,' she said quietly. 'I know about the breakdown, Mum. After the baby. Keeping a diary was part of your treatment when you were in hospital, and you must have carried on when you came out.'

'No.' The voice was firm, the movement assured. Bobbi shook her head. 'I didn't write those things.' She closed the diary. 'This isn't mine. I didn't write those things.'

For a long moment, neither of them spoke.

'I understand this is difficult.' Jo stood up. She went back to her handbag and took the photograph out. 'Do you remember I showed you this before?' she said, standing tall in front of her mother, stretching it towards her. 'At the memory café? You said it wasn't your writing, but it was found in your purse. And the date on the back... April. That's only six months before you were admitted into hospital.

As if the photograph were a torch shining in her eyes, Bobbi turned away. 'I can't think,' she said, the thumb beginning to rub. 'I can't think.' Her lips were thin, a wisp of bubbles escaping as she spoke.

Timid as a cornered mouse, Bobbi had curled herself into her chair and it infuriated Jo. All she wanted was an answer. It wasn't much to ask, not after over forty years. 'It's not fair,' she said quietly. 'If this was my brother or sister, don't you think I had a right to know? Don't you think you could have told me? Or Dad? Why didn't anyone tell me?'

Still Bobbi didn't turn.

'I know what happened, Mum.'

'No.'

'I know that you were sick.'

'Stop!'

But she didn't. Because if she did, she'd never know. She'd never fully understand why Bobbi had never come home again. And she'd never really be able to answer the question, not the way she yearned to. Had her mother ever loved her? Had she just been too ill to show it? Could Bobbi still be a mother, and could she still be a daughter?

'I know the baby died,' she said. 'I know that's why you went into hospital. There's no shame in it, Mum. I just want—'

'Too fast,' Bobbi cried. She turned her head sideways and pushed it against the back of the armchair and covered her exposed ear with her good hand. 'I don't want to talk about it.'

'Why didn't you tell me? Was it because I was a child? I grew up, Mum! You could have talked to me then. You could... It's not fair!' she exploded. 'It's not fair that I was never told! You left. You were sick, and then you just left, and you never told me! You never explained yourself!' And then it came. The question that all other questions had always been leading to. 'Why? Why did you leave me?'

'No.' Bobbi turned, her eyes pale and watery, moving with confusion and managing to stay still at the same time. 'I didn't do that,' she said. 'I didn't leave you.'

'*You did!*' The words bounced off the walls. 'How can you say you didn't? You left me, and Dad.'

'I made a promise,' Bobbi whispered. Her hand flapped at her face like a wounded wing. 'I made a promise.'

'You left us, Mum! Don't you think I deserved an explanation? Don't you think someone could have told me what was going on?'

'It was better...' Bobbi's thumb worked furiously, her lips moved too, small anguished shapes that produced no sound. 'I was better—'

'*On your own!*' Jo cried. 'So you keep saying. But what about me! Why didn't anyone stop and think about me? That it might not have been better for me!'

There was no answer, and Jo was glad. She didn't want to

hear an answer to a question she'd never asked before, and never would again. Asking it had meant diving deep into a well of memory she'd spent her whole life skimming the surface of. And she didn't, she knew now, have the reserves to explore places the sun had never reached. Nights when the loneliness had been a physical thing that lay beside her, hard edged, unyielding, as she'd listened to the hiss of another can of beer opened, the stumbling as her father weaved his way around the cottage. All those times, she had tried and failed to piece together the jigsaw of why her mother had left. She didn't want to go back to the misery of irreconcilable emotions. Wolves tearing her apart. The yearning to see her mother, the bitter disappointment when another uncomfortable visit had ended, the shameful relief as her father drove her away, her mother becoming ever smaller, ever distant in the background.

'It doesn't matter,' she sighed. 'None of this matters any more. I was going to tell you over the weekend, but you might as well know now. We have an appointment at a care home on Monday. So you'll never have to talk about it again.' And she turned and left the room.

46

Was that me? Did I write those things? All those years I blamed him as well as myself for everything that happened, but if it was me, if I wrote those things then I did need help. The first night was the worst. The woman in the bed next to me cried and cried. Her lip was cut. She'd been fighting. They said she had cut someone with a knife. Joanne is so angry with me. Surely I should remember more. Why did I say that? Why did I tell her I was better on my own, without my child? It was because he told me that I was. I can see it. I was in the bathroom. There was no field of gold then, so it was winter. He came in, and he didn't knock, he never knocked. When he saw my stomach, he knew. I can see him. I can feel him holding me. On my arm, things that gripped my skin. I can't think of the name, a part of him that gripped my skin and hurt. He told me I was a bad nurse. No, that's not right. I was a mother. A bad mother. He told me I couldn't look after my child. He told me that he would give me another chance if I gave up the baby, and that he would leave and take Joanne if I didn't. He made me choose and now she says I'm going into a home. If I go into a home I'll never get out. I'll never see him again and I want to see him. I want to see him before I die. I don't remember but I remember that I held him. I held him for as long as I could, his hair was so fair, it was gold and I asked the nurse to cut a tiny piece and she was kind, and then they took him. He was three hours old. Surely I should remember more. I left him there. That's where I left my son. That's where he is.

47

Nikki's gender reveal. The most important event of her business so far. The sun was shining, the forecast fantastic and she could barely lift her head from the pillow. Barely drag herself to the bathroom, where she stood under the shower for a long time, trying to shake the dullness. She dried her hair and put her make-up on, every line and sag of her face magnified. She looked her age, she felt triple it.

Outside the closed door of Bobbi's bedroom, she paused, hand raised to knock. Coffee first. She would face her mother after coffee.

But when she went into the kitchen, Bobbi was already there. Sitting at the kitchen table. She had managed to dress herself in a pretty flowered blouse and a pair of lightweight trousers. Even the buttons were done up. It must have taken ages.

'I didn't use the toaster,' she said, spreading a thick layer of marmalade onto a slice of bread.

Framed in the doorway, Jo paused. Last night she'd taken her heart out and placed it on her mother's sleeve, and once again she had been rejected. She'd gone to bed on a promise and woken to the same vow. Never again would she make herself so vulnerable. But last night she'd also thrown a grenade and walked out before she could see the damage it would do. Had Bobbi remembered? 'OK,' she said, and moved across to fill the kettle.

By the time she had made her coffee, Bobbi was on to her third piece of bread. 'I will go to the memory café today,' she said, breaking the silence as she put her knife down and wiped her hands.

Jo turned.

'So you can call and cancel the person coming.'

'The carer?'

'That's right.' Bobbi nodded. 'The person.'

'OK.' Her mother was acting as if nothing had happened last night. As if she hadn't been shown a photograph of her lost baby, as if she hadn't been told Jo was taking her to see a care home with the obvious intention of – one day, soon enough – leaving her there. Because that was what had happened, and in the end the conversation hadn't been difficult and it hadn't been delicate. It hadn't even been a conversation. She held her cup at her lips, hiding her face. Perhaps Bobbi didn't remember. And perhaps she did, and had decided to just say nothing. Neither explanation would surprise her. In fact, the only surprise Jo felt was that she had expected something different. 'I'll drive you,' she said. It was difficult. The memory café didn't start until eleven and she'd promised Nikki she'd be there early. She threw the last of her coffee into the sink and, machine-like, rinsed the cup. 'It's on my way. I have to pick up the cake, and then I can drop you there.' She could drop Bobbi a little early. That wouldn't do any harm.

'She's having a baby?'

'Who?' Jo turned.

'Vera's sister?'

'That's right.' And although she watched Bobbi's face carefully as her mother picked up her bread, nothing was revealed. Not a flicker of remembered joy, not a shadow of painful regret for her own lost child.

48

'Are you sure you'll be OK?'

The room in which the café took place was empty, and there was no sign of either Violet or her enormous welcome board.

'I'll be fine,' Bobbi said.

'Shall I get you a chair?' Guilt surged. Last night had been awful. The best she could do was hope that her mother really had forgotten.

'There are plenty of...' Clutching her handbag, Bobbi waved at the thing she couldn't name.

'Chairs?'

'I'm capable of finding somewhere to sit.'

'Yes. I know.'

It was the longest conversation they'd had since leaving the bungalow. She didn't ask again. She watched as Bobbi made her way across the room, taking a seat much closer to what would become the stage than where they had sat last time. Now relief soared. At least with Bobbi here, she could get on with her job.

49

Which couldn't have been going better, because walking out onto Nikki's huge deck, her legs almost buckled. Everything looked perfect! Following her thorough instructions, Amy, who helped decorate, had draped the bunting perfectly. Not so low that guests had to duck, and not too high so it lost visibility. Jules, her caterer and Tom, her barman / DJ, had set the table and bar exactly right. The starched linen tablecloth fell in neat folds, and the champagne flutes had been arranged in precision gridlines. Carefully she took the cake from the box and laid it in the centre of the table. *Boots or Bows! Soon We'll Know!* she read, smiling. Yes, soon enough everyone would know the sex of a baby that would not be born for several weeks. And suddenly it all seemed so unfair. How one life could be so celebrated, and another not even remembered.

'Jo! You're here!' The tap on her shoulder was electric. It was Nikki, dressed in a white chiffon dress and a floral tiara. Like an escaped fairy.

'I'm so sorry,' she said. 'I sent Vera a text. My mother—'

'It's fine. Vera explained. We understand, Jo. Honestly.

Oh!' Nikki clapped her hands together. 'The cake!' she cried, as she caught sight of it. 'Everything in fact! Everything looks fabulous!' She flung her arms around Jo's neck. 'And the cupcakes are just gorgeous! I'm so happy!' Jo smiled, a well of emotion surging. Nikki's bare shoulders were warm as they embraced, her skin soft as a child's. She'd never know. She would never know if her own sibling would have worn boots or bows, because the world kept turning and rivers kept flowing on to the sea and if the best she could do in the meantime was make people happy, then that was OK. It felt OK. And Nikki was happy. Nikki who had lost her mother too. She pulled back, straightening her blouse. And Toby was wrong. And Toby was wrong. Those cupcakes wouldn't taste of emptiness, they would be sweet and light and every last mouthful would satisfy.

'Everything OK?' Vera appeared behind Nikki. In the drainpipe white jeans, but a different t-shirt, Jo noticed. The Grateful Dead. A concession to the fact that she was a guest, and not the cleaner.

'Everything is great,' she said. 'Go and enjoy the party.'

With Nikki and Vera welcoming the first guests, Jo turned to carry on her inspection. In the middle of the manicured lawn, mounted on a raised platform, stood a table. Amy had tethered clouds and clouds of pink and blue balloons to either side. Above it all floated a massive football-shaped piñata. It was perfect.

Still, a ripple of anxiety arose. It hadn't happened yet, but she was waiting for the day something went wrong. Like the smoke gun failing to fire, or the piñata not breaking. Once, she'd done a much smaller-scale reveal where a drunk mother-in-law had let go of the balloons holding the coloured confetti. The atmosphere had slid off a cliff as everyone watched in embarrassed silence, those balloons carrying their secret to the stars. She scanned the few guests already on the deck. Andi's mum stood to one side sipping what looked like orange juice, her face set in a grin-and-bear-it-expression. She could, Jo surmised, be trusted. Settled onto lounger chairs were an elderly couple. Andi's grandparents? No problem there either. And Nikki's family today consisted only of Vera. The major players looked like they would behave. As long as she kept her eye on the ball, which she always did, there was no reason to panic. She could, and should, settle back and enjoy what she had worked so very hard for. Calm returning, she picked up the smoke gun that lay on the table. It would be filled with edible smoke. Who has that, she thought as she laid it back down. She smiled. In the whole of East Anglia, who had edible celebration smoke at their parties? Andi would break the piñata by kicking a football at it. Then Nikki would fire the smoke gun. It would be another successful gig, from Party Girl – the most efficient, the most innovative, the friendliest service in the area. She would stay, as she had promised, mingle, hand out some cards, chat up a few potential customers and then when it was safe slip away to pick Bobbi up from the memory café.

By the time she had completed her tour, Andi's team-mates were arriving, along with impossibly glamorous-looking partners. Faces she vaguely recognised from the gossip pages of the local paper. Women with time and money. Women who loved parties. She stood at the edge of the deck, tapping the arm of her sunglasses against her lips. It was a gold-mine. She was standing at the entrance of a gold-mine.

Over by the bar, several men had gathered, already knocking back champagne. Jo watched them. Andi, she could see, was smack-bang in the middle. Timing at these parties was everything. Too long a wait, too much alcohol served, and people forgot why they were there. That didn't matter if they didn't have a central role to play, like that of the father-to-be. Someone would need to keep an eye on Andi, at least until the reveal was over. In the back pocket of her jeans she felt the thrum of her phone. She took it out. Nikki had just posted on Instagram. There were already fifteen likes. Dozens of 🩶🩶🩶🩶.

I say boy!

I say girl!

I say twins!

It looks beautiful.

Love the piñata.

I love this! They must do our anniversary.

Jo clicked on the profile of the last comment. The woman was married to a midfielder at Norwich United. Scrolling down, she counted one... two... three... kids! Now she was *in* the gold-mine, falling head first, images of eighteenth birthdays, graduations, engagements, tumbling beside her. She bit down on her lip and opened up her phone, ready to make a note of the woman's name. By the time she looked back up, the deck had started to fill.

Within another twenty minutes, it was crammed. Around thirty Nikki had said. More like fifty, Jo thought, as she made her way through the crowd. Faces pressed in from all sides, and waves of cloying perfume caught in her throat. The music was a little too loud, the laughter a little too easy. It was time to find Nikki, and get on with the reveal while the guests remembered the reason they'd been invited in the first place.

Across at the bar, Andi swayed. There was no sign of Tom. 'Excuse me,' she said pushing uselessly against a tall woman with hair extensions so long she could have made a rope bridge from them and swung herself across. The woman turned, her hair whipping Jo's face. 'Are you JoJo Swainson, from Party Girl?'

'I am,' she answered, the smile instant.

'Fabulous! I'm looking for someone to organise my Christmas party. It's just a small thing. About two hundred.'

But Jo's smile had faded. Through the crowd, a gap had opened up, and she could see Andi more clearly than ever. He was visibly drunk. Stuffing a card into the woman's hand, she excused herself and moved away, watching as the man next to Andi refilled his glass. Tom was nowhere in sight.

She found Nikki in the kitchen. Her flower crown had slipped, the dandelion stalks wilting like cooked spaghetti. Tom was there too, collecting ice. 'We need to do the reveal,' she whispered. 'Get Andi ready.'

Tom nodded, the ice bucket clinking as he left.

'I'm nervous,' Nikki whispered.

'It'll be fine.' She hooked her arm through Nikki's, steering her onto the deck and through the crowd. She was a woman on a mission. Get this baby revealed, get the piñata smashed, the smoke gun fired. Get the crowd cheering and Nikki celebrating her moment... After that, it was up to them.

They reached a quieter space, at the edge of the deck, where Jo stopped. She was looking along the length of the garden to where Tom had moved Andi. Watching, as Tom put a football in Andi's hands, as Andi put the ball down, took a step back... and fell over. She squeezed her eyes shut, rubbed her forehead. 'I know you had your heart set on Andi breaking the piñata,' she said, 'but—'

'He's too drunk,' Nikki finished, because she too was watching.

'He's too drunk,' Vera echoed. She'd come from nowhere.

'It's not that bad,' Jo said brightly. 'Let's forget the piñata and just do the smoke gun, and the cake.'

Nikki's eyes brimmed tears.

'The gun is pretty spectacular,' Jo urged. Judging by the rising noise from the crowd on the deck, if they didn't get on and do the reveal soon, no one would care if it was a boy or a girl, or a baby giraffe. 'Gun?'

Nikki nodded.

In her back pocket, Jo felt the buzz of her phone. She ignored it.

'I'll get Andi some water,' Vera muttered.

But Andi didn't want water. The pupils of his eyes were huge as he thrust the glass back at Jo. '*You think I can't hit that?*' he sneered, his arm making loops as he tried to focus on the piñata.

Standing next to him, Vera slapped it down.

And next to Vera, Jo bit the inside of her mouth so hard she could taste the tang of blood. Two sores now, one either side. She, too, was seething with irritation. Andi was too young, too rich and too stupid. But she was too old, too single and her mortgage – because it was *her* mortgage now – was too big. It depended upon this party going well. A party that was threatening to descend into a family bust-up. 'I've got it,' she said to Vera, who shaking her head, was already backing away.

Jo picked up the smoke gun. 'It's really simple. The

switch is here. It couldn't actually be simpler. One switch. *Fire.*'

'I'm ready,' Nikki breathed, her hand on her chest.

'Great,' Jo turned, signalling to Tom who was back on the deck. Half a moment later, the music died and a heavy silence rose. 'It's OK,' she said, because Nikki's face had drained. She understood. Every party had these moments. Loaded with expectation, vulnerable from all sides. Would it go well? Would it work? Her phone buzzed again. Stepping aside, Jo pulled it from her pocket. It was her mother. She glanced up. The crowd on the deck stood waiting, behind the table Nikki stood waiting, and in her hand her phone buzzed. Nikki knew what to do. 'Mum?' she said as she clamped her hand over her ear and turned away to answer the call.

'Not quite,' a man's voice said. 'But she is here. My wife is just making her a cup of tea.'

'What? I don't understand—'

'My name is William Porter,' the man interrupted. 'And I live in Broadfields Park, off Mill Lane. The apartments used to be a part of a hospital. Your mother rang our bell. She's very confused. She says she was looking for maternity.'

'But she's at the community centre.' Jo had her head down, pacing further along the garden now, one hand still over her free ear. She'd left Bobbi at the community centre. She had watched her mother take a chair, sit herself comfortably so much further to the front. 'Besides,' she added lamely, 'the maternity hospital doesn't exist any more.'

'Well, I don't know about that,' William Porter said. 'I know that this development used to be a hospital though I don't think it had anything to do with maternity. Anyway, it's all apartments now and your mother rang our bell. Can you come and get her?'

For the briefest moment, Jo didn't speak. Couldn't speak. She turned back to the party. Nikki had the gun ready. Andi... Jo squinted. Where was Andi?

'She's wearing a sling. Roberta Carter? Or Bobbi, she said she likes to be known as. I had an aunt called Roberta...' The voice drifted off.

Jo's mouth hung open. Andi had moved to crouch behind the table; she watched horrified as he slipped off the only item of clothing he was still wearing. His boxer shorts.

'This is your mother, right?'

Someone screamed.

'Look, I appreciate you're at a party...'

'I'm not at a party,' she whispered, her voice dry with disbelief.

Andi had stepped out from behind the table, naked as the day he was born.

'But she's getting distressed.'

'No,' Jo mouthed. 'No, please...'

'*It's a boy!*' Andi shouted.

Like a huge and fragile balloon, a gasp went up, floating from the crowd on the deck, hovering over Jo's head.

'*It's a boy!*' Andi yelled again.

And the pop that burst the balloon was Nikki, firing her gun, edible smoke rising as a cloud, settling as blue snow all along her arms.

And then time slowed, got pulled apart like dough in a baker's hands.

Vera marching across the lawn... '*Sa kuradi idioot! See on viimane kord...*' and reaching Andi in long strides, her fist rising, moving forward, making contact... Andi stumbling, knees bowed, arms flailing.

Falling.

'... If it's not too inconvenient...' William Porter was saying.

50

There wasn't anything she could have done…

She couldn't physically have stopped people from leaving…

Jules was still there, to help with cleaning up. And Tom.

There really wasn't…

Heavy with despair, Jo took her foot off the accelerator, slowing as she turned the car onto Mill Lane. It didn't matter which way she spun it, she'd be doomed to rented unicorns and disposable plates forever now. The party had been a disaster, and it had been a disaster because she had allowed herself to lose focus. She wasn't even there now, picking up the pieces. With a flurry of apologies to Nikki, and a rushed explanation to Jules, she had had to leave. She hadn't even had time to find Vera. Her business was going to be over before it had properly begun.

She glanced down at her phone. No calls. William Porter had said Bobbi was getting distressed, but there had been no more calls. *Distress.* As Jo said the word out loud the night before replayed itself. The way her mother had pressed her head against the back of the chair, put her hand over her ear, how she had recoiled in *distress.*

How she hadn't even seen. Worse. How she carried on, insistent and oblivious. Cruel.

Mill Lane was long, and driving past the white-pink of cherry trees in bloom and gardens displaying scarlet tulips, images of the party faded. Nikki's unconstrained weeping and Vera's dark anger, the way that even though the music returned, the atmosphere didn't, the way the crowd had trickled away, leaving Andi's mother, alone on the deck, still clutching her orange juice. Until only one thing remained. Her mother, head pressed against the back of the chair, hand over her ear, recoiling in *distress.*

Eventually, a bronze belfry tower rose sombrely above a canopy of budding green, and she remembered where she was driving to, and why. A sign appeared, Broadfields Park. She put the indicator on and turned into the wide, shingled drive of what had once been a hospital.

William Porter answered his buzzer almost immediately. 'I'll come down,' he said, not waiting for her response. He sounded keen, overly friendly. Perhaps, she thought, as she turned and looked across at the landscaped gardens, he was compensating for his impatience earlier. Or perhaps he was just happy to be getting rid of Bobbi.

'Jo?'

'Yes. William?'

He nodded. 'You made it then.'

'I made it,' she said, smiling at the slightly built, balding man who had answered the door.

'I'm sorry to drag you away from your party.'

'Oh don't worry about that!' She waved a hand. 'Not at all.'

'This way.' And he stood back to let her in.

The hallway she stepped into was magnificent. A large square space, with a parquet floor and a huge domed ceiling. On the left-hand side, a dog-legged staircase led to a landing where a beautiful arched window radiated light.

'The design was intentional,' William said, noting perhaps the way she had paused to take it in. 'There was an emphasis on fresh air and sunlight. Really rather progressive considering.'

Jo frowned. She was about to ask, but something else was bothering her. She turned back to the solid front door. 'How did my mother get in?'

William shrugged. 'We don't know. My wife found her on the landing, right there. He indicated the arched window. She was standing there, looking out. Probably someone was leaving, and she just slipped in.'

'Probably.' Jo nodded. She followed William up the stairs and along a handsome corridor, where more windows overlooked the grounds. 'It is lovely.'

'Isn't it? The wooded area was planted as part of the therapy as well. Who would have thought that an old lunatic asylum would make such lovely apartments?'

'Lunatic?' Her fingers tingled.

'This building was part of the old psychiatric hospital.'

'Broadfields... Broadfields Hospital?'

'That's right,' William said cheerily. 'I'd hate to think what went on once upon a time. Here we are!' And he turned and opened the door of his apartment.

She'd barely had a moment to assimilate his words before she saw Bobbi. Perched on the edge of a handsome pale blue sofa, her thumb rubbing her fingertips, she sat staring across the room. On the sofa opposite, a smartly dressed woman watched her. A tea tray lay on the table between them, the biscuits untouched. When the woman looked up, Jo smiled.

'Thank you,' she said. 'I'm so sorry for the trouble.'

The woman nodded. A polite, limited movement

'Mum?' Jo turned away. This wasn't the old maternity hospital. Her mother had got it very wrong. Jo needed to get her out of here, fast. Away from a place of such memories. Or feelings. She was remembering Violet at the memory café. *If they don't remember they've been, they will remember the good feelings.* What would her mother be feeling now? It couldn't be good. It couldn't possibly be good. 'Mum?'

Bobbi didn't respond. She didn't turn, and she didn't speak.

'She's been like that for the last twenty minutes,' William said. 'I'm afraid we can't get a word out of her. Strange, she was talking when she first came in.'

'She's frightened,' Jo whispered. She could see it, plain as day.

'Of us?' William chuckled.

Jo moved across and knelt down in front of her mother. This close, she could see that Bobbi had something pressed to her chest. She hadn't noticed before, but she could see it now. She was close enough to read the writing: April 1982. She'd returned the photograph to her own handbag last night. She was sure of that. Bobbi, she thought, as she laid her hand over her mother's, must have taken it. With the pressure from Jo's hand, Bobbi's thumb stopped moving, but she didn't turn. She didn't acknowledge Jo, she didn't even seem to be aware of her presence. Still she stared across the room, her eyes fixed in fear.

Jo turned to see.

Her mother was looking at a wooden cabinet. It was a colossal piece of furniture, heavy wood, with full-length doors of grid-worked iron. She was looking and looking, and she wouldn't turn, no matter how much Jo stroked her hand, how softly she whispered, *Mum.*

'She's fascinated by it,' the woman said.

William rocked back on his heels. 'It is a pretty impressive piece. The old armoire.'

'It was probably used to store medicines,' his wife said, although Jo hadn't asked.

'We got it with the apartment. They were going to skip it! Can you believe that?'

'No,' Jo breathed. She couldn't believe it. She couldn't believe where they were and what was happening. For all she knew, they could be sitting in the same room in which her mother had spent the worst weeks of her life. Consumed with grief, locked away with strangers. A time inhabiting the space between sanity and madness. They could even be looking at, admiring, the place where the drugs that had so blighted her mother's life had been stored. For all she knew. Because what did she know? What did she really know? 'Mum,' she said again. 'It's me, Joanne. I've come to take you home.'

And finally, the trance broke. Bobbi turned, her eyes wide with fear. 'How did I get here?'

'It doesn't matter. Let's go home.'

Bobbi shook her head. 'I don't want to be here.'

'I know. It's OK.'

'It wasn't my fault.'

'Of course it wasn't.' Jo stared. At the back of her neck a fresher air chilled. How much she wanted to know! How strong was the desire to fling open this door that was opening in her mother's mind. To push through and see everything! She was – they were – closer than they had ever been, because whatever Bobbi was referring to, whatever *was not her fault* did not take place last night. She was sure of that. Bobbi was not talking about what had happened last night. But she could also feel the eggshell frailness of her mother's wrist-bone, and Bobbi was only sat here now, facing down ghosts of the past, because of last night. Because Jo had been deaf and blind. 'It wasn't anyone's fault,' she whispered, closing that door oh-so-softly. 'If anything, Mum, it's my fault. I shouldn't have shown you the diary. I shouldn't have made you read it.'

From behind came a soft cough. 'We'll give you a few minutes,' William said.

'Thank you.' Jo nodded, watching as William took his wife's arm and steered her towards a door through which Jo glimpsed what must have been the kitchen.

'They made us line up.'

She turned back to her mother. 'I'm sorry, Mum. I shouldn't have pushed.'

'They waited until we had swallowed everything.'

'Mum.'

'There was a woman in the next bed. She hated the bangs. She screamed every time.'

'Bangs?'

'The fireworks,' Bobbi whispered. 'I watched from the window. On the stairs.'

Jo's head dropped. So this *was* the place her mother had gone to. The place her eight-year-old self had hoped she would not come back from.

'I was glad to take the tablets.' Bobbi was looking straight at her. 'They made me forget.'

'It's OK.' Jo stroked her mother's hand. 'It's all OK now.'

'I forgot. I forgot I wrote those things.'

'I'm glad you did. You don't need to remember.'

'But you found it again.'

'I shouldn't have. I shouldn't have gone looking.'

'Where did you find it?'

Still holding her mother's hand, she fell back on her knees. 'In the shed,' she said quietly. 'With my old stuff. Drawings from when I was little.'

'Your things? I put it with your things?'

'You must have.'

Bobbi shook her head. 'I was sick. I didn't remember how sick I was.'

'I know. It's OK, Mum. I know.'

And suddenly Bobbi leaned forward, her hand trembling as she stroked Jo's cheek. 'I was trying to get better, Joanne. You were my baby. I was trying to get better for you. I was trying to get back to you'.

Jo laid her hand against her mother's, pressing it to her face. She wanted to hold it there. She wanted to feel the touch of the papery skin forever. All her life she had held one undeniable truth. Her mother had left. There had never been room for any other truth. But Bobbi had just said it: she had tried to come back. Words that flattened a wall she hadn't been able to see through or climb over. The boxing away of her childhood had been an act of preservation. Not rejection. The revelation was bone-deep and bitter-sweet. 'Let's get home,' she said, her voice thick with emotion. 'Let me take you home.'

'I'm going back for him.' Bobbi's eyes were clear, inches from her own.

'The baby's gone, Mum.' She was crying now. 'The baby's gone.'

'I'm going back for him too.'

'The baby died,' she pleaded. 'There's nothing to go back for.'

'No.' Bobbi shook her head. 'He said he would leave.'

Jo didn't speak. The clarity of her mother's gaze could not be refused.

'He said he would leave, and take you, if I kept him. He made me choose.'

Slowly she lowered Bobbi's hand. These were the words that had ended the diary. 'Me?' she whispered. 'Dad said he would leave, and take me?'

'I had to choose.'

'You're confused, Mum.' But her mother looked as lucid and calm as Jo had ever seen her. It was she that was confused. 'You're freezing cold,' she said. But she meant herself. She was cold.

'No.' And with a strength she wouldn't have believed, had she not felt it, Bobbi pulled her hand away and turned, a trail of clear mucus clinging to her nose like a stalactite in a cave

A long moment passed. Because she didn't know what else to do, she felt deep into the pocket of her jacket, found a scrap of tissue and reached up to wipe her mother's nose. It was like wiping the face of a statue. 'I don't know what to do,' she whispered. 'I don't know how to help, Mum. I can't bring him back. Do you know where he's buried? Maybe—'

'My baby didn't die,' Bobbi said as she turned back and looked directly at Jo. 'I'm not losing my mind, Joanne. I'm not losing my mind.'

'Mum, the doctor said...' Jo paused. What *had* Dr Dandicott said? *Loss. I do suspect that there may have been a loss.* Such a soft-syllabled, ambiguous phrase and she remembered now how tentative she'd thought the words were, a tiptoeing. 'Let's get you home,' she said, inching her hand forward to take the photograph resting now on Bobbi's lap.

And, as she helped her mother to her feet, she studied it carefully, the tiny, scrunched face of her brother. Because her mother had said 'him'... *I'm going back for him too.* And as she looked, her heart began to fold, halves to quarters, quarters to eighths, eighths to sixteenths, until it was nothing more than a tiny acorn in her chest, an acorn the size of a newborn's live and beating heart.

51

Sweat pooling at her back, Jo flung the bedcovers off, thrust an arm into the cool air and stared at the ceiling. She had no idea what time it was. Three a.m.? Four? Through the open window she could hear the whispering of the garden, sense the nearly-white light of a blue moon. She stretched her arms above her head and circled her wrists. The clicking louder than castanets. Reaching for her phone, she checked the time. Four-thirty.

She sat up, found her dressing gown and without turning the lights on, opened her bedroom door. Immediately a welcome draught of fresh air hit her face, deliciously cool. Along her arm, goosebumps sprung like molehills. Tying the belt of her gown, she made her way along the darkened hallway. Bobbi's bedroom door was half open. Jo went to close it. The air this far along the hall was even fresher, as if a door was open to outside. She frowned and instead of closing the bedroom door, peered around it. The bed was empty. Moments passed. What she was looking at didn't make sense, so her mind refused to accommodate it, sending instead the image of the empty bed back, again and again, as if the next time it would include her mother, tucked up, where she should have been.

And still she stared.

If the stream of cool air on her neck hadn't distracted her, she might have stood longer. It came from the direction of the kitchen and as soon as she put the light on, she saw. The back door was wide open. *Mum?* But only a whispering from the lilac's shivering leaves came back as answer. Hugging her gown, she made her way out of the door, along the path and out to the garden.

Bobbi was sitting on a patio chair. A curved, small figure, darkly shaped against the pale square of the garden fence. She wore a dressing gown; she didn't stir as Jo approached.

'Mum,' she whispered, wary of breaking the spell.

'You've come back.' Bobbi turned.

'I've come back,' she said, 'and I'm not leaving.' Pulling a chair close, Jo sat down. 'What are you doing out here?' Bobbi had been exhausted. When they had arrived home, she had refused dinner, choosing instead to go straight to bed. Jo had been relieved; her mother had looked older, more fragile than ever.

'I came to look,' Bobbi said, and she raised a hand to the moon. 'I came to look at it.'

Jo too, raised her chin. It was as big a moon as she'd ever seen. A luminescent silver-white, patterned all over with soft ochre. And somewhere, a sea of deep tranquility. No wonder her sleep had been light, no wonder Bobbi too had wakened. 'The moon?'

'Moon.' As if it were a flavour and not a word, Bobbi held onto the sound. 'I thought if I came and looked closer, I'd remember.' She stopped talking and it seemed to Jo that she was doing exactly that, looking as closely as she could at a celestial object hundreds of thousands of miles away. 'I couldn't find the name.'

'Moon,' Jo whispered.

'Moon. That's it.' Bobbi nodded. 'What happens,' she said, 'what happens when they're all gone, Joanne?'

'When what's all gone?'

'The words. Moon. Grass. Sky. Flower... What happens when I can't remember. Will they still be there?'

For the longest moment Jo didn't speak. Her mother had never asked such a question of her, which of course was not a question at all. It was a plea. A petition for a reassurance that she didn't know how to give. How could she? How could anyone understand the isolation of being trapped in a world you could no longer name? 'The grass will still be there,' she started, quietly. 'When you walk on it, it will feel the same. The sky will still be there. What exists, still exists.' It felt right. These things went beyond names.

'His name was Liam.'

'Liam.' Now it was her turn to hold onto the resonance. *Liam.*

'He was born at four minutes past six on the seventh of April, 1982. Seven pounds, three ounces. Fifty-one centimetres.' Bobbi's jawline was sharp in the soft light. All the blurriness, the hesitancy that had so defined her, gone. She sat now, her spine straight, her eyes unblinking. 'I believe they kept the name.'

'They?' Jo whispered, she barely dared move.

Across the lawn came the shrill chirp of an unseen grasshopper.

'I've been writing things down.'

Jo didn't speak. She looked down at her hands in her lap and what she was thinking was how unimportant words were, in the end. How last time she had used far too many of them, far too quickly. Thrown them up into the air like a deck of cards and expected her mother to sort them – *demanded* that she decode and understand them, play them back. When all the time she hadn't needed to say anything. Only to listen and let Bobbi pick her own way back. And now she had. Liam. Born at four minutes past six, seven pounds three ounces, fifty-one centimetres. He had lived.

'I'm beginning to remember,' Bobbi said, and her voice was hesitant again. Boulder-size gaps between sentences. 'I did write those things. I blamed your father, but I see now. I was sick. I did need help.'

'What happened?' she whispered. 'To Liam.'

'They took him away. He was three hours old and they took him away.'

'Adopted?'

Bobbi nodded. 'Your father said he wouldn't raise another man's child.' She turned. 'Liam wasn't your father's child, Joanne. I'm sorry.'

Jo sat. The words, and the story they carried, slotting in the last rungs of a ladder, complete now, between herself and her mother. 'I remember,' she said. 'I remember being in the bath, and the doorbell rang. I remember the cigarette smoke. And Dad never smoked.'

Bobbi shook her head. 'No, your father never smoked.'

Silver light fringed the black spires of foxgloves, and the outline of the shed was dark. That forgotten place where so much had been boxed up and hidden away.

'He was a very controlling man, Joanne. Your father.'

She sat, staring across the shimmering grass, neither confirming nor denying what she had no knowledge of. He hadn't tried to control her. He had, in fact, been indifferent rather than controlling. Or he'd been drunk. But he had looked after her. And he had stayed. That was what had mattered then.

And yet, he had exerted more control over her life than she could ever have known, until this moment. He had denied her her mother, and a brother. Too proud to raise another man's child. He had made her mother choose. He hadn't given Jo any choice at all.

'He never would let me learn to drive.' Bobbi turned to her. 'I wanted to drive, but he wouldn't let me learn.'

Leaning forward, Jo made a steeple of her hands, elbows resting on her knees as tears streamed down her face. 'Did you ever love him,' she said. She had to know. For his sake, and for hers. To put to rest the ghost of that lonely father and his lonely child, she had to know.

'I did.' Bobbi curled into her dressing gown, wrapping it tighter. 'In the beginning, I loved him very much. I remember we laughed a lot. He made me laugh. I used to sing, and he came to see me. He bought me flowers.'

'I didn't know.' Her voice was a whisper. She didn't know, hadn't known that her mother used to sing, that her father had bought her flowers, that once upon a time they had loved each other, just as once upon a time Toby and she had loved each other. They too had laughed a lot, in the beginning. 'This other man?' she said. 'Did you love this other man?' The question was clumsy. A hammer, to break a delicate shell. But she didn't have any other tool.

'I was lonely,' Bobbi said. 'I was lonely at that cottage.'

Jo nodded. She had loved the cottage. The huge skies, the spread of land in all directions, broken only by stacks of wheat piled like giant lego bricks, the beet factory on a distant skyline. Every morning walking to school she had felt as if she could keep going to the first horizon and then the horizon after that. To the end of the world, because the world had seemed so available, so easy to explore. It had been why getting on a plane and flying away had always felt so easy. But if she had walked to school, where had Bobbi walked to? Where had she gone? Who had she talked to? There had been no neighbours. None at all.

'You were free as a bird there,' Bobbi said.

Jo turned. 'And you were caged? Is that why you never came back? After the hospital?'

Her mother's smile was small and sad. She lifted her hand and it shook as her fingers traced the line of her brow. 'I remember the day I first saw it. The cottage. I thought it was too far away from everything. I thought we were only coming to look, but your father had already signed the papers. Decided.'

'Without telling you?'

'Yes.' Bobbi nodded. 'Without telling me.'

She nodded, she leaned back and lifted her chin. Her father had died young, only fifty-five. And suddenly it seemed preposterous. The idea that she should have thought she had known either of her parents. She would be forty-nine on her next birthday, and who she was now was not who she was on her last birthday. She wouldn't be married for a start. She was changing. Life had changed her, and in a place where she had felt free, her mother had felt caged.

'I'm cold.' Bobbi looked down at her dressing gown. 'Where's my jacket?' And looking up at Jo, her eyes emptied.

'Mum?'

Her mother's face was blank as a wall.

'Mum? It's me. Joanne.'

'Joanne?' Bobbi repeated the word.

And it was just a word, emptiness echoing as the wide-open space of a memory voided opened up.

52

The next morning Jo was woken by the tinny cheerfulness of Kool & The Gang, urging her to *Celebrate good times*. And again, *Celebrate good times, come on—*

'Hello.' Lightning quick, she rolled over, snatched at her phone and swiped right.

'Jo?' a cheerful voice said. 'This is Lindsey!'

'Lindsey?' Despite the speed of her movement, her voice was slow with sleep.

'From Ashdown House? I'm just ringing to give you a little heads up, before our appointment later today.'

Heads up? Scrabbling up onto her elbow, she blinked at the wall opposite. Her eyes felt dry as dust and blinking again, she could feel the edge of plastic. She'd fallen asleep with her lenses in. She looked down. And her t-shirt on.

'Presuming your mother likes us, I would be in a position to offer her a place from next week.'

Lindsey. Ashdown House. The pieces fell into place.

'That's welcome news, I expect?' Lindsey said.

Clutching the phone at her ear, she fell back on the pillow. There was a time, not so long ago, when she wouldn't have hesitated. *Of course,* she would have said. Very welcome. Now, she couldn't find any words to express what she was feeling. She didn't know. Apart from sweaty and exhausted, she didn't know how she felt about the fact that soon, she could walk away. Deliver her mother up to the care of Ashdown House, satisfied that she had done all that had been required. All that could have been expected. '... Yes.' The word climbed out, so reluctant was she to say it. The call ended, and she lay, arms stretched above her head, staring at the ceiling.

Last night, Bobbi had fallen into the dense fog of dementia, and Jo hadn't been enough. Sitting shoulder to shoulder, under a moon they had caught and named together, her physical presence had not been enough. Her mother had not known her.

Nothing had been said, she'd guided Bobbi back to bed, made sure she was comfortable, and then lain awake for hours. And although sleep had eventually come, it had been awkward and fitful. Her hand still tingled with pins and needles where she'd lain on it and her neck was stiff as a rod. The situation could not continue. And after yesterday wasn't it clear that Bobbi would be better off in the safety of a place like Ashdown House. Better off living with people who could look after her properly. Who wouldn't drop her off like an unwanted package leaving her to roam the streets vulnerable and lost. From the hallway came the sound of a key scraping in the lock. Vera. Exactly on time, as always. Yes, Bobbi would be better off with almost anyone other than her own daughter.

She pushed into the pillow and pulled the duvet over

her head. She had nothing else to do today anyway. After the fiasco yesterday at Nikki's party, who would be interested in hiring her?

53

By the time she had hauled herself out of bed and into the kitchen, Vera had filled the dishwasher and made a pot of coffee.

'Morning.' Jo settled herself at the table.

Vera nodded. She was wearing sunglasses, the silver foil packet in her hands crackling loudly as she wrestled it open.

'Are you OK?' Jo frowned. She'd left the party so quickly, anything could have happened. Andi, she was thinking, could have returned Vera's punch. He probably did. Hence the sunglasses. 'Did something happen, Vera?'

'How is Bobbi?' Vera batted the question away. 'They said you had to go and pick her up.'

'She's OK. She's tired.'

'I thought she was at the memory café.'

Jo leaned her elbows on the table and dropped her head into her hands. 'It's a long story,' she said, through a mop of hair. 'How's Nikki?'

'Fine.' Whatever Vera had been fighting with gave up. The packet popped open. 'Just don't ask about Andi.'

'I won't.' She looked up. 'He's the last thing on my mind right now.'

'I wish I could say the same.' Vera tipped the contents of the packet onto a plate and plonked the plate onto the table. 'I picked them up on the way,' she said. 'I thought we needed them. Just save the crocodiles for me. Here.' And now she handed Jo a cup of coffee.

Looking up through her hands, Jo smiled. The plate was piled high with chocolate animals. 'Thank you,' she whispered, and picked up an elephant. But she didn't eat it; she was looking at Vera, at the sunglasses. 'What happened?' she said. 'Please don't tell me he hit you, Vera?'

'Andi?'

Jo nodded. She tapped at her eye. 'Why the glasses?'

'He didn't hit me.' Dipping her head, Vera removed the sunglasses.

'Oh. I see.' Slowly, Jo put the biscuit back on the plate, her fingertips sticky with chocolate. There was no bruising, no imprint of violence at Vera's eyes, just a tell-tale puffiness. Vera had been crying. And it was almost impossible to imagine in this stoic mountain of a woman. 'You've been crying? she said softly.

Vera nodded. She put a fist to her mouth, blinking furiously. 'I can't live there any more,' she whispered. 'I left not long after you, Jo. Nikki started blaming herself for what happened and I couldn't listen to it, so I went to a friend's house. She has to stand up to him. Or not. Either way, I have to leave.'

'Oh, Vera.' Jo stood up. She wiped her hands clean and put them on Vera's shoulders. 'If it's anyone's fault,' she said firmly, 'it's mine. I'm the party planner. It's up to me to keep things running smoothly. I got distracted. I took my eye off the ball and—'

'It was Andi's fault,' Vera said bluntly. 'It's as simple as that.'

'It was my party to—'

'No.' Vera shook her head. 'It was Andi who did what he did. And your mother needed you, Jo. She needed you.'

'Yes.' She sat back down. There was nothing to add. Bobbi had needed her. And although it was impossible to know what might have happened had she ignored the call, kept her attention focused, what wasn't impossible was the truth of understanding that the quantum of calm she felt this morning came from knowing that she *had* answered. Her shoulders sagged, her back rounded, as any ounce of argument remaining gave up and left in a huge sigh of resignation. A sharp pinging sound sliced through her thoughts, made her lift her head.

Vera was swiping at her phone. 'So greedy!' she muttered.

'What are you looking at?'

'Somewhere to live. I have a notification set up.' Vera turned the screen around. 'Look at it! The site is called My Cosy Space. They should call it My Coffin Space! Not enough room to lie down. No bath, no smokers, no pets, no cheap either!'

Leaning forward, Jo peered at the image on Vera's phone. The room was tiny. It would have fitted into Nikki's house a hundred times over. 'Can't you ask Nikki?'

'For help? That means asking *him*.' Vera shook her head. '*Never!*' And putting her phone down, she turned and poured out a cup of coffee for herself. 'You're not going to work today?'

Leaning back, she sighed, stretched her arms forward and turned her hands over and looked at them. 'Not today,

Vera. Or tomorrow. Or ever again, I don't think. Not after yesterday. Who is going to want to hire me now?'

'Is it that bad?'

And now it was Jo's turn to shrug. 'I don't know, yet. I'll see when I check emails and bookings. But...' She stood up, both hands wrapped around her cup. 'Before all that, the first thing I'm going to do is check on Bobbi. Then...' The words fell away, and the ground scooped from under her feet. She put a hand out to the chair, coffee splashing over her wrist. 'My parents,' she heard herself saying, as the cup was eased from her hands. 'They kept secrets, Vera. They kept secrets.' She was back on the chair, with no idea how that had happened.

Vera's hand was on her arm. 'We all keep secrets, Jo.'

'No.' Jo shook her head, her voice pale and urgent. 'Not like this. These are the kinds of secrets that change things, Vera. They change everything.'

'Well, I know about those kinds of secrets too,' Vera whispered.

'Can I show you something?' It felt right. Because Vera wasn't a tank. She wore the amour she did because of the life she had lived. And looking at her now, hearing the soft whisper, *I know about those kinds of secrets too,* Jo felt overwhelmed with gratitude. Diane was thousands of miles away, wrapped in the glow of her new grandchild. And Toby? Toby had gone. But Vera was here. Vera who had come into her life like a gift she hadn't known she needed. 'I'd really like to show you something.'

'My brother,' she said as she handed the photograph to Vera. 'My mother's secret. And my father's. Born at four minutes past six on the seventh of April, 1982. Seven pounds, three ounces. Fifty one centimetres.'

Vera held it for a long time before she looked up and said, 'You didn't know before yesterday?'

'I'd been trying to find out.' She shrugged. 'That's what I was doing, the day you saw me going through Bobbi's wardrobe.'

'When was this?'

'You don't remember? You didn't wonder what I was doing?'

'No.'

Jo smiled. She hadn't even questioned it – Vera's assumption, her guilt. She'd worn it willingly. She'd been wearing it forever. Guilt that her mother had left. Guilt that she hadn't cried. She reached her hands upwards to stretch her body and her mind. She wanted to know what she was thinking, give it space. It hadn't been easy to start lifting the veil that had shrouded her mother's life, to even understand that there had been a veil. Goosebumps raised a trail along her arms. What if Bobbi had never fallen? What if she had gone to her grave with that photograph snuggled in the folds of her purse? Would Jo ever have found out? Or would she have gone to her own grave, blinded by a fixed idea of who her mother was that wasn't right, wasn't whole. 'That photo,' she said quietly, 'was in Bobbi's handbag, the day she fell. They thought it was her grandchild. It wasn't, of course because…' Pausing, Jo looked up at Vera, her smile small and sad. She'd been about to say, *because I don't have children,* but the thought had hit a wall. A wall made up of Vera's words: *we all keep secrets.* What had she said in response? *These are the kinds of secrets, that change things.* She'd never said her secret out loud, but Toby had come to guess it anyway. And it had changed things for both of them. She hadn't wanted children. 'I thought the baby had died,' she said, as Vera handed the photograph back. 'I don't know why. And yesterday, Bobbi told me that it hadn't. She's been saying it all along, Vera.' Jo looked up. 'All along, she's been telling me that she isn't losing her mind. I just didn't believe her.'

Vera nodded. 'Last week, I couldn't find my cigarettes and Bobbi said they were on top of the wheelie bin. When I told her I always keep them in my pocket, she said the same thing. *I'm not losing my mind.* You know where they were?'

'On top of the bin?'

'On top of the bin.'

'Just because she can't remember some things, doesn't mean that she doesn't remember anything, Jo.'

'I see that now.' For a long moment they held each other's eye, the moment broken only by the sound of the dishwasher's churning. 'I just don't understand why I wasn't told,' she whispered. 'And I don't think I ever will.'

Carefully, Vera turned and picked up her cup. 'My father,' she said, 'he never told me that my mother was going to die.'

Jo looked at her.

'In the end, my mother told me herself. This was her secret, Jo. The one that changed everything.' Vera shrugged.

Through glassy tears, Jo smiled. 'Nikki said that she was envious of you, because you got to know your mother. She talked about how close you were.'

'We were very close.' Vera looked at Jo. 'I watched her die. It's why I never wanted children myself. I saw what it meant to her, to have to leave us. Especially Nikki, so young. I never wanted to risk that. History can sometimes repeat itself.' Her hands, Jo saw, shook as she brought her cup to her lips and took a slow, calibrated sip of coffee.

'I know,' Jo whispered. Her throat was rock hard and at the same time tender as if the flesh had been sliced open.

'It's the same for me,' she managed, before she had to lower her head and take such a deep breath her whole body shuddered. 'Until yesterday,' she said, 'I truly believed my mother didn't love me, and this is a hard thing to admit.' She paused, took a small gasp. It was the hardest thing. So hard it branded her with shame. So hard she had never, not even to Toby, said it out loud. 'I was terrified of doing the same, Vera. Of becoming a mother to a child I didn't love.'

'Jo.' Vera's voice was a feather. It landed on her shoulder, nudging her to lift her chin and look up.

'I've never told anyone that,' she said.

'But now you have.'

'Now I have,' she whispered. Now, she really had.

From the hallway came the sound of paper thrust through the letterbox, the slap of the post landing on the carpet, the thin clatter of the box closing behind.

'Do you still think that?' Vera said. 'That she doesn't love you?' She didn't wait for an answer. 'Bobbi's always asking after you. She's always asking where you are, when you're coming back.'

'No.' Shaking her head, Jo said it again, louder. '*No.*' She was thinking of the way Bobbi had stroked her cheek yesterday. 'I was her baby, she—' But her voice broke. She put a hand to her mouth, tears rolling down her cheeks. 'She was sick, Vera. When I was a child, my mother was very sick, and she tried. She tried to get better. I just never knew.' Her head dropped again, her shoulders shuddering with each sob. 'I never knew,' she whispered. 'I never knew.'

Long moments passed. Vera handed her a tissue, waiting until she had blown her nose and wiped her face. 'What are you going to do?' she said.

'About this?' Jo picked up the photograph. 'I don't know.'

'Would you like my advice?' But again, Vera didn't wait

for an answer. 'Spend today with your mother, Jo. Sit in the sun with her, while you still can.'

It was good advice. And she was so tired, it was welcome advice. Spend the day, sitting with Bobbi in the garden? Standing up, she pushed the chair under the table and waited a moment. If it was a choice between taking her mother to see a care home, or sitting in the sun with her, it was crystal clear. She would – they would – sit in the sun, together. Nothing felt more right. 'I have an appointment,' she said. 'I'm supposed to be taking Bobbi to see a care home today.'

'OK.' The disappointment that passed across Vera's face was unmistakable.

'I'm sorry,' Jo said. 'I really am, Vera. I can cancel...' She sighed. 'But at some point, I'll have to make a decision. Especially after yesterday.'

Vera nodded. 'I understand.'

'I'll have to sell the bungalow.'

'It's OK, Jo.'

'The fees are... well...' But before she could say any more, she was interrupted by a laugh and then the throaty yell of the opening rap of the Spice Girls' 'Wannabe'. A ringtone reserved for Diane... Who should be sound asleep, six hours behind and four thousand miles away in Chicago.

54

'Where are you?' Diane said, firing off the question before Jo had the phone at her ear.

'I'm at my mother's.' Head down, Jo walked along the hallway. The urgency in Diane's voice was irritating. After everything that had happened. It made her feel as if Diane expected Jo to be at her beck and call when needed, but had it been the other way around...

'I'm standing outside your house, Jo. And there's a For Sale sign. What is going on?'

'Oh.' Jo paused. 'Wait a moment. I'm going to take this outside.' And opening the back door, she stepped into a morning that was warm and fresh, perfumed with the honey- rich scent of the first roses. 'Aren't you meant to be in Chicago?'

'I was and now I'm not. What's going on, Jo?'

'Well congratulations, Grandma! How's Rachel doing?'

The pause on the other end of the line didn't go unnoticed. But Jo wasn't ready to start. She didn't know where to start.

'Thank you,' Diane said eventually. 'And since you ask, my daughter has turned into a marsupial.'

'Marsupial?

'She's got the baby strapped to her day and night. Like a kangaroo. The fourth trimester, she calls it. Well she can call it what she likes, but she could have told me before I flew thousands of miles to heat up lasagne, and hang around like a spare wheel! Not that I said anything. God, Jo, you'd think no one had ever had a baby before! And do not talk to me about their apartment. You can't move for gadgets. They've spent a fortune! I don't know why, considering she never puts it down. Honestly, I had more space and more sleep on the plane back than I've had in the last week. It's a relief actually. I feel relieved to be able to leave them to it. Anyway...' Diane took a deep breath. '*Now* are you going to answer my question? And before you do, here's another one! Why the hell didn't you tell me?'

One arm wrapped around her waist, the other holding her phone, Jo looked up at the sky. 'How did you find out?'

'I rang Toby.'

'You rang him? Why?'

'Well, I couldn't get hold of you, and I wanted to discuss your new-found fame. And obviously he told me. I don't know what to say, Jo. I'm so sorry. I really am.'

The breeze was fresh on her face as she listened. 'It's OK,' she said, for Diane's sake more than her own.

'I know you'd been having difficulties. I didn't realise it was that bad.'

'Neither did I. But it's OK. It really is, Di. I'm OK.'

'We need to meet.'

'I'm not sure there's much to say.'

'Well... we don't have to talk about that... *yet*. But we need to meet. I want to hear all about it! Can we start with

Vera? I presume it was Vera? That was an impressive right hook!'

'Vera?'

'*And* we need to discuss what you're going to do with all the publicity. You'll have to act fast, Jo. Yesterday's news and all that. This beats *The Gazette* hands down—'

'*Stop!*' Jo raised her palm. 'Di! I have no idea what you're talking about.'

In the pause that opened up, Jo could almost see it, the shock that had momentarily silenced Diane. So big and round it was.

'*You don't know?*'

'No!' She wanted to laugh. 'No Di, I *really* don't know.'

'You went viral, Jo! That party you did for the footballer's wife? You're all over Instagram! Haven't you seen?'

She did a confused half turn, looking out at the garden, turning back to the bungalow. 'I don't have notifications...'

'Party Girl is going to be inundated! You can't buy this kind of publicity. That's why I rang Toby in the first place.'

Jo didn't speak. Her eyes had fixed on the frame of the kitchen window as her mind struggled to shuffle yesterday into a readable order. The memory café... Nikki's party... Andi naked... Vera...

'Open Instagram,' Diane urged. '*Now!*'

55

Of course someone had filmed it. Andi's stunt. Vera's punch. Yes, it had gone viral.

'Are you looking?' Diane said. She sounded as excited as a teenager at a pop concert. 'Can you see?'

'I can but...' Her hands were shaking and her head felt so light, one tip forward and it might fall off. Overnight, Party Girl's Instagram account had accrued nearly thirty thousand followers. Diane was right. She could never have paid for this. Never.

'And if you take a look at Norwich United's website, Andi's football shirt has sold out. So they'll be happy too.'

'Really, Di?'

'What can I say?' Diane laughed. 'It's a long flight. I was bored.'

Jo smiled.

'So when can we meet? I want to hear all about it.'

'Aren't you tired?'

'I have time,' Diane said. 'I'm going to collapse later, but I'm fine now.

Jo was still looking at the kitchen window. Bobbi would

probably sleep a long time after last night, but to meet Diane, and tell her about the party, would be to tell her about Broadfields, would be to tell her about Liam... She paused, her hand at her lip as she bit down on it. *Liam.* No longer, *the baby*. He had a name, a date of birth. And he was alive. 'It's a long story,' she said. 'And I'm really not sure where to start.'

'Why don't you start here, Jo. Judging by the length of the grass on your front lawn, I'd say you could do with starting here.'

'My house?'

'Yes,' Diane said. '*Your* house. You need to come home, Jo.'

56

Diane was sitting on the grass, her suitcase and handbag by the front door. 'Where are the butterflies?' she called, as Jo got out of her car. 'I loved them. Toby hasn't taken the butterflies, has he?'

'I took them,' she said. And looking across to the empty spaces where they had once stood, she added. 'And I'm glad I did. I've needed them.'

In a move that had all the elegance of a carthorse, Diane twisted onto her knees, elbows wide, arms shaking as she hefted herself to her feet. Shuffling sideways, she gasped as she creaked her spine straight. 'My knees! I wasn't built for long haul at twenty-four, never mind fifty-four.'

'I didn't realise you'd come straight from the airport.'

'Where else would I go!' Diane said and pulled Jo into a hug.

Inside, the house was a portrait, a still-life, displaying the unused props of lives that had moved on. The shoe rack, so neat in its emptiness, the undisturbed plumpness of sofa cushions, the perfect lines of carpet tread no longer trodden. Jo dropped her keys in the bowl on the sideboard and the clatter was loud. Then she took off her shoes, took a deep breath and went into the kitchen, where it was all exactly as she remembered. His silhouette, his voice, *I'm here, JoJo.* The fear in his eyes he hadn't been able to hide. It had been so difficult for him to tell her, and she wondered now, as she stood and looked at the space they had once shared, if he hadn't found the courage, would she?

'You OK?' Diane's hand was on her shoulder.

Jo nodded, but she didn't move.

'I'll put the kettle on,' Diane said. 'I know where everything is.'

57

'What are you going to do?' Diane said, as she put the photograph down on the bench and stood to fill the cafetière for a second time.

Jo smiled. 'Vera suggested I sit in the sun with Bobbi. While I still can. And I think I will. At least today, I will.'

'It's not a bad suggestion.'

'It's a good suggestion.' Jo nodded. She looked down at the bench and folded her arms. 'But I'm going to find him,' she said. 'I have a date of birth now, a place, a name. If he's out there, I'm going to find him, Di. Before it's too late.'

Neither of them spoke. There was no need for words, no need for anyone to say what *too late* meant.

'Start with the adoption register,' Diane said. 'He might have put himself on there, and if not, you can put yourself on.'

'Me? Or Bobbi?'

'Either of you.'

'I can put myself on it?'

'Of course you can! You're his family too, Jo.' Diane pushed the plunger down and carried it across. And the smell of fresh coffee was the aroma of possibility, the unveiling of a new day, a new beginning. That baby was her family, and she was his. Somewhere, out there, she had family.

Diane picked up the photograph again. 'He'd be about forty? Forty-one?'

'What if he's no longer alive?'

Diane shrugged.

'Or if he doesn't want to meet?'

Diane shrugged again.

'Or if he hasn't forgiven her?'

'This isn't a movie, Jo. He's probably a middle manager living around the corner with a receding hairline and three kids. And if he wants to meet... great. And if he doesn't, well at least you tried. You don't have to say anything to your mother until you know.'

'No.' Jo picked up her coffee. Diane was right of course. She didn't have to tell Bobbi.

'Just like you didn't say anything to me.'

Looking up, she held Diane's eye. 'It felt too much,' she said and waited for a moment to find more. But there was no more. Trying to find the space to slot her worries into her friend's busy life had simply felt too much.

'I would have dropped everything,' Diane reached across and squeezed her hand. 'You know I would.'

'Would you?' Jo smiled. 'Think about it, Di. You've got your family, your grandchildren, your own parents, Simon's father. Could you really have dropped everything?'

'No.' Diane's voice was small. 'No,' she said again. 'I'm not sure I could have.' Briefly, she closed her eyes, squeezing back tears. 'It's hard, isn't it? Always trying to please everyone. Sometimes I feel as if I'm being pulled in six different directions.'

'Too hard.' Jo nodded.

'Not like when we were young.'

'Not at all like when we were young.'

And looking at each other, they smiled again.

Diane leaned back, her shoulders rising as she took an enormous breath. 'Well, I'm glad you've told me now.'

'Me too,' Jo said. 'But you look exhausted, Di.'

'I am exhausted.'

'I was supposed to be taking Bobbi to see a care home today.' Jo stood and took the cups across to the sink. 'But I think I'm going to take Vera's advice. It can wait, can't it?'

'Has it been decided then? We haven't even had that conversation with Simon's dad.'

'I can't see any other option. She doesn't want to go, but…' The words fell heavy as leaden balloons. Jo turned the tap on and began rinsing the cups. 'It wasn't so much a conversation,' she started, but the memory of Bobbi pressed against the chair, her hand at her ear, had her turning off the tap, standing at the sink frozen with shame.

'Take Vera's advice, Jo.' Diane's voice was gentle, she was at her side now, her hand on Jo's shoulder. 'No need to decide anything today.'

'No. Not today.'

'One thing that can't wait. I need to text Simon and tell him I'm on my way and then I need the bathroom.'

Jo smiled. 'You know where it is.'

As Diane took her phone out, Jo took a tea towel and dried the cups as carefully as if they were precious porcelain. Then she put them back in the cupboard, along with the other cups, careful to keep the bright pattern facing outward. And looking at them she thought of Lizzie and her teapots, her *whimsicals.* She'd missed them, these cups. These silly things, that weren't silly at all. That she'd chosen for their cheeriness, that she enjoyed looking at, enjoyed drinking from, that gave her a small pleasure at the beginning of every day. Hands on hips she looked across the kitchen, through the wide-open doors to the living room. Diane had been right. She had needed to come home. It wasn't so difficult to bear, because suddenly the ghost of her husband seemed to have grown so quiet and so small. Maybe he was still there in the corner of a kitchen drawer, in the restaurant cards he collected. Or maybe in the sideboard where there was bound to be a stray golf tee, an open packet of throat lozenges. But these were hidden places. He wasn't visible in the wide pale walls that reflected seas of dappling sunshine, the elegant furniture and tasteful fittings she had chosen... That she would soon have to leave behind in order to start all over... Somewhere else. The thought brought new tears, and she sat heavily, her hand pinching her nose as she shook her head and tried to stop them.

'Oh, Jo.' Diane put her phone down.

'It's not him,' Jo whispered. 'It's the house. I'm going to miss the house more than him.'

'Can't you keep it?'

'I can't see how. The mortgage is too much.'

Diane didn't speak. 'I wish I could help,' Diane said quietly. 'I really wish I could.'

'I know.' Jo smiled. 'I know you do.'

And then Diane's hands were on her shoulders, heavy and warm. 'One thing at a time, Jo. It's the only way. One thing at a time. I'm popping to the bathroom and then we're going. Me to bed, you to sit in the sun.'

'OK,' she sniffed. 'OK.'

And with Diane upstairs, Jo went through to the living room, to the patio doors, and stood looking out at the garden, the blank canvas Toby and she were supposed to have been filling together. The space where the summer-house was supposed to go. What she had said was true. She would miss the house more than Toby, and she thought of Vera, swiping through rooms the size of broom cupboards. She understood. She might have a bigger budget, but facing down the thought of having to do the same, of starting again, was like facing down a rockface. Sighing, she went to the hall and took her phone from her bag. She might as well get started. Might as well look the thing in the eye, get some idea of what she could afford. On auto-pilot, she opened email first.

She had seventy-three new messages.

Seventy-three.

Forehead furrowed in disbelief, she opened her inbox. There they were, all seventy-three of them, all enquiries for the services of Party Girl. One with a date two years away. So many that Toby's *Something for you to sign* mail had dropped off the first page, off the second page and was now completely out of sight. 'Di!' she yelled up the stairs. 'Di, you're never going to believe this...'

58

'Oh my God!' Diane looked up from Jo's phone. She was sitting in the passenger seat of Jo's car, scrolling through, as Jo clipped her belt on. 'You have to answer the mail from Lauren Watson first,' she said. 'I'm googling her now! She's married to Joe Watson, and she has a hundred thousand followers on Instagram. This is huge Jo! You have enough work here to keep you going for months. I'm sure you could...' She stopped talking.

'Keep the house?' Jo finished.

'Could you?'

Hands on the steering wheel, Jo shivered. She wasn't sure what the feeling was. Excitement? Fear? She hadn't read even a quarter of the messages, but Diane was right. It was huge, and there was enough work there to keep Party Girl going not for months, but for years. She wasn't in the land of unicorns now. The names she'd briefly read through were names she'd recognised as those of the wives of Andi's teammates. Almost as if... She turned, and looked at Diane. 'Do you think it's deliberate?' she said. 'Do you think they all want to book me because of what happened? Do you think they got together and—'

'Of course they did!' Diane laughed. Holding up the phone, she said, 'Do you think this is a coincidence? Women stick together, Jo. They look out for each other.'

Jo nodded. Leaning forward she put the key in the ignition. Vera had listened, and Diane had listened. And now the wives and girlfriends of Andi's teammates were looking out for her. She had all the support she needed from the women in her life, and that included the one woman whose support she had needed above all others. Her mother had put her hand on her cheek, she had said those words, *I was trying to get back to you*. Wasn't it time? If her mother had tried so hard, wasn't it time she made it easy and stayed close enough never to get lost again?

59

But any idea of sitting in the sun vanished as soon as she walked into the bungalow. Bobbi was sitting in the armchair closest to the living-room door. She had her jacket and shoes on, her handbag on her lap.

'Are you going somewhere?' Jo said.

'We're going to look at the home.' Her mother's eyes were clear as air. 'Had you forgotten? I've been waiting for you.'

'No,' she said, and then, 'It's me.' And she didn't know why she'd said that. Nothing about Bobbi's voice or manner was suggesting that she didn't know who she was talking to, or where she was. There had been no pause, no hesitant, *You're back.*

Bobbi nodded. 'I know it's you.

'Did you sleep well?' The question was so tentative, it struggled to find legs, it wobbled, it almost fell.

'Very well.'

'Did you see the moon? It was a full moon.'

And now Bobbi turned. 'We saw it together, Joanne.'

. . .

Ashdown House managed to appear both imposing and welcoming. A dignified Edwardian building, with huge bay windows that displayed boxes of sky-blue lobelia and deep pink petunias. By the front door a handsome pewter planter caught the light, winking its burnished hue, and to one side of the well-kept lawn a stately cypress swayed slightly.

As she turned the engine off, Jo glanced at her mother. There were so many questions she hadn't been able to bring herself to ask. Last night had felt like the beginning of something, but right now felt uncomfortably close to an ending. 'Are you sure you want to do this?' she said. It wasn't the first time she had asked. It wasn't the second time either. 'We can always come back.'

Bobbi nodded, her free hand fumbling for the door handle. 'I'm sure,' she said, and it wasn't the first time she'd said that either.

The bell was answered within moments. A heavy black door swinging open to reveal a tiny woman.

'Lindsey?'

'That's me! Joanne. Roberta. Come in. Come in.' And stepping back, Lindsey made a loose circular wave to usher them through the door.

Jo hesitated. Everything about Lindsey required a pause. Her hair was an improbable blue-black, scooped up into a knot and teased into spikes. Her eye make-up was equally vivacious. Pearl-blue and mauve eyeshadow, thick black eyebrows. She had three gold hoops in each ear, two gold necklaces and various rings. She was clearly a woman who believed in adornment.

'I'm so glad you could make it!' Lindsey's voice was breathless as she came forward again and put her hand on

Bobbi's elbow to guide her over the doorstep. 'You were with Dr Dandicott, weren't you? He's lovely, isn't he? Quite a few of our residents have been under his care. I'll bet you're glad you had him!' She turned now to Jo. 'I'll bet you're glad your mother had him, aren't you? To be honest you've caught us smack-bang in the middle of coffee. But don't worry, we've got some lovely pastries. Are you hungry? Come in, do come in!'

They were standing in the path of a human barrage of goodwill, against which resistance was impossible.

'Now!' Lindsey turned, pressing her hands together in silent praise. 'What we like to do with our visitors is start with a tour. You can take all the time you need! Make sure you get a feel of the place. It's such a big decision. I mean, it's Mum, isn't it?' she said, and beamed at Bobbi. 'There's no one more important.'

No one more important. Jo smiled. The words rang true. Who was more important in her life now than Bobbi?

'Would you like to follow me to the lounge?'

With Lindsey leading, they walked to the end of the hallway and turned right into a longer, darker corridor. Halfway along stood a wheelchair, a young girl behind, draped over the handles, her head bent as she swiped her phone.

'*Becky!*' Lindsey barked.

Jo startled.

So did the girl whose hands jerked, flipping her phone like a baton. 'Sorry, I... I was just checking a message what come...' The girl stopped talking, or the look on Lindsey's face stopped her talking. 'Sorry,' she whispered, again, and she leaned forward to help what Jo could see now was the occupant of the wheelchair. Whoever it was had a sweater over their head, one arm in, one arm out, the top of the skull poking out like an acorn from its shell.

'That man in the chair,' Lindsey stage-whispered as they walked past. 'He was head of maths at a secondary school. These youngsters need reminding.'

Jo nodded. She was thinking of Vera, how it was the other way round. How Vera had taken it upon herself, every morning, to do the reminding. *Hello Bobbi, it's me, Vera. I've come to take care of you today*. She glanced at Bobbi, but her mother's face was unreadable, and she had no idea if she might have been thinking the same.

'Our lounge!' Lindsey declared proudly as they rounded another corner.

They stood at the entrance to a huge room. It had four floor-to-ceiling windows that overlooked the garden, and a high ceiling with beautifully ornate coving. Green was the theme. Serene, orderly. Across one wall, huge cream letters spelled out *WELCOME TO OUR HOME.*

Armchairs had been arranged around the room. All occupied. One woman was sleeping, as well she might, Jo thought, because her chair sat in a shaft of delicious sunlight. She looked cosy; thick support socks and sheepskin slippers peeking out from the metal walking frame in front of her chair like the noses of hibernating animals.

'As I said, you've come at coffee time.' Lindsey indicated the far wall.

Across the room an elegant sideboard had been set with cups and saucers, teaspoons in place. To the end a silver urn, and next to it a silver jug. Presumably milk. In the middle sat a large plate of appetising pastries, pains au chocolat, pains aux raisins, croissants. Jo's stomach rumbled.

'Would you like a coffee?' Lindsey said. 'And a pastry of course.'

Another coffee? At least it would keep her awake.

But the pastry was delicious and the coffee piping hot, and as they sat in a sunny corner, Jo noticed how with her good hand Bobbi had lifted her cup to admire the china.

'I like to do things properly,' Lindsey said. 'This is a home, after all.'

'It's very nice,' Bobbi said, her head moving as she took in the expanse of the room. 'Very nice indeed.'

Jo looked too, but, holding the delicate china, her arms were heavy. The room was nice, Lindsey was nice, the cups were very nice. Why then did everything feel so dull? Why, as she watched Bobbi lean across to talk to the woman in the chair next to her, did she feel as if she'd placed herself and her mother in the path of a current they would be unable to resist. A force that would sweep them both so far downstream there could never be a return.

They finished their coffee and moved on to the dining room. It was another large light-filled space. The round tables were each laid for four, with cream tablecloths and floral table mats that matched the curtains, napkins folded like lilies into the glasses. The colours were soothing creams and greens that were echoed in the botanical prints on the wall.

'We have a rotating four-week menu,' Lindsey said, nodding towards the open hatch of the kitchen. 'All our meals are freshly prepared on the premises and there's always someone on hand to assist.'

'With the washing up?' Bobbi asked.

Lindsey laughed. 'Oh, there's no washing up here, Bobbi. It is OK if I call you that, isn't it?'

'Bobbi is fine.' Jo could see the sudden stiffness of the movement, the small discomfort it betrayed.

'No washing up ever again! That's good news I expect.' Lindsey beamed.

Jo took a step back. The bonhomie was too much. The shortening of her mother's name was too much.

'Now then! On to what we like to call our residents' private space.'

'The bedrooms?'

'That's right,' Lindsey said and her smile was infinitesimally tighter.

The room they were shown was small, but clean. A single bed, bridged by a narrow table on wheels, and a single wardrobe that matched the single chest of drawers. Marginally bigger, Jo thought as she looked around, than the room Vera had been looking at on My Cosy Space. She thought of her own house. The dining room, with the table that no one ate at now. The spacious bedrooms upstairs. She watched as her mother walked across to the window and stood looking out.

'It depends on finances of course,' Lindsey was saying, tilting her head and lowering her voice. 'There are variations in size, but no baths I'm afraid.' She nodded at the ensuite bathroom. 'Walk-in showers are so much safer.'

'No baths, no smokers, no pets.'

'I'm sorry?'

'Nothing.' Jo shook her head. 'Just a thing... I heard.'

Lindsey smiled brightly. 'Would you like to see the garden? It's really beautiful.'

'Of course.'

Lindsey was right again. The garden was magnificent. Exactly how she might have directed a landscaper to work her own garden, if she had wanted a landscape. The lawn sloped away to a wall beyond which lay farmland. An oak tree marked the far corner, and hydrangeas, azaleas and rhododendrons filled the beds. There were several benches, all sheltered by trellises.

'Well, what do you think?' Lindsey said.

Jo nodded. Bobbi had moved away to admire a large hydrangea. She watched her mother, how she raised her hand to trace the outlines of lime-coloured petals, and how her mother's hand shook. The garden was indeed beautiful. A space that had been designed for peace, quiet, and above all, to be sat in, walked in, looked at. This wasn't somewhere Bobbi would ever come indoors from with dirt under her fingernails. She tipped her head back to the sky, a well of emotion rising.

'Can we sit a moment?' she heard herself saying as she looked at Lindsey. The question felt ridiculous. Like a child asking permission to go to the toilet. But the need to press pause was overwhelming, the desire to step out of the current, and trace a path back. There was a reason she hadn't wanted to do this today, and it was there in the tingling of her fingertips, the hardness at the back of her throat. 'I'd like to take a moment with my mother,' she said, because when had she ever done that?

'Naturally.' Lindsey smiled. 'Of course.'

She waited until Lindsey had disappeared around the corner of the house, choosing a bench as close to the boundary wall, as far from the house, as she could find. She wanted to look back, to see it as a whole, this place that could become her mother's home for the rest of her life. She didn't speak until Bobbi was sitting comfortably beside her and then she turned. 'Do you like it?'

Bobbi nodded. 'It's a nice house. The garden's lovely.'

'It is, isn't it.' Jo followed her mother's gaze and for a moment, they sat side by side, taking in the loveliness of a garden neither of them would ever have a hand in caring for.

'Do you think you want to come and live here, Mum?'

Bobbi's head trembled slightly. 'It's for the best,' she said. 'Yesterday... I don't know...' Her voice drifted into a silence that felt impossible to break. Silence that was, despite the fresh summer air, suffocatingly thick.

Jo laid her hands in her lap and looked down at them. *We saw it together, Joanne.* Nothing more had been said about the events of yesterday. For all she knew, it was the only thing Bobbi remembered. 'Do you remember what happened?' she said, her voice careful. 'Do you remember me coming to get you from that apartment?'

Bobbi turned. Her thumb working across her fingers, as she shook her head. 'I'm scared,' she whispered. 'It scares me, Joanne.'

'I know, Mum. I know.'

'Don't cry.'

She hadn't known. Until she felt her mother's hand fleetingly cover her own, felt the tears there; she hadn't known they had fallen.

'I'll be safe here. It's for the best.'

'*No.*' Jo clenched the edge of the seat and her head lowered as she fixed her sight on the lawn. 'You always say that. Whenever I tried to ask you, Mum, you always said that. But it's not for the best.' Showing her mother to that small room. Laying her suitcase on that small bed... and then walking away, was not for the best. 'Don't you think,' she whispered, 'that we've done enough leaving. You and me?' It was hard to speak, her voice was low and strangled. 'Last night, you told me about Liam.' And once again she felt her mother's hand, firmer this time, as it came back to cover her own.

'He was born on the—'

'Seventh of April,' Bobbi said.

Jo turned. 'Seven pounds and three ounces.'

'Fifty-one centimetres.' Bobbi smiled, her eyes wet, the gleam of the tears they held so bright against her papery skin.

'You told me, Mum. You told me everything.'

'I'm glad.' Bobbi nodded. 'I'm glad I did. I'm glad you know now.' At the far end of the garden, the oak tree seemed to shiver and from deep within its leaves a magpie flew straight up, the purplish-blue sheen of its wings unmistakable. Jo watched. What had it stolen? she wondered. What had that bird snatched from the heart of the oak? Folding her fingers through her mother's, she turned. 'Why didn't you tell me? We've had so many years to make things right. I don't understand... why you never told me.'

But Bobbi only shook her head, her eyes seas of sorrow.

'I thought you didn't love me. That if you could leave me, then you didn't love me.'

'No, Joanne. No. I wasn't well.'

'That's how it felt,' she whispered. 'That's always been how it felt.'

Bobbi squeezed her hand. 'You've been away too. You've been away a long time.'

Jo didn't speak. What could she say? She had been away. For most of her life she had been as far away as possible. She took a deep breath, lifting her shoulders and pulling herself straight, ready to try, to keep trying... but Bobbi was first.

'I didn't tell you because I promised. You could have died that day, and it would have been my fault.'

'Died?' She looked up.

The expression on her mother's face was one of calm determination. Her eyes were lucid and it was clear that there would be no doubt, nothing forgotten, about what she was going to say.

'That day... When we had our party... It was a wedding. I can't remember... a big wedding and your father brought you home. He found you walking along the road. A long way... you walked so far.'

Her mind raced. There had been no parties. She couldn't remember a single party.

'I made myself a promise, that I would never do anything that might make you walk away from me again—'

'But I didn't... I wouldn't...' Jo's voice trailed off. 'We had a party?'

'You were in the bath, we both were, and he came, our guest with the tractor, and you went outside, you were in your party dress. The tea was laid out in the garden. All ready, and I made you wait. You had to wait for me, and you waited and waited... and then I couldn't find you... oh, Joanne.' Turning, Bobbi's eyes were huge, breathing a fear that still lived. 'What had I done?' she whispered. 'I was so scared... I looked and looked... You could have died... He looked with me, and when your father found you...'

Jo sat, the pressure of her mother's hand on hers uncomfortably strong now, vice like.

'I was being punished. You were safe, and I'd been lucky. But he knew, Joanne. Your father knew what had happened, and then... and then it wasn't his baby, and that's why Liam was taken away, and I wasn't well...' The vice tightened. 'If I'd told you I might not have been so lucky again. If I told you about the baby, you might never have come back.'

The word that echoed was *lucky*. But what was lucky about a daughter who'd sat hoping her mother would not come home, who'd grown up and flown as far away as possible, as often as possible? *Lucky*. She couldn't even say the word. It was a dull weight, a soft and heavy blow that left her numb. It didn't matter that she didn't understand what

Bobbi was saying. She hadn't died. She was still here, and so was Bobbi, and that was what mattered. 'Were you scared?' she whispered. A question that answered itself as her mother turned and nodded, and Jo saw the fear, old as it was new, in her eyes. 'Were you scared of telling me?'

'Yes.' Bobbi nodded, and her hand fluttering to her cheek was as fragile as her voice. 'And then time passed and I couldn't tell you. I didn't know how.'

'I wouldn't have judged you, Mum. I wouldn't...' Jo stopped talking and her head dropped so low it almost nestled in her mother's lap. The weight of understanding was heavy as an executioner's axe. In the beginning she'd been a child, capable of understanding only childish things. Later she'd been a prickly teenager, later still, a defensive adult, always ready to hold up her trump card: *my mother left*. Acceptance was something to learn; perspective couldn't have been rushed. Choices, she was only just beginning to know, belong to times and places, more than the people who make them. And didn't times and places change like the wind? 'I'm sorry,' she whispered. 'I stayed away too, Mum. I didn't know how not to stay away.' And then she felt it. No axe, just the stroke of a mother's touch, Bobbi's hand on the back of her head. 'Would you like to try and find him?' she said, sitting up to meet her mother's eye. 'Would you like me to help you find him?'

Bobbi didn't speak. She didn't say yes and she didn't say no. She didn't say anything.

'It's easy to try. We can...' Her voice faltered. What she was seeing in her mother's face was a reflection of all the questions she had asked Diane.

What if he's no longer alive? Or if he doesn't want to meet? Or if he hasn't forgiven me?

'You'll still have me,' she said. 'Whatever happens, you'll still have me.'

'Joanne.' Bobbi raised her hand and placed it on Jo's cheek.

A breeze blew in. She felt it on her face, at the back of her neck. 'I don't want to leave you here.'

'I know.'

'It's not for the best.'

'Joanne.'

'Come and live with me, Mum. Please. Let me take care of you, like you once took care of me.'

'What about Vera?'

'Well…' Jo paused, but there was no need. What she was about to say felt as natural and right as the order of the seasons. Vera needed a home and Bobbi needed Vera, and she had a home and she, too, needed Vera. 'I'm going to ask Vera to come as well,' she said. 'Would you like that?'

'Oh.' Bobbi's eyes lightened. 'I would,' she said. 'I would like that.'

'Good.' She took her mother's hand and held it and as Bobbi looked at her and smiled, she felt a stilling of the water. This was no turning back of the river's flow, but it was, if only for a while, a quieting of the current. A moment in which she, and Bobbi, might just be still together. 'Let's go home,' she said. 'Vera said I should sit in the sun today. Would you like to sit in the sun with me?'

'But you're married, Joanne.'

The question was as hesitant as it was unexpected. And as Jo looked at her mother's open face, she almost laughed. 'Not any more,' she said. 'Toby and I are getting divorced.'

'Toby?' Bobbi's eyes moved with confusion.

'Toby.' Jo smiled. In all the weeks that had passed, Bobbi had never asked about Toby. She had, Jo assumed, forgotten him. And it felt natural, because there had been moments that had stretched into minutes and hours when she too had quite forgotten she had a husband. Sitting back, she squeezed her mother's hand. 'He wanted a family. He's left me for someone else. Someone he's having a baby with.'

And now when Bobbi looked at her, the confusion had gone. In its place, a clear and perfect clarity. 'Are you sorry,' she said. 'Are you sorry you didn't have children, Joanne?'

Jo's eyes widened in surprise. The lucidity of both the question, and the questioner. She shook her head. How could she have explained it? How frightened she'd been, the idea she hadn't been able to shake, that it was genetic and that she too might be capable of leaving her own child. She couldn't. She would never even try. She looked away across the lawn. The only thing in her life she was sorry for was that she hadn't stayed close enough to find that photograph earlier. 'No,' she whispered. 'I'm really not.'

'And I'm not sorry that I did.' Bobbi patted her hand. 'There are many sadnesses in my life, many regrets. But I don't regret you. No, my children are not among them.'

60

And finally, she was able to take Vera's advice.

She positioned two reclining sun chairs in dappled sunlight, and she sat. With Jo at home, Vera had taken the opportunity to 'go shopping'. *Just a few essentials,* she'd said, and Jo hadn't asked any more. The excuse was clear. What was also clear, with her phone buzzing non-stop, and Bobbi shuffling in and out of the kitchen, was that the space she needed for the conversation she wanted to have with Vera wasn't available anyway. It could wait until Bobbi was settled for the evening, because of course there was always the possibility that Vera would not want to continue. The thought was the only grey cloud in an otherwise perfect blue sky. She busied herself with finding her mother's sunhat, keeping her water glass filled, and when Bobbi snoozed, scrolling through her inbox. Diane was right, the income potential was enormous.

At some point she must have fallen asleep herself. She woke to her mother's voice.

'Smells lovely, doesn't it?' Bobbi had a stalk of lavender pressed to her nose. 'My favourite flower,' she said.

'Lavender?'

'Is it?' Bobbi looked at the stalk. 'Is it lavender?'

Jo smiled. So now she knew. Lavender was her mother's favourite flower. She watched as Bobbi turned back to continue her perimeter shuffle of the garden, stopping here and there to touch an overhanging branch, rubbing the leaves between her fingers like a blind person. That was how it was now, she thought. Her mother's increasing blindness was of the mind, not the eyes.

By late afternoon, she was sprawled on her back, the chair fully reclined. Heat, combined with fatigue, had worked its spell. Sweat beaded her upper lip, and her phone, hidden underneath the chair, buzzed away unseen.

She dreamed. Vivid scenes in which she was tasked to find something in a house filled with many rooms. But the rooms kept changing, and she didn't know what she was supposed to find. She just knew that she had to keep looking, that she couldn't ever stop looking. It was only as she felt the coolness of a shadow fall across her face and she heard Vera's voice that she opened her dry, dry eyes.

'Jo?' Vera was holding up a frozen steak and kidney pie. 'I found this in the freezer.'

With difficulty, Jo pushed herself up. Her arm, where she'd been sleeping on it, was tingly and weak. Nursing it to her chest she squinted at the icy packet Vera held. If there was anything she couldn't face right now it was the internal organs of a dead animal.

'OK.' Vera read her face. 'I'll think of something else. Go back to sleep.'

'I'll go shopping,' she said, but she was already falling back, her eyes heavy, and anyway hadn't Vera gone shopping herself...

The next thing she knew Vera was shouting for her to

answer the door, and as she sat up and looked at her watch, she realised she'd slept the afternoon away. 'Shall I get it?' she yelled back.

'I'm with Bobbi.' Vera's voice floated out of the bathroom window.

Jo got out of the sun chair, her legs weak with a satisfied exhaustion, wobbled to her feet, straightened her bra straps and stumbled to the door.

61

'Nikki?'

'Hi JoJo.' Nikki stood on the doorstep, holding three huge pizza boxes. Her cheeks were gaunt and there were deep shadows underneath her eyes. Poor Nikki. Poor... A rich cheesy smell filled her nostrils. Her eyes went to the pizza boxes.

'I'm so sorry!' Nikki cried. 'I was too scared to ring you! Here, take these!' She thrust the boxes into Jo's hands and burst into tears. 'Vera said I had to come. She said I had to grow a pair, and come over right now. She said you needed pizza.'

'Vera said that?' Jo ran a hand through her hair, a smile forming. Her stomach growled. The pizza boxes were very warm and it was a wise, wise woman who understood the difference between an offal-for-dinner-day and a pizza-for-dinner day. Who understood when chocolate animal biscuits were needed, and when they were not. But, *sorry*? Frowning, she looked at Nikki. 'What on earth are you sorry for?'

'For ruining your business!' Nikki whimpered. 'The

party! Andi doing what... Showing his... here were children there, JoJo! Your reputation!'

'Oh, Nikki.' Jo's smile was wide and warm. Nikki was such a child. A child, expecting a child, and the boxes were so warm they burned and the cheesy smell was twisting her stomach like a wrench. Sweat ran cold down the back of her knees. Poor Nikki. She was married to a man with the impulse control of a five-year-old, the kind of man who... her breath caught in her throat. Dumping the pizzas on the hall table, she threw her arms around Nikki and held her tight. The kind of man, she'd been thinking, who could one day walk out on her as easily as if he were leaving a shop. The way Toby had walked out on her. But that simply wasn't right. Toby hadn't left on impulse. Everything he'd said had been true. Things had been difficult, and she hadn't talked to him. She'd fallen back on platitudes. *It wasn't meant to be; if it doesn't happen, it doesn't happen...* Redirected her energy onto fairy lights. It was ironic. She'd spent so much time and effort on the external accruements of a contented life, she'd never even guessed the depths of his discontent. 'You haven't anything to be sorry for,' she said. 'Nothing at all.'

'I haven't ruined your business?'

'On the contrary.' Jo pulled back, her hands on Nikki's shoulders. 'I've had more publicity than I could have paid for in a hundred years. And my inbox is full. Mostly from Andi's teammates' wives and girlfriends.'

'Really?' Nikki sniffed.

'Haven't you looked, Nikki? It went viral.'

'I didn't dare,' Nikki whispered. 'I'm so embarrassed. It was my first party. I don't know the other women very well and...' Looking down at her swollen belly, she said, 'He's an idiot, I know, JoJo. But I don't want to be on my own. And now, Vera says she's leaving... What am I going to do? I'm really scared.'

'I know.' She squeezed Nikki's hands. 'I know.' It was scary. To be young, and facing raising a child alone, to be middle-aged and facing the second half of your life alone, to be at the end of your life, completely alone, as you forgot everyone and everything that had mattered. 'Life is scary,' she said. 'But it's all we have.' From the table, the smell of cheese wafted a consolation.

'And pizza,' Nikki said quietly. 'We have pizza.'

'We do.' Jo laughed. 'Your sister,' she said, 'is a genius.' And the feeling of joy was so sudden and so real, she wanted to tip her head back and laugh. She had just spent the first afternoon of her adult life with her mother, doing nothing more than snoozing in the sun. Her business was set to explode, and she could stay in the beautiful home she had created for herself as much as for the husband who had left. The last emotion she had energy and time for was fear. And once again she drew Nikki into an embrace, her voice choking as she said, 'You asked me what you should do? You need to do what your mother did, Nikki. We all have to do what she did.'

'I don't understand,'

As she spoke she could feel the warmth of Nikki's tears against her own cheek.

'You have to be brave,' she said. 'You have to look it in the eye and face it. Everything that comes your way.' And pulling out of the embrace, she held Nikki's eye. 'That's all you can do. Do you think you can?'

Nikki nodded. 'I think so. But it's Vera I'm worried about, JoJo. She showed me this place she's going to rent. It's awful... I can't...'

'It's OK,' Jo interrupted. 'It's going to be OK.' So that's

where Vera had disappeared to. 'Come in,' she said. 'I don't think either of us needs to be worried about Vera, but let's have some pizza first.'

She ushered Nikki into the garden and introduced her to Bobbi, then she took the pizzas into the kitchen, where Vera was getting plates ready.

'Pizza was a great idea.'

Vera nodded. Her face implacable.

Jo took two glasses from the cupboard and a bottle of wine from the fridge. 'Thank you,' she said, as she filled a glass and handed it to Vera. 'Thank you for this morning. And thank you for asking Nikki to come.'

Again, Vera nodded, eyeing the glass suspiciously.

'I went back to my house today,' Jo said. 'For the first time.'

'OK.'

'That's where I was this morning.'

'OK.'

'And I know where you were this afternoon, Vera. And it doesn't make sense.'

'What doesn't make sense?'

'I've asked Bobbi to come and live with me.'

Vera's eyes widened. 'What about the care home?'

'It was lovely,' Jo nodded. 'It really was very nice, but it doesn't make sense that Bobbi should go and live there, when I have a home she can live in. And...' She took a deep breath. 'It doesn't make sense either, that you should go and live in a shoebox, when I have a home you can live in.'

'Jo.'

Raising her hand, Jo stopped any objections Vera was about to voice. 'You can pay your way by continuing to care for Bobbi. Just like you are now, Vera. It's not charity. This isn't charity.'

'I don't know...'

'It's a beautiful house, Vera. There's so much space. But it's not a home. It needs people. It needs a family.'

'I'm not your family, Jo.'

Jo smiled. 'Who says, Vera? The last few weeks have been the most difficult of my life, and you've been there for me every day. If that's not family, I don't know what is.'

'Well...' Vera looked down at her glass. 'I have really enjoyed looking after Bobbi and...' She paused. 'And talking to you, Jo. I've been lonely, to be honest. Sometimes, I've been lonely.' A soft blush spread across Vera's cheeks. She was, Jo realised, shy.

'There's a saying in this country,' Jo said. 'You can choose your friends, but you can't choose your family.'

Vera looked up. 'My country too.'

'Well, I don't see why that should be. I don't see why I can't choose my family, and invite them into my home. Will you come?'

Vera smiled, a lop-sided turning up of the mouth. 'Do you have a dog?' she said.

'A dog?'

'No dog poo. I won't come if I have to clean up dog poo. That's my only condition.'

Jo laughed. 'I don't have a dog!'

'Then, I'll come.'

62

With the arrangement confirmed, they made their way out to the garden, arms full with plates of pizza and glasses of wine. Bobbi and Nikki sat side by side, deep in conversation. God knows what they were talking about, Jo thought as she turned the garden path and saw them. The conversation looked lively. She stood very still. From the moment she had introduced them, Bobbi had warmed to Nikki instantly, and that, she had instinctively felt, was because of Nikki's pregnancy. Now she was sure. The way her mother kept putting her hand to Nikki's bump. And Nikki, so accommodating in her innocence, didn't seem to mind.

'You two looked as if you were having a great conversation,' she said, laying the plates on the table.

'We were! Gosh, I'm starving.' Nikki took a large slice, wafting the heat away with her hand. 'I've just been showing Bobbi Instagram,' she said. 'You'll never believe it, the local news station want me to come and do an interview.'

'Are you going to be on the television?' Bobbi said.

Nikki laughed. 'Maybe.'

Vera took a slice of pizza, sat down, slipped the button of her jeans free, and lifted her face to the dipping sun. 'This is the life,' she murmured.

'I wanted to be an actress,' Bobbi said. 'I used to sing. I was in a show on stage once.'

Jo turned. 'Was that when you met Dad?' she said. 'When he bought you flowers?'

'Flowers?' Bobbi frowned. 'Who has flowers?'

Jo smiled. She took a sip of her wine, the spicy plummy notes lingering on her tongue. Lavender was her mother's favorite flower and she had once been in a show on the stage. She had had a baby boy, who was taken away from her, when he was three hours old. All these things she knew now. If she was praying, she was praying for the river to slow, for the sea to recede, for more time.

63

The email came four days before her mother was due to come and live with her. Forty-two years after she had left.

Jo read it through twice before it registered. Diane had been right. Liam lived an hour away. All these years and he had been closer to Bobbi than she had. Yes, he did want to meet. He had put himself on the register, like so many adopted children, only after he became a father himself. Jo had two nieces and a nephew! He'd wondered all his life who he was, and where he came from, who his parents were.

Leaning back, she looked across at Bobbi, sitting in her usual armchair. More than two months had passed since she'd added both her own and her mother's details to the register. So much had happened. Bobbi's sling was gone, so now she had both thumbs to run over her fingertips. Nikki was a mother... and Toby a father. Diane was a three-times grandmother as of a week ago. The dining room of her house had been converted into a bedroom with an ensuite. The solar butterflies were back in place. Vera had already moved in, coming over to help with Bobbi every morning.

Bobbi's bungalow had sold on the first day and, everything packed, they were due to complete and move at the weekend. Just in time for her forty-ninth birthday, for which of course she had organised a party. The smallest party she had ever planned. Everything was ready. She'd splashed out on both a summerhouse and a landscaper, and of course, a whole new set of lights, nailed everywhere she could reach. But it didn't matter how many lights she strung, she'd never managed to bring the moon back. Bobbi was fading. Vera reported it, and Jo could see it.

Why didn't you try? As she looked at her mother, the question she would never ask floated between them. Lizzie had spoken of the detachment the drugs caused. Dr Dandicott of the smallest of tasks being like mountains to climb. Or was it the fear she'd seen in Bobbi's eyes that day at Ashdown House? Was that what had stopped her mother trying to find her baby? Fear that he would reject her? Or fear that Jo herself would reject her? Cupping her face to hide her tears, she read on... His parents? – and he apologised for being so direct – were they still alive? If so, he was very much looking forward to getting to know all of his family.

Jo closed her eyes. She hadn't thought of this. How to tell him? How to tell her brother that the opportunity of building a relationship with his mother would be a race against time, a race that he had probably already lost. How could anyone find the words for that?

64

Two days later, early, and nervous, Jo kept her back to the wall, her jacket folded and her handbag on the chair opposite as she awaited Liam's arrival. She couldn't have been more prepared to flee if she'd been Al Capone.

At the next table two children blew froth from their tiny drinks, cautious at first, becoming bolder as the woman with them sat and swiped at her phone. They blew and laughed and giggled, until one cloud of froth sailed across and landed in the other child's drink. The woman looked up. 'Stop it, you two,' she said. 'You want me to be able to tell your mum how good you've been, don't you?'

Jo watched. She'd assumed the children were with their mother. She'd assumed wrong. She nursed her latte and waited.

The children and the woman left, a workman in a high-viz jacket took their place, and, although she had studiously clocked every single man of an appropriate age coming through the door, when a dark-haired man, holding a cup and a packet of biscuits, approached her table and said softly, 'Jo? I'm Liam', she was speechless with surprise, her cup rattling loudly in the saucer as she struggled to put it down whilst standing to greet him. Liam the baby was a middle-aged man, thick around the middle, with peppered streaks of grey in his hair.

No, she could not have picked him out of a line-up. He could have passed her in the street, and perhaps already had a thousand times, and she would never have known. Maybe he had her (their) mother's nose, and the same arch of brow. Maybe once, the same jaw. Faces change. Her mother's jawline sagged, so now it was hard to know. Hard to see. He was a stranger. Their handshake was awkward and tentative. Jo sat down.

As if he sensed that she needed time just to look, Liam busied himself opening the biscuits. 'I can't resist sweet stuff,' he said. 'My kids barely get a look in at the biscuit tin.'

'I'm the same.' Jo smiled. 'And Bobbi. It must run in the family.'

'Bobbi?'

'My... our mother.'

'I see.'

'Sometimes...' Jo paused, heat rising in her face. 'I haven't always called her Mum.'

'Are you alright?' Liam was reaching for a napkin.

She didn't know why he was asking, and then she felt it, the tell-tale salty wetness on the top of her lip. When she put her hand to her cheek, she was surprised to find it wet. 'I'm sorry.' She took the napkin. It was patterned with cherries. 'You look like her.' Because now she'd had the chance, she could see he did look like Bobbi. He did look like his mother.

Liam put his fist to his mouth and coughed. 'I don't want

to get all emotional,' he said, 'but I was really scared I'd never get to know her.'

And for a long moment neither of them spoke.

'So you have kids?' Jo said. Now wasn't the moment to explain.

'Three. How about you?'

'No.' She answered with a smile.

Liam smiled too. 'Well, my three are very excited to meet you.'

'Really?' She was thinking of the children at the next table. How she'd presumed they'd been with their mother. They could have been with their auntie, and that could have been her. She could have been, could still be, the auntie on shopping trips, the auntie on special visits. 'I'd love to meet them too,' she said. Then, 'Actually it's my birthday at the weekend. It's nothing special, just a barbeque, but perhaps, you could... Or maybe it's—'

'We'd love to,' Liam said. 'If I haven't jumped the gun? I mean, if that was an invitation?'

Jo smiled. 'It was an invitation,' she said. 'It definitely was.'

'And our mother?'

Our. The word jolted.

'When do you think it would be possible to meet her? Will she be there, at the weekend?'

'She lives with me. Well, she's coming to live with me. She's moving in just a couple of days. She'll be there.'

'That's lovely.' Liam leaned back in his chair. He had a wistful look about his eyes. 'You must be very close,' he said.

Jo nodded. What else could she have done? For the time that was left, whatever time was left, she was more than willing to share her mother. But her past? That was something she would carry alone. 'There's something I need to explain,' she said. 'It's difficult. Too difficult to have done so by email. I don't really know where to start.'

'At the beginning?' Liam smiled. 'Once upon a time?'

'Once upon a time,' she echoed. Where was that? Where was the loose thread that fate had snatched at, beginning the slow unravelling of her mother's mind? To find it meant unpicking the stitches of Bobbi's life. A life she still knew precious little about. Time was running out. So much was already lost. No river ever flowed back out of the sea. She could only start with the few pebbles left behind. Their mother had been a window-dresser. She'd sung on stage and been given flowers by a man she had loved. She did not live happily ever after.

65

Standing at the window of what was now Bobbi's room, Jo stood watching the Wych elm at the end of the front garden. She was thinking about the evening Toby had left. The way she had assumed he'd parked on the road because he'd be leaving early in the morning. How, after he had gone, she had sat in the semi-darkness for hours, numbed into stillness. How her house had become a prison, the light and spaciousness reflecting back her loneliness. Those first days when the shock had been a hammer, when the only future she could envisage for herself was a future hollow with loneliness. He had left to start a new life, while she, it had felt, had been left to simply live out the remainder of hers. And it seemed strange now. Strange and sad, that she should have been so scared.

On the window-ledge several items had been placed. A tiny plastic carriage, a Holly Hobbie rag doll. Bits and pieces she'd taken out from the box that had lived in Bobbi's garden shed. The hope had been that they would help her mother to remember. It was a hope she was struggling to keep alive. As summer had crept on, and the light had crept out, so had Bobbi. Her appetite was failing, most days she struggled to recall who Jo was. She was, Jo knew, leaving.

From her pocket she felt the thrum of her phone registering a message. It was from Liam.

Arriving in five.

How many times, she thought now as she picked up the tiny plastic carriage and turned it over. How many times had she explained to Bobbi that she had found Liam? That he wanted to meet her? That he was coming to meet her? Only once had there been a flicker of recognition in Bobbi's eyes. *Liam,* she had said. *Seventh of April.* But the next day had been to start from scratch. The seventh of April had meant nothing. Liam had meant nothing.

The plastic of the carriage was brittle with age, sharp against her fingertips. She put it back down and, going into the hallway, looked at herself in the mirror. Liam knew. She'd tried as best she could to keep his expectations realistic. But she didn't know herself. Like oases in the desert, Bobbi's mind retained pools of lucidity. Impossible as it was to believe, perhaps she would look at this slightly overweight, slightly balding middle-aged man and see in him the baby son of three hours.

66

'Mum?' Bobbi was in the living room watching TV. She was dressed in a smart rose-coloured blouse that Vera had helped her pick out. Along with matching earrings and brooch. Not once had she asked why, although Jo had reminded her several times. *It's my birthday, Mum. I'm having a few friends over. And Liam is coming.* Every time Bobbi had simply looked at her and smiled. No questions, no register of interest. Nothing.

'Mum,' she tried again. She went over and turned the sound down. Then, standing in front of the screen to block it, she said, 'I'm going to turn it off now. There's someone to see you.'

'Turn it off?'

'Do you remember I told you that today is my birthday?'

Bobbi looked up, her lips shaping a soft *b*.

'And I said someone is coming to see you.'

'Me?'

'Yes, you, Mum. Not me. This person is coming to see you.' As she spoke, Jo looked to the doorway. *OK,* she mouthed, and Liam appeared. 'This is Liam. This is who has come to see you.'

'Liam.' Bobbi roped her hands together, fingers twisting, thumbs rubbing. 'Liam,' she said, watching not the doorway, watching Jo. Her eyes breathing confusion.

'I found him,' Jo whispered. 'I found him, Mum. Look.' And she turned and held her arm up and Liam took a step into the room.

Bobbi turned.

'It's your baby,' Jo said. 'It's him, Mum.'

And then Liam was all the way into the room, on his knee by Bobbi's chair, his hand stretched out.

'Liam,' Bobbi said, her mouth moving, ready to shape a thousand words her mind could not deliver. 'Liam,' she said again, and, watching, there was no doubt in Jo's mind. Her mother knew.

67

In the kitchen Jo topped up her champagne and, picking a cherry tomato from a huge bowl of fresh salad, stood listening to the sounds of her garden. Vera had used some kind of magical dressing, the tartness of lemon and the peppery smoothness of olive oil coated her tongue.

She'd left Liam alone with Bobbi, and had just taken Susie her sister-in-law (her sister in law!), and her nieces and nephew, out to the garden to introduce them to everyone. They would in time meet Bobbi. *In time,* Susie had repeated to her youngest, who, beside himself with excitement, had protested loudly at being relocated and then immediately become distracted by the sight of a human so much tinier than himself. Cash, Nikki and Andi's newborn son. Nikki was a semi-permanent feature at the house, visiting almost every day. Many late-summer evenings, Jo had come home to find everyone in the garden. Nikki, Vera and Bobbi, who was usually holding the baby, Nikki keeping a close protective arm nearby. It hadn't made her envious.

She hadn't been jealous. She had felt only the relief of a good decision made, the joy that comes from other people's joy. Because holding that baby, Bobbi had seemed joyous. Freed from a mind that had become chained, released into lucid moments of happiness.

Andi, of course, she'd seen much less of. Still the transformation was clear. For the first time in his life, he needed the help of a middle-aged woman. And it had amused Jo no end to see the humility as he'd handed his fretting son over to Vera's implacable calm. Karma, she had thought as she watched, was a woman in the prime of her life.

She walked across to the window and looked out. Never had her house and garden looked lovelier. It was alive. Strings of solar lights glowed in the twilight, the butterflies shone, all six of them. She'd bought four more. And everyone she needed gathered together.

Andi came in, opened the fridge, took out a bottle and popped it into the microwave.

'Kash?'

He nodded. 'Last one before bedtime.'

Jo smiled. As Andi left, Vera and Diane came in. Jo nodded at Andi's departing back. 'He's a different man,' she whispered.

Vera laughed. 'Because Nikki's a different woman.'

'That's true.' Jo smiled. Nikki had taken her advice and run with it. She'd kicked Andi out and started divorce proceedings. Whether she would ever have followed through, Jo didn't know. It didn't matter. Andi had taken fright, and sobered up in more ways than one. They were two different people in a different marriage.

'How is it going?' Diane whispered. She nodded across at the closed door of the living room.

'I don't think they'll hear us.' Jo smiled.

'Did she know him?' Vera said.

'She knew the name.' Now Jo looked at the closed door. 'If she's able to understand that he is her baby, if she even remembers the baby any more, I don't know.' She shook her head, unable for a moment to speak. 'It just came too late.'

'You did everything you could, Jo.' Diane put her hand on Jo's arm.

'Did I?'

'Yes.' Vera said. 'Don't tell yourself anything else.'

Jo nodded. Whatever she was going to say, whatever she was thinking, was cut off by the clanging chimes of the doorbell. She frowned. Everyone was here. The party was small and intimate and there wasn't anyone she could think of who would be ringing the door now.

It was Toby.

Never had she seen him so dishevelled. He had deep circles under his eyes, his hair was in need of a cut and the shirt he wore had a large white stain on the shoulder.

'I wanted to give you this,' he said, and placed a long package into her arms. 'In person.' His mouth had twisted with the effort of contained emotion. He thrust his hands in his pockets and nodded. 'And I just wanted to say happy birthday, Jo. That's all.'

Jo looked down at the parcel. She was struggling to contain her own emotion. There was no point in inviting him into what had once been his home; he hadn't come to be invited in. She knew that and that was why they were both trying not to cry. 'What is it?' she whispered.

'Something for your office. I heard business is good.'

'Business is great.'

'Well... I guessed as much. The house... And of course, I saw the video.'

Jo laughed. 'The whole world saw the video.'

He smiled. 'How is your mother?'

'She's... She's as well as can be expected. She's living here now actually.'

Toby's face opened with surprise. 'That's good,' he said. 'If that's what you want, Jo, I'm glad.'

'It is what I want. Very much so.'

'OK.' Toby nodded at the package. 'Well, open it.'

The paper came off quickly, the plaque slipping into her hand, a beautiful burnished brass, that read: *Party Girl Ltd.* She gasped. 'Toby, it's lovely!'

Toby shrugged. 'I'd always planned to give you this. It was going to have your name as well. And then... Then I wasn't sure what name you'd be using. I didn't want to assume... The divorce thing was clumsy, Jo. Really clumsy. I'm sorry.'

Jo held the plaque up. 'Party Girl Ltd,' she read. 'I haven't even thought about what name I'm going to use.' She was thinking of Bobbi. All her lost words, all the things she could no longer name. 'It doesn't matter,' she said, and she turned to look at him. 'Losing my married name doesn't mean I've lost our marriage, Toby. The time we spent together... That still exists. It always will.'

Toby didn't speak. He tried to, but, shaking his head, he gave up and when he looked at her, his eyes were full of tears.

'Are you happy?' she said, wiping away her own tears.

'I am,' he whispered. 'I really am.'

She laughed. 'Well, you look dreadful.'

'I know.' He looked down at his shirt. 'I meant to change but...'

'But,' she finished.

'What about you? Are you happy?'

Jo didn't answer. She lifted her chin and listened. From

the garden, she could hear children laughing, a baby fussing, adults talking. The sound of a family. A family she knew she would never leave. 'Yes I am,' she said, hugging the plaque to her chest. 'I'm very happy.'

THE END

ALSO BY CARY J HANSSON

☆☆☆☆☆ 'Achingly sad, but beautiful.'

☆☆☆☆☆ 'Beautifully and boldly crafted.'

☆☆☆☆☆ ' Few people write female friendship as well as Hansson.'

Ebook available: Here

For paperback order through any good bookshop or my website, www.caryjhansson.com using ISBN:978-9152786017

Back to her future is the compelling first novel in *The Gen X* Series of women's contemporary fiction.

ALSO BY CARY J HANSSON

The award-winning, best-selling Midlife Trilogy. Start with book one: A Midlife holiday

'Totally addictive reading.'

'Bridget Jones meets Shirley Valentine.'

'It's sad, it's funny, it's every woman's life.'

'Heart-warming, heart-breaking and hilarious.'

'I feel as though I am part of their friendship group now.'

Looking for paperbacks?

Order through my website or any good bookshop using these ISBNs

A Midlife Holiday ISBN: 978 91 987 5873 3

A Midlife Baby ISBN: 978 91 9875 8795

A Midlife Gamble ISBN: 978 91 9875 8771

AFTERWORD

Thank you for reading.

Gaining exposure as an author relies upon word-of-mouth, so if you have enjoyed the book do tell your friends. Or gift them a copy! And please do consider leaving a review or rating at the site you purchased from. It really helps.

If you're interested in having me participate in your reading group, drop me a line through social media. (Instagram)

If you're interested in Writing for Wellness you can find out more on my website:

www.caryjhansson.com

Printed in Great Britain
by Amazon